Praise for
Remind Me How This Ends

'Bursting with humour and heart, Gabrielle Tozer reflects the pain, pressures and pleasures of life between high school and what comes next.'

Will Kostakis, award-winning author of
The First Third and *The Sidekicks*

'Tender and tough, this gorgeous story of love, loss and friendship will pull you in heart-first.'

Fiona Wood, award-winning author of *Wildlife* and *Cloudwish*

'Being 18 is hard as nails and Gabrielle Tozer captures the spirit of impending adulthood perfectly. *Remind Me How This Ends* is a beautifully written read that tells us it's okay to have no idea what comes next — it's the adventure in finding out that's the most exciting part.'

Mel Evans, *Cosmopolitan Australia*

'A tale full of heart with characters who — by the final page — feel like friends. Milo Dark is the boy next door I always wanted. Gabrielle Tozer has delivered a story with depth and heart. Milo and Layla have stayed in my head long after the final page.'

Rebecca Sparrow, author of
Ask Me Anything and *Find Your Tribe*

'How refreshing to read a book in which the real love story is the one between a young girl and her mum. It's rare to see grief explored in teen fiction, rarer still to see it handled in such a nuanced way.'

Dannielle Miller, author of *Loveability* and
CEO of Enlighten Education and Goodfellas

Praise for
The Intern and *Faking It*

'*The Intern* is a page turner that left me wanting more of Tozer's work.'

JJ McConnachie, *NZ Booklovers*

'If you loved *The Devil Wears Prada*, I have a sneaking suspicion you'll dive right into *The Intern* ... I loved this fun, cheeky read, as well as the genuine heart at its core.'

Lauren Sams, author of
Crazy, Busy, Guilty and *She's Having Her Baby*

'*The Intern* is an upbeat tale with a loveable heroine who is both physically clumsy and academically clever, which sets it apart from the usual teen fantasy fare.'

Kerryn Goldsworthy, *Sydney Morning Herald*

'Gabrielle Tozer nails it with *Faking It* — it's fun, sassy, endearing, and an accurate account of magazine life with a hilarious twist.'

Lucy Cousins, *Dolly* and *Cleo*

'Funny, entertaining and engaging ... Both *The Intern* and *Faking It* are highly recommended for readers looking for entertaining contemporary fiction for teens that is both light-hearted and insightful.'

Susan Whelan, *Kids' Book Review*

REMIND ME HOW THIS ENDS

GABRIELLE TOZER

Angus&Robertson
An imprint of HarperCollins*Children'sBooks*

Angus&Robertson
An imprint of HarperCollins*Publishers*, Australia

First published in Australia in 2017
by HarperCollins*Publishers* Australia Pty Limited
ABN 36 009 913 517
harpercollins.com.au

HarperCollins*Publishers*
Level 13, 201 Elizabeth Street, Sydney NSW 2000, Australia
Unit D1, 63 Apollo Drive, Rosedale, Auckland 0632, New Zealand
A 53, Sector 57, Noida, UP, India
1 London Bridge Street, London SE1 9GF, United Kingdom
2 Bloor Street East, 20th floor, Toronto, Ontario M4W 1A8, Canada
195 Broadway, New York NY 10007, USA

National Library of Australia Cataloguing-in-Publication entry:

Tozer, Gabrielle, author.
    Remind me how this ends / Gabrielle Tozer.
    978 1 4607 5168 8 (pbk)
    978 1 4607 0656 5 (epub)
    For young adults.
    Summer romance — Fiction.
    Young adult fiction.
A823.4

Cover design by Hazel Lam, HarperCollins Design Studio
Cover image by Pixel Stories / Stocksy.com (Image #891936)
Typeset by HarperCollins Design Studio
Printed and bound in Australia by McPherson's Printing Group
The papers used by HarperCollins in the manufacture of this book are a
natural, recyclable product made from wood grown in sustainable plantation
forests. The fibre source and manufacturing processes meet recognised
international environmental standards, and carry certification.

For my not-quite loves,
nearly-right loves and missed-timing loves,
some of you know who you are ...

But most of all, this is for my
first reader and forever love,
JT

REMIND ME HOW THIS ENDS

Milo

It's barely past seven but the party's already messy: sticky carpet, cigarette smoke spiralling in the air, tinny music bleating out of a speaker that no-one seems to care sounds rubbish. Everyone's leaning against torn op-shop couches, leaning against the walls, leaning against each other. Everyone except two girls doing cartwheels outside on the grass — and me. I hesitate in the doorway, wondering if it's too late to do a runner, and see a pile of puke decorating the steps at the entrance to the uni residences' rec centre. Not surprising really: homemade punch's been flowing for hours.

Through the stench and drooping streamers, from a couch on the other side of the room, Sal spots me and waves me over. She's cross-legged, barefoot and laughing with three guys slurping from plastic cups. They're in uniform: deep V-necks, thongs, lashings of sunburn across the nose. If we were in Durnan, Sal would've avoided them, shrugged them off as douchebag poster boys. But we're not in Durnan, not even close. A red bra peeks out from beneath her singlet. I haven't seen it before, or maybe I haven't paid enough attention.

I give her a wave — *on my way* — and squeeze past a table stocked with undercooked sausage rolls, tripping over a spray-painted sign that's fallen from the ceiling: *Happy Valentine's Day, loser!* I smirk. Tell me about it.

By the time I reach Sal, I'm drenched in someone else's punch. She leaps to her feet, passes me a cup and introduces me to the group, but I forget their names immediately, except the tallest guy — a gum-chewing second-year law student called Woody who can burp the first verse of *Bohemian Rhapsody* and has already kissed two girls tonight, according to one of the first-years who's migrated to our corner.

When everyone slides back into their own conversations, Sal steps in closer to clink our cups together. 'You're here.'

'Yeah, sorry, hot water dropped out, and Mum rang to check I got in alright, then I sorta got lost finding this joint and …' I cut myself off. 'Yeah, I'm here. Hey.'

'How great is this?' Sal says. 'We can pretend you live here — that we're freshers together. We're not cheesy Valentine's Day people anyway, are we?'

I shrug. 'Nah, all good.'

I don't remind her that only four hours earlier, I'd organised a date for us for tonight, before her 'slight change of plans'. The kind of date she's always pestering me to organise — without party pies soaked in punch.

Laughter erupts from the rest of the group. A massive grin has spread across Woody's face.

2

'What? What did I miss?' Sal asks, grabbing a nearby girl's arm.

'Just my famous Chewbacca impression, dear Sal,' Woody says. 'Don't worry, I'll do it again just for you.'

Sal laughs as she readjusts her cut-offs. I wait for her to tell him she's never seen a *Star Wars* film, not even after two years of me begging, but she doesn't. Instead, she tosses her ponytail, like girls do in the movies when they're pretending to be blasé but really just want to show off their hair. Sal's is strawberry-blonde, flowing, shiny — the kind that gets in the way when you're fooling around.

Woody repeats the impression, throwing an extra growl in her direction, and the group cheers.

A girl with lipstick as bright as a traffic cone pushes through our group to top up Sal's cup before wandering off to splash punch over someone else.

'That's Jamie,' Sal tells me. 'Apparently she fell down two flights of stairs after the last punch party. She's a scream. Oh, and her and Woody used to date, like a hundred years ago.'

'Ah, right. Cool.'

I take a swig, realising it's the first time we've met new people who don't already know us as a couple. In Durnan, we've been a package deal since we were sixteen. I was her first kiss, she was my first kiss that meant something, and we were voted 'most likely to get married' at our Year 12 formal three months ago. While everyone else was hooking up and breaking up, we were 'Milo and Sal'. We just *were*.

A hand claps on my shoulder. Woody's back.

'So, Miles, we're all wondering, how'd you pull this top chick?' he asks, snaking an arm around me. 'She's a legend, our Sal, a fine specimen.'

Miles. Chick. Our Sal. Specimen. I force a laugh. 'Er, well —'

'Woody, it's *Milo*,' Sal cuts in.

He slurps his drink. 'What did I say?'

'Miles.' Sal elbows him. 'It's Milo, with an "o". I told you that last night.'

Last night?

'Okay, so what's the story, Milo with an "o"?' Woody asks. 'The boys around campus've been nursing broken hearts since finding out this little fresher is off-limits.'

'Ignore him,' Sal says. 'There are no broken hearts. Although maybe there'll be some broken bones if certain people don't watch themselves.' She elbows Woody again, this time throwing him a smirk too.

A second fake laugh is out before I can stop it. Woody doesn't notice — he's already charged off to a beer-skolling contest on the lawn.

His question thumps in my head, probably 'cos I never 'pulled' Sal. We got together when our pushiest mates interfered during recess in Year 11. I was playing basketball when two of her friends — both gossips, both perpetually single — dragged me off the court. 'Sally likes you, do you like her?' they asked me, giggling, as my mates pissed themselves. I remember shrugging. I didn't like her, not like that, but I didn't *not* like her, which seemed good enough at the time. I didn't know anything about her other than that she sat in front of me in chemistry, plaited and unplaited her hair whenever she was supposed to be taking notes, and ate meatballs and pasta for lunch when most of our year was throwing away half-eaten sandwiches. But she was a girl — a girl who had the hots for me apparently — so I worked out how to like her. *Fast*. One week of awkward conversations, one week of sweaty hand-holding, one week of kissing each other so hard I had to sneak some of Mum's lip balm later, one week of grinding our school–uniform–covered bodies against each other whenever her parents were home late from work, and that was that — I'd fallen into my first relationship. Our friends did all the work and I let them. It was all mapped out for me. Not exactly the stuff of fairy tales.

Sal drags me over to sit on the couch. 'Hey,' she says, 'loving life?'

I give a thumbs-up 'cos it feels like less of a lie that way.

'Oi, bitches! Coming in.' Jamie wedges between us, tugging on my shirt. 'Alright, Milo, real-talk time. Tell me everything I need to know. Who are you, what are you doing, and why aren't you coming here to play with us? And ... go!'

I rattle through the boring stuff — *eighteen, live in Durnan, Sal's boyfriend of two years, doing the long-distance thing while she's studying in Canberra* — to disguise the fact I don't have answers for most of her other questions. She may as well have asked me to multiply 47,201 by 13,546, subtract 391 and divide by 31 without a calculator. The answer? Who the hell knows.

'Yeah, but why are you still in dumb-ass Durnan?' Jamie interrupts. 'Three hours away with nothing going on? You may as well be on Mars. Sal says it's a hole packed with halfwits. Right, Sal?'

Sal shakes her head. 'That's not exactly what I said.'

I shrug. 'Just taking some time.'

There it is. I've said that line so much since last year, I almost believe it.

'Whaddya mean?' Jamie asks, leaning in. Her breath reeks of cigarettes so I pull back a little. 'To do what?'

Sal answers before I can admit I have no freakin' idea. 'He's working for his parents and then he might join us next year. Or even next semester. Either way, he'll get here. Right, Milo?'

Sal seems to have a whole publicity campaign down, spinning the truth so I don't seem like such a dud of a boyfriend. She's so confident, so happy, so unlike the Sal who reversed out of my driveway two weeks ago. That Sal whispered, 'Tell me I'm going to make friends and learn how to fold a fitted sheet and ace my subjects and find a café that makes the perfect poached egg. Tell me I'm going to be fine.' When I told her, 'You're going to kill it,' she was so overwhelmed with nerves that she burst into tears. Now, it's like she's someone who's never been anxious in her life.

'You're saving money, Milo? Oh damn, you're rich, aren't you? Hey, Milo's rich, everyone!' Jamie claps her hands together. 'Do you live in a McMansion with a pool and a tennis court and a pantry big enough to hook up in?' Her body slants towards me like the Leaning Tower of Pisa and she pokes me in the chest. ''Cos you should. You should, Milo.'

Burp. Her eyes bulge. Her hand rushes to her mouth.

'You okay?' Sal asks. 'J?'

Jamie nods, her chin now smudged with lipstick, before hurling red chunks all over my jeans.

* * *

Woody is a human skyscraper so it's no surprise his shorts bunch up on me, giving me the appeal of a mouldy cucumber. I wriggle around on the tiles to try to disguise my knobbly knees, but can't get comfortable — especially with about thirty of us jammed into the kitchen on Sal's residence's floor, which now stinks of burnt cheese.

'You look fine, stop worrying,' Sal says as she butters up a round of toasted sandwiches. 'Besides, everyone here on ressies wants to get into Woody's pants, and look at you — nailed it first time.'

'They do?' *Everyone*. She's said it herself.

She pecks me on the lips. 'Obviously not *every*one.'

'I know.'

I don't know shit.

Now the punch party's fizzled out, the night has somehow morphed into a blow-by-blow of Woody's shenanigans. How many girls he's kissed tonight (six), how many girls he's turned down tonight (two), and how many girls he's kissed since Orientation Week (thirteen). Jamie, perked up with a second wind, inputs all the data onto a piece of butcher's paper that stretches across the kitchen floor. The others all cheer as she tapes it to the wall, crooked, while I gnaw on my toastie and digest the fact I don't even know that many girls.

'Bed?' Sal whispers.

'Nah, I'm not that tired,' I reply, before noticing her raised eyebrow. 'Oh. *Bed*. Yeah, definitely bed.'

Milo

The sink's tap in the corner of her room is dripping. My head spins as I pick at the Blu-tack on the wall behind me, alternating between breathing in time with the leak and with Sal snoring next to me.

Drip, drip, drip.

Sharing the single bed is like trying to sleep in a matchbox. My left foot hangs over the edge, poking out through the sheets, while my right foot presses against Sal's leg. I struggle to breathe through her hair, which is damp with sweat and twisted up in her singlet.

Drip, drip, drip.

My left arm is flopped over Sal's body, resting in the curve of her lower back, while my right arm has nowhere to go, so I switch between squashing it between our bodies and curling it up near my face.

Drip, drip, drip.

Jamie's words ring in my ears: *Why are you still in dumb-ass Durnan?*

Four knocks strike Sal's door, so soft I wonder if I'm hallucinating.

'Sal,' a deep voice says. 'Sal. It's me.'

Not hallucinating. Someone's out there.

I nudge Sal to wake up, but she murmurs, 'I don't know where the baking paper is, Mum,' and hugs her pillow tighter.

Three more knocks, this time they're louder. I tug at my boxers, which hang low around my hips, and hobble towards the crack of light squeezing under the door. Bleary-eyed, I poke my head out to see Woody, who's also in his boxers.

'Ah, hey.' I try not to make eye contact with the dusting of hair coating his chest.

'Damn, sorry, bro, forgot you were here.'

'Yeah, still here. What's up?'

'Locked myself out again.'

'Ah, shit.'

'Yeah, yeah …' He runs his fingers through his hair. 'You know what, security can sort me out. Yeah, I'll call the big fellas, they'll get it done.'

'You sure, man?'

'Yeah, bro, all good. My bad. I'll, ah, I'll see ya later, yeah.'

Woody collects a bucket of fried chicken from the floor, then disappears down the hallway towards the fire exit.

Too wired to sleep, I fumble in the dark for my phone and head for the kitchen. Plastic cups half-filled with punch litter the coffee table and the telly is pumping infomercials. I crash down on the ratty couch between an inflatable palm tree and a torn-open packet of chips.

'Overwhelmed? Lost? Something missing in your life?' a lady with a frozen smile chirps, drilling into me through the screen. 'Sounds like you need the Supermop 33-20 to clean up your mess!'

I turn off the telly and stuff a handful of soggy chips in my mouth, stomach churning as I remember Woody standing half-naked in Sal's doorway.

I reckon I'm going to need more than a Supermop.

* * *

The line of passengers waiting to climb aboard the coach to Durnan wraps around the side of the bus station. Sal and I sit side by side on a bench, waiting until the last minute before I have to get on. I've scoffed a bacon and egg roll that tasted like it'd been sitting out all night. Sal's only taken a few bites from hers.

'Better get going,' I say, pointing to the shrinking line. 'Alright, um, well, I love you.'

The sentence flip-flops out like I'm mumbling a secret. We've only been saying it for a few months so it still feels alien hearing it come from my mouth, like I'm the cheesy hero in one of the trashy rom-coms Mum watches when she's hogging the remote.

Maybe 'cos the first time I said it was by mistake.

We were watching re-runs of *The Simpsons* in the dark in my room and Sal cracked a joke so I mumbled, 'Ohhh, you,' through a mouth of chocolate and she turned and whispered, 'Oh my God, Milo, I love you too.' Then she kissed me fast and hard on the lips, then my neck, then my lips again, and we missed the rest of the episode. We've never stopped saying it after that night and I've never told her about the mix-up. Besides, she texted all her friends what I'd said — what she thought I'd said — five minutes after she removed her tongue from the back of my throat.

Sal gives me a hug as the bus rumbles behind us. 'You had fun last night, yeah?'

'Yeah. Yeah. It's just … this distance thing …'

'Don't tell me it's too hard already?' She laughs. 'Forget what Jamie said. She was off her head.'

'Yeah, I know, but you're right: I'm a halfwit. I've *stayed*. And you've already got this whole other life.'

'It's not an "other life" — it's my life. You're a part of that.'

'You heard what Trent said before you left.'

'You've lost it. Just 'cos your brother's footy mates can't handle long-distance doesn't mean we can't do it. It's only three hours. Besides, we'll talk lots.' She pauses. 'Unless you don't want to do it?'

'I never said that.' I kiss her lips. 'Text you when I get home, yeah?'

'You better.'

'And you're back soon to pick up the rest of your stuff?'

'A whole weekend,' she says with a nod. 'None of this one-night-only business.'

It's not until later when I'm crashing out on the bus that I realise she never said, 'I love you too.'

Milo

Trent sniffs his armpit. 'Geez, I'm ponging up a storm. Can you hurry up and get in, bro? I've gotta get back for a shower before Warrick's kicks off.'

'Serious?' I ask through the car window. 'But it's only nine thirty in the morning.'

'Whatever, I'm meeting the boys for pre-drinks.' He grunts, revving the engine. 'Just get in the car, ya clown.'

I clamber in and slam the door. The only thing worse than working at our family bookstore on a Saturday is getting a lift there with Trent when he hasn't showered after two hours at the gym. The Durnan tip smells more appealing than Trent on a Saturday. I'll be lucky to make it three blocks without commando-rolling out of the car.

'Don't give me that look,' he says, turning up the radio. 'I'm driving you around like a chauffeur. You should be tipping me the big bucks. Or, I don't know, getting your licence like the rest of us.'

'Yeah, yeah. This was *your* shift, remember? I'm doing you a favour.'

He swears as he reverses out the driveway. 'Fine, I owe you one if that'll shut you up.' He throws a stick of gum into my lap — an order, not a request. I wish I had a bar of soap to peg at him. 'Hey, how's Sal going in old Canberra town? You two have a lovers' tiff? You've been acting like an even bigger weirdo all week.'

I pop the gum in my mouth and start grinding. 'Nah, it's good. She's good.'

'Damn straight. She was a sort the last time I saw her.'

I snort.

'What? It's not my fault she got smoking hot. It's science.'

'You're a knob, man.'

Trent pushes his palm against the horn, payback to the learner driver in the car crawling ahead of us. He turns back to me. 'You were always batting above your average with her, bro — we all knew it. You were just lucky she never did.'

I don't say anything, just keep chewing.

'It's gotta sting that she's gone,' he adds. 'And you're still here, bludging off the parentals.'

'Righto. Remind me who does your laundry?'

He laughs. 'Yeah, but we're talking about you, bro, 'cos Sal's off doing who knows what.' I catch him smirking in my direction. 'Literally.'

My jaw tightens as I turn up the radio, but it's not enough to block out Trent's ribbing. The truth is: Sal left in such a rush she probably didn't even slow down for the usual salute to the *Thank you for visiting Durnan* sign. And I stayed to sink into the semitrailer-sized pile of crap that is my new life. No idea what to do, no idea where to go, no idea how I missed the memo everyone else got to get their lives together. Not even Durnan High's careers advisor could help me. Nothing she suggested felt right. Although she's a careers advisor who not-so-secretly resents that she never made it as a musical-theatre star, so I don't reckon I could've trusted her advice anyway. Despite her urging me to 'just do anything' — *er, no thanks, Mrs Fletcher* — I wound up missing the cut-off date so didn't apply anywhere.

The rest of our year fled town at such high speeds you'd swear a cyclone was nipping at their bums. Uni, TAFE, travel, jobs — they've all left for something. My mate Steve sped off in his ute to Bathurst Uni with a 'Guess I'll see ya, Dark,' like the past six years counted for nothing. Another mate, Murph, got into University of Technology Sydney, but reckons he'll visit his dad heaps and still come round to see me. He's probably lying, even if he doesn't know it yet.

That's the thing about Durnan. Most of its residents live and die here, but if someone leaves, they don't come back.

Trent swears as he slaps the steering wheel. 'Oi!' he yells out his window at a bearded bloke driving a minivan. 'Where's your blinker, mate?'

He taps my arm. 'Don't freak about Sal, bro. I'm playing. She ain't a cheater.'

The gum is now flavourless rubber in my mouth. 'I'm not freaked.'

'Good. That's good. Well … I'm pretty sure she's not.' He notices my filthy expression. 'Relax. I'm *sure* she's not. Well, ninety per cent sure. She is a long way from home, bro.'

Next time I'm hitchhiking to work.

* * *

It's a quiet Saturday at The Little Bookshop.

I squiz at the notes and coins in the till. Almost the same as when I opened up this morning. Dad won't be happy when he runs the numbers after I close, which means we're all in for a lecture at dinner.

Despite working his way through half the books in our self-improvement section, Dad's signs of self-improvement so far are zero. In fact, he might even be worse, because now if we have a good day, he's upset because he wanted it to be a great day. We have enough — money, food, clothes, house — but *enough* isn't enough for him any more. The man's one inspirational quote away from mutating into a walking, talking Instagram feed.

Those books should really come with a thirty-day money-back guarantee.

Still, Mum steps up the marketing for the bookshop, we all take turns serving at the front counter — even Trent pitches in when he's not talking me into covering his shifts.

I don't need a self-proclaimed guru to know why the shop's empty today. Half the town's probably seeking refuge at home in the air-conditioning or cooling off in their above-ground pools, while the other half are probably watching my old team at the cricket ground, sweating it out with soggy egg and lettuce sandwiches on their laps and fighting for the scraps of shade bordering the field. I quit playing when a chunk of our team bailed out of Durnan. It wasn't that great without Steve and Murph taking the piss out of everything with me.

With no-one to serve in the shop, I return to scrolling through my phone, whizzing through my friends' picture-perfect lives in London, Sydney, Melbourne, Newcastle — everyone is everywhere except Durnan. I look at a photo album of one of Sal's mates who's doing an exchange in Scotland. Damn. Should've thought of that. Then I'd be oceans away from Trent's stirring and foul BO.

That's the thing. Everyone else is doing stuff. Real stuff. The sort of stuff you can brag about. Studying law and accounting and nursing and actuarial science. I don't even know what that is, but it sounds hard core. A guy I used to play cricket with has already scored an internship at a radio station in Wollongong. A girl I've known since Year 8 moved to the city and is starring in a commercial for dry shampoo, whatever the hell that is, but she's on telly so she's doing alright. And it looks like Steve has a girlfriend. Steve's never had a girlfriend, not unless you count groping Rebecca Clifford's boobs, outside her top, for about thirty seconds at a house party in Year 10.

Some people say they want the truth, but I reckon they only want to know the good stuff. The highlight reel. Wake me when the world's ready for the lowlight reel. No prospects for the future because I'm paralysed by decision fatigue? Freakin' oath. Working weekends instead of having a life? Kill me now. Overbearing parents? Yep. Girlfriend living hundreds of kilometres away and probably never coming back? You know it. Annoying brother? Tick, tick, tick. No mates because they had the brains to rack off? Cha-ching. No amount of cropping, filtering or hashtagging photos can frame my current existence any differently. It sucks, filters and all, so the fewer people who know about my sad little reality in Durnan, the better. If I'm stuck here while I work out what I'm supposed to be doing with my life, then I'm staying incognito.

'Friggin' hell, is that you, Milo Dark?'

Or not.

I lock eyes on a shaggy blonde mop. A shaggy blonde mop with a dimple wedged in her chin and thick lashes all gloopy with mascara. My vision adjusts to take in the full picture. Faint streaks of pink and purple run through the yellow nest, jarring with the black regrowth radiating from the middle of her scalp.

Jesus. It's her.

'*Layla?*'

'Yeah, 'course it's me,' she says, with a smile just big enough that I spot the sizeable gap between her front two teeth. I'd forgotten about that gap. 'Hey.'

'Er, hey,' I echo, still in shock. 'How's it going?'

'It's okay, it's good. So your family still runs this place, huh?'

'Yeah, we do, we're here.'

She walks around to my side of the counter and drags me into a hug. Her hair smells of coconut and her Cons tread on mine. It's over in a second. When she leans back against the counter, her top rises up above the belt looped through her jeans, revealing a sliver of caramel skin. Real olive brown, not the usual Durnan tandoori fake tan. The top is so stretched it looks like she's jammed herself into a younger sister's clothes, but I know she's an only child.

'It's been ages,' I manage to add. 'What's doing with you?'

Her fingertips drum the counter. Her nails are blue, chipped, chewed down. 'Good question. This and that, I suppose. Nothing to tell.'

'Nothing to tell after five years?' I pause, then rush in with, 'It's gotta be that long, yeah?'

Her bottom lip quivers, so fast I almost miss it. 'Five years, huh? There you go.'

'I think it is.'

I know it is. I wait for her to say something, anything, about that day. I wonder if I should — one of us should — but before I can, she frames my face with her fingers, sizing me up.

'You look exactly the same,' she says. 'It's blowing my mind.'

I snort, kinda embarrassed, kinda annoyed. I've still got the pimples, but who doesn't? Surely I've grown up a bit in her eyes? Surely I look just a *bit* better? Taller, at least.

19

'Well,' she concedes with a smile, as though she's read my mind, looking me up and down again through those lashes, 'maybe you've changed … a little.'

'Well … you look … I don't know …' The words spurt out in staccato bursts. Not sure why. I was never tongue-tied around her.

'Here we go. Hit me with it.'

'Different,' I say, voice cracking. I hope she doesn't notice, but she usually noticed everything, especially the stuff you didn't want her to. If you had a booger hanging out of your nose, Layla wouldn't just notice it — she'd notice it and point it out in front of everyone.

'I look *different*?' she says. 'Smooth, as always, although I guess you're not wrong.' She points to her hair like it's the only change. I don't mention the skinny jeans or the red staining her lips. 'You look like you've seen a ghost. It's just me, dude — former neighbour extraordinaire, not to mention head nurse in Doctors and Nurses.'

'Jesus. Don't remind me.'

'That I've seen you naked?' Her lips pucker as she struggles to hold in a laugh. 'Back then barely counted. Not like seeing each other naked now. Hypothetically, of course.'

'Of course.' She's not blushing, but heat spreads over my cheeks and down my neck. I gulp. 'So you're really back?'

I sound like a moron but I never thought I'd see Layla Montgomery again. Never even imagined it. Not when they've been off having mysterious adventures for half a decade.

'Just crashing at a share house,' she says. 'You wouldn't know them. I'm back, just not … back-back.'

Her voice trails off, as though that explains everything. It doesn't explain anything, especially why she's not staying with her dad. Mum told me he moved back to Durnan with a new girlfriend last year. I kinda get the vagueness though. Living in this town comes with a disclaimer, an in-case-of-emergency exit strategy, 'cos it's the plan B, maybe the plan C, never the plan A.

'Anyway, how's my boy Trenticles?' she asks. 'And your parents? I guess it's been five years since I've seen them too.'

'They're all the same really … although Dad's like a wannabe Tony Robbins these days.'

Layla laughs. 'Whaddya mean?'

'Don't ask. Trust me.'

'Sounds grim.' She pauses. 'And our treehouse? I miss it.'

Our treehouse. I thought she would've forgotten. 'Um, it's still there, but I heard the Perkinses are knocking the tree down.'

'They can't do that!'

'They want a pool.'

'Okay, they *can* … but they shouldn't. I'm egging their house.'

Now it's my turn to laugh. 'You're back five minutes and … You know what, you're the one who's exactly the same.'

'Yeah?' she says, tucking her hair behind her ears. 'Maybe I'll egg your face.'

'Maybe you will.' I smirk. 'Why are you even here? Like, *here*? After a book?'

'Nah, not really. Don't read much any more.'

I remember how Layla used to fill her schoolbag with so many books her shoulders ached. She'd lend them to me, I'd forget to return them to the library, the cycle continued.

'Er, wait, forget what I just said ...' She dumps her handbag on the counter to empty out the contents — mints, sunglasses, wallet, loose teabags, a notebook, tissues — before shoving a crumpled sheet of paper into my hand. 'I'm looking for work.'

'For real? Here?'

I read the first few lines of her CV: four and a half months at a bakery in Cooma. Two months stacking shelves at a supermarket in Berry. Three weeks delivering junk mail in Campbelltown. Five days at a pet shelter in Port Macquarie. I've had pimples more committed than her.

'Yeah. Books. Reading. Words. I can't get enough.'

I raise an eyebrow.

'Fine.' She sighs. 'No-one's hiring. This place is my second-last stop — before Joe's.'

'The new charcoal-chicken joint? Dire.'

'You're telling me.'

'Sorry, dude, hiring freeze. Probably 'cos Dad's got me and Trent for personal slaves.'

Layla groans. 'I can't believe you're forcing me to go to Joe's. You might almost be as bad as this town, Milo Dark.'

I grin, folding up her CV. 'Not at all new information.'

Jingle, jingle, jingle. The front door swings open. A solid guy ambles in, smacking gum around in his mouth. He's about Trent's age, maybe older, but I can't quite place him.

'Babe,' he says, twirling car keys in his hand. 'Ya ready?'

'Kurt!' she almost hisses. 'What are you doing?'

'Can we get going?' He spots me standing there like a dork. 'Hey.'

I give a little nod. 'Hey.'

Layla stays glued to the spot. 'Just give me a sec.'

'Babe, my mates are bugging me. Two minutes or I've gotta leave without ya. Sorry, but I can't keep them waiting, you know that,' he adds, storming out the door.

'But it's my friggin' car!' she shouts after him. She swivels back to me, avoiding eye contact, her cheeks flushed.

'He seems nice,' I say, hoping it doesn't sound as weak as it feels.

'Don't. Don't even …'

'Did he go to Durnan High?'

'Yeah, few years above us and he left early — sparkie apprenticeship. Does odds and ends now. Stuff like that. We met a while back … anyway, I should go,' she says, cutting herself off as though she's trying to stop me from asking anything else. 'Say hi to your fam from me.' She pauses. 'Or maybe that's too weird, it has been ages …'

As she hovers in the doorway, hands resting behind her on the glass, she looks like she's going to say something significant, like the words are so big and important they're fizzing up in her mouth.

'I, ah … bye, I guess.'

Maybe not.

'Yeah, bye.'

I manage to get the words out just before the door swings closed behind her. She's gone. In and out of my life, just like that.

Ten bucks says I never see Layla Montgomery again.

* * *

Milo: *Hey Layla, sorry for the late msg. Got your number from the CV. You left your sunnies at the shop*
Milo: *It's Milo Dark by the way*

Layla

Music pulsates through the house. My bedroom walls hum with vibrations and the floorboards shake. I imagine Kurt and our housemates thrashing around in the lounge room. The furniture'll be pushed to one side to create a dance floor, their hair'll be damp and the room'll reek of sweat. It's Saturday night so they'll be happy — well, happy enough to forget everything in their lives that's making them unhappy — and they'll keep telling each other they haven't been *this* happy in ages. Kurt'll be pounding the ground with his feet and punching the air with his fists and he'll have forgotten why we even fought this afternoon. Ryan'll be sucking on a homemade bong, probably in the laundry so he doesn't have to share it with the others. Jay and Mel will be feeling each other up on the balcony and wondering when Kurt's going to come in and make up with me so they can get some privacy.

I burrow down deeper into the mattress and jam in my earphones, but it's not enough to block out the noise. I pull the sheet over my head a little tighter.

My phone buzzes. Two unread messages. Both from Milo.

Before this afternoon, he was a discoloured memory with blurred edges and a washed-out palette. Yet five minutes with him and everything came back to me in an instant. I remember riding our bikes around the river until our thighs ached, and sprinting across grass riddled with bindis to catch the Mr Whippy van. He had hair the colour of dust and dirt and once let me dye it royal blue for the athletics carnival. He was my partner-in-crime in convincing the kids across the road that a witch lived in the rundown double-storey house around the corner. When I argued with Mum and Dad, sometimes it was about how long I could stay up 'cos Milo was a special guest and, in my opinion, I shouldn't have to sleep at all when he was visiting from next door.

I reread his messages.

Milo doesn't know it — there's no way he can — but one look at his face also awakened a million memories of Mum. Memories I've spent five years trying to block out. Like how when we were busted playing Doctors and Nurses, Mum sent Milo home and gave me an educational talk so detailed I became the go-to girl in the playground whenever someone whispered, 'Where do babies come from?' How when I beat him at ping-pong, Mum hollered from the sidelines as though I'd taken out gold at the Olympics.

The last time I saw him was at Mum's funeral. He was hiding behind Trent as they shuffled down the aisle out of the church with its light grey walls and dark grey carpet. Everything was grey and drab that day.

Everything except our clothes.

Mum hated black, so her closest friends requested everyone wear colour to the service. The bigger and bolder the better. Dad forgot, so Jen, Milo's mum, took off her lime-green shawl and wrapped it around his shoulders to hide his wrinkled charcoal suit.

At Mum's request in her will, we also had to suffer Mr Agiostratitis struggling through Europe's *The Final Countdown* on the organ. I thought his vocal cords might snap as he squeaked and squawked for the higher notes. I reckon I even saw Dad, who was almost crumpled over next to me in the front row, hide a smile during that. Mum would've loved the sight of the stickybeaks and snobs turning up their noses at her unorthodox super-eighties' pop selection too. Friggin' loved it.

I read over Milo's unnecessary apology laced through his texts. I want my sunglasses, I do, but I don't know if I can see him again now that my chest aches a little more than it did yesterday. It's not his fault that he makes me feel like this — that he's triggered this. It's all so intertwined, so smudged together. But me and Milo aren't ten any more. His ear isn't pressed up against my bathroom door while he waits to hear from Mum if my stomach has stopped hurting from eating too much ice-cream so I can go to the skate park with him. He can't make me feel better by letting me paint his toenails with her purple nail polish, or daring me to jump from the top tower at the pool while Mum takes photos from the grass below, even though he's too scared to do it himself.

He has his own life now, his own mess to wade through. Some things are the way they are, no matter how much you wish they weren't.

I delete the messages.

I can always buy new sunnies.

* * *

The floorboards creak as Kurt tiptoes to the bed. He snuggles next to me, T-shirt damp with sweat, his hand finding mine.

'You awake, babe?'

'Yeah.'

'We missed ya out there.' He doesn't wait for a response. 'I know I blew up at ya before. Sorry, babe. This whole work sitch's got me stressed. I don't wanna stuff it up, ya know?'

I clear my throat, unsure how to reply.

Sparkie jobs seem to have dried up in Durnan, but he's not talking about that kind of work. He's talking about the other thing. The thing I can't even say out loud 'cos it's so unlike anything I used to be that I don't even know how I ended up here. Kurt and I are pretty broke — the kind of broke that's got us eating noodles every night and diving for stray gold coins on the ground — so he's been dealing on the side. 'Just a little pot,' he told me in a calm, cool voice, like it's not totally breaking the law. 'Just for a little bit 'til we're set up.'

I believed him too, at first. Yet now he's getting stressed about it. Now he's calling it work. Like it's natural to be doing this. Like I should be alright with it. But the secret's heavy on my shoulders.

Kurt raises an eyebrow, sensing my discomfort. 'It won't be for much longer. Promise. And it brings in money, doesn't it?'

I shrug.

'You know it does. Easy money too, no big deal. My folks can't spare a cent — they're still up to their eyeballs in Temora — and one of us has to keep things afloat. Right now, that's me.'

'*Hey*. I'm trying. This town is *hard*.'

'Take a breath, yeah? I didn't force ya to come here. Ya followed me, babe, and it's adding extra pressure on me. Don't forget that.'

My jaw tightens at the mention of pressure. I had nowhere else to go. No choice.

When your dad drags you through nine high schools in five years, covering almost every kilometre of New South Wales from Albury to Lismore, you don't exactly end up with mates you can count on — just a stack of almost-strangers telling you to, 'Follow me!' and, 'Add me as a friend!' on social media. I deleted any trace of my online self after the fourth school. Most people didn't even bother wishing me happy birthday anyway. Dad's final move was halfway through last year — back to Durnan, so he and his girlfriend, Shirin, could rent a house before he headed off to the mines. Somehow, he was content to live back here again. He's discovered peace, but he hasn't taught me how to find it.

When Dad asked me to join them and return to Durnan High — Milo's school, *Mum's* old school — to finish Year 12, I refused. I couldn't go back. Not when I've spent all these years running from everything to do with her. I've been an expert at staying away. I couldn't handle the thought of looking everyone in the eye. My old friends. My old teachers. People who used to believe I'd go on to do great things — whatever that means now — or at least go on to do more than this. More than this life.

But most of all, I couldn't face the idea of returning to Durnan High without Mum. She'd walked every hallway of that school.

I begged Dad to stay with me in Sydney, but he wouldn't listen. Or maybe he couldn't bear to dredge up all the reasons he'd left Durnan in the first place. He just packed up our stuff and went without me; and left me his old bomb of a sedan — something to ease his mind.

My cousin let me sleep on his couch for a while, so I never used the word 'homeless', or even thought about it like that — I was so relieved I wasn't sleeping in the car like I've seen people do on the news — but I didn't have a home. I didn't have a fixed address where people could send me mail. I didn't have a wardrobe to hang my clothes in, or a favourite chair at the dinner table. We didn't even have a dinner table — we ate curried egg toasties on our laps in front of a tiny old TV that didn't get all the channels. And I didn't have a key, so I'd wait on the doorstep until my cousin or his girlfriend got home from uni to let me in.

After a while, I started cutting school because I was the girl without a mum *or* dad and no-one let me forget it. Girls would say, 'Hey, Layla, where's ya mum?' or mutter, 'Little orphan Layla' behind me in the canteen line to see how long it'd take me to crack. And I always cracked, swearing or slapping or shoving just as a teacher walked around the corner. I swear they timed it like that. The girls'd get a warning, I'd get detention.

I dropped out of Year 12 with four months to go. It was hard to care about writing essays or handing in assignments on time when half my days were spent missing my dad, and the other half were spent hating him for leaving me.

My cousin's girlfriend got sick of me being there all the time without chipping in, so the couch-surfing continued. I stayed on my cousin's friend's couch for a few weeks. Then his girlfriend's couch for a week. When that didn't work out, I was onto *her* friend's couch — which was also Kurt's couch. A boy from home, of all the possibilities. Turns out Durnan's a hard town to outrun, even when you're hundreds of kilometres away, because everyone seems to know someone from that little place on the map. And before long I was creeping into Kurt's room to whisper under the covers with him once his housemate was asleep.

Kurt left Durnan a few years ago. He grew up on the other side of town — the wrong side, depending on who you ask — so our lives never overlapped as kids. He told me he'd never go back, and for that reason he was the perfect escape. He was also spontaneous and free, a place to stay and someone to talk to, and no-one stuck by me like he did. But none of that mattered as much as the fact that he didn't have what everyone else from my past had: history. Then he announced his plan to move in with his mate Ryan and sort out sparkie work in Durnan, and the cracks formed. My choices felt non-existent. I couldn't afford to stay in Sydney alone, so I followed him and he let me. Before then, I'd never followed anyone.

But a lot of things are different from before. Now *I'm* on the wrong side.

'Babe,' Kurt says, snapping me back, 'that came out wrong. Ya know I want ya here.' He sighs. 'I've gotta ask again: have ya reached out to your dad or step-mum? Maybe we need to borrow some cash, just to get another top-up since Chrissie, ya know? Then we can do this right. They said they'd —'

'I know what they said, but they're not made of money. And they're not married.'

'Huh?'

'She's not my step-mum. She's just ... Shirin. And no, I can't call them. I won't.'

Boxing Day with Dad and Shirin was a nightmare. I endured two hours of pushing soggy beans and burnt potatoes around my plate while attempting to duck questions I didn't have answers to. Why I dropped out of school before sitting the exams, living with a boy they barely knew, waiting until late on Christmas Day to tell them I'd moved back to Durnan in mid-December, having zero idea of what to do next — and all before Shirin served up the pav and cream. I stopped listening when they suggested repeating Year 12.

The part that stung most was hearing all this from the man who'd bailed on me. Who'd cocooned himself in grief after Mum's death, pushing everyone away. Dad dissolved into a shadow, losing himself in anything that didn't involve her. That counted me out — I looked too much like her. The same nose, frizzy mahogany-brown hair, olive skin.

Kurt sighs again, just in case I missed his annoyance that I won't call Dad to stick my hand out for money.

'It was just an idea,' he says, grabbing his pillow and standing up. 'I'm gonna sleep on the couch, babe. You're way too on edge.'

I sit up. Anger throbs in my chest, sharp and hot. 'Yeah? Well, stop calling them "mates" like you mean something to them.'

He stops, his frame filling the doorway. 'What?'

'The customers. You called them "mates" today.'

'So?'

'They don't care about you — only if your pot's any good.' It's out there now. I've said it.

He scoffs. 'Have ya forgotten how we got together?'

'Once. *Barely once.* And I liked you.'

'Yeah, you did.'

A moment of stillness.

Kurt comes back to bed and wraps his arm around me. I let him. The tension evaporates, like someone's pricked the air with a pin.

'By the way, I remember,' he adds, kissing the base of my neck. 'I know what's really going on. Five years tomorrow, right? I know ya think I've forgotten, but I haven't.'

I snuggle into him. He's forgotten my birthday and my phone number, but when it comes to Mum he never does.

'I reckon you should go,' he continues. 'Don't people talk about "getting closure" or something?'

Here we go again. The urge to put me back together. I wonder whether I have a *Fix Me* sign taped to my back.

'It won't help her come back. What's the point?'

'C'mon, we're in Durnan.'

I know what he's really saying. *The cemetery is barely fifteen blocks away. We're that close we can probably see it if we get up on the roof. What are you waiting for?*

'I've seen photos,' I say. 'Looks the same as the hundreds of other graves — depressing.'

'Yeah, but it's hers.'

That sinks in as Kurt waffles on about visiting the grave in the morning so we can go to brunch together afterwards.

'Why would I *want* to go?' My words are soaked in frustration. 'Why would I want to imagine her body, her mouth, her hair covered in dirt?'

'Lay, shit, stop that.'

'Why would I put myself through it?' I ask, overpowered by a raging blackness. This is what happens when I remember. It's why I don't want to remember. 'No-one seems to get that I have no choice but to live without her, yet everyone keeps trying to make me look back. She's gone. Stuff brunch.'

'We don't have to go, not if ya don't want to ... it's fine.' He says it in a way that suggests it's not fine. 'And you're right — stuff brunch. Stuff bacon and eggs. And sausages.'

'And pancakes.' It sounds so ridiculous that I don't know whether to burst into tears or crack up laughing. 'And stupid little muffins. They never have enough blueberries in them.'

'And corn fritters. Stuff corn fritters.'

'No, you love those things.' By now my body's aching with exhaustion. 'I think I need an exorcism.'

'Go to sleep, babe. It'll be better tomorrow.'

There's a deafening pause, like he's remembered all over again that tomorrow is *the* day.

A warm orange light floods one corner of the room. The bedside lamp is on, the sheets are crumpled and Kurt is out of bed. I watch him as he walks to the two-metre-wide whiteboard we've hung on the wall and scribbles the words *And stuff omelettes*.

The whiteboard is our way of stitching things up. Kurt started it with a post-it note scribbled with a cartoon version of him holding a bunch of flowers, then we progressed to a shared notebook, which we filled with so many messages and drawings that we splurged on the whiteboard when we arrived in Durnan.

He crawls back into bed and my body feels heavy, like I'm being pulled down into the mattress. I wait for him to drift off before I close my eyes to shut out the black.

Layla

Even from the car park I can see the rose bushes in bloom at the Durnan Lawn Cemetery. Pinks and reds and whites dance alongside the manicured grass, which is the same shade as the rows of eucalyptus trees lining the edges. If I didn't know better, I'd think it was a normal garden — the kind where people get wedding photos taken or have their first kiss. Not the kind where graves are dug and people are buried, remembered, forgotten.

My right boot kicks at the gravel in the car park, my right hand tightens around a bunch of wilting gerberas. Mum hated gerberas, but the florist kept probing me with questions about 'the special someone' getting the flowers, so I grabbed the closest bunch, threw some money at her and ran out of the shop without waiting for my change. The whole morning's been a last-minute decision; an impulsive effort to wipe the eternal look of concern off Kurt's face.

'Coming?' Kurt asks, gesturing to the cemetery's front entrance.

He's wearing his fanciest outfit — a crushed jacket, pants that need the hem taken down, a white shirt and a stripy tie that neither of us knows how to do up properly. I'm in boots and a dress I've worn a million times to special occasions — Christmases, presentation nights, birthday dinners. Now it's the cemetery dress. I wish I was wearing something I like less so I could toss it in the bin afterwards.

'Ready?'

Kurt tries again, but my feet won't budge. When I announced over a cold piece of toast that morning that I'd changed my mind, I didn't imagine this. I didn't think it could feel so ordinary. The sun is out, toasting our skin — a usual Durnan February afternoon. Birds dance in a fountain just metres from the entrance, while flies buzz near my nose and seek refuge on the back of Kurt's jacket. It's the weekend, so less than a kilometre away kids are probably bellyflopping into the Durnan River, floating on tyres in the water and dangling from the rope swing. It's all so summery and normal in every way except one. Today is the day I'm visiting Mum's grave for the first time.

I dawdle behind Kurt to the entrance and he slows down so we can walk in together. I drag my feet some more. The distance between us widens as the cemetery looms ahead — rows and rows of dead parents, grandparents, sweethearts, children.

'Screw this. What's another year.' I spin on my heel and stride back towards the car.

Kurt yells for me to wait up, but I don't turn around. Instead, I pick up the pace. Blisters burn my ankles as my boots crunch on the gravel. I'm running, sprinting, I don't ever want to stop moving.

Out of the corner of my eye, I spot a garbage bin overflowing with flowers, garden clippings and coffee cups. I toss the gerberas in, pushing them down so they're blended into the rest of the rubbish.

Mum would've hated them anyway.

* * *

Kurt's phone buzzes for a third time. He glances at the screen. 'It's a mate,' he tells me. It's usually a mate.

The car engine is off but his fingers stay wrapped around the wheel. We haven't left the cemetery, but the visit is over; it's just that neither of us has called it.

I elbow him from the passenger seat. 'Text them back.'

'Yeah right. Not after that.'

He thinks I'm losing it. Maybe I am.

'Listen for a sec,' I say, hoping to distract him. 'I can't eat another packet of noodles for dinner. We need money, and if it's easy like you say, then maybe …' I shrug. 'I dunno … maybe it's what needs to happen while we keep looking for other work.'

Maybe. I don't know any more.

Kurt's phone rings. I snatch it from him and answer it. Kurt swears and tries to take it back from me, but I pull away so he can't reach.

'All good,' I say into it. 'Kyla, is it? He'll be right there.' I give Kurt a thumbs-up. 'Yeah, text him the address if he doesn't already have it. Easy. Done.'

I pass him the phone.

'What was that?'

I turn on the radio. 'Just doing your job.'

Kurt turns it off. 'Ya hate it though.'

I don't disagree.

'Lay ... are ya even gonna acknowledge what happened before?'

I clear my throat. 'I'm fine. Hey, can you drop me in town before you do your thing? I think I want to window-shop for a bit.'

'Didn't a counsellor say ya should talk about this sorta stuff?'

'We are talking. And that counsellor was the one who needed her head checked.'

I only got two sessions in before Dad dragged us away from Durnan. After that, it was like school: we never stayed anywhere long enough for me to settle in, and I got tired of telling my story to new doctors. Besides, after the first few towns, Dad forgot to chase it up and I wasn't about to remind him.

'I'm serious,' Kurt says in the most serious voice he can muster. 'I reckon ya should try talking about it with someone again. With me even.'

I don't bother telling him that sometimes there isn't anything to say. He talked over me the last time I tried explaining it feels like everyone's forcing me me to tick off all the right grief boxes.

He chews his bottom lip. 'I just ... I reckon you're making a mistake. She's right there.' He points towards the graves. 'Literally there. You're so close.'

His words sting every inch of me, but I'm too exhausted to fight back today. If he can't get that she's *not* there, not in the way I need, then there's no point.

'Anyway,' I say, almost holding in my breath to try to keep it together, 'let's stop at home so I can change out of this stupid dress.'

As we drive off, I don't look back towards the graves, not even for a second.

Milo

It takes Sal fourteen minutes and twenty-five seconds of talking about lectures, bar nights and first-year hazing before she admits she's cancelling her weekend in Durnan. She takes twice as many words as she needs to get it out, which somehow makes it worse.

'You're angry, aren't you?' she says. 'You haven't said anything for like a minute.'

'No, I'm not, it's just … I mean … it's kinda been planned for ages.' The aim is to sound chilled, to be the relaxed, cool boyfriend, but there's a sharpness to my tone.

It's a Sunday afternoon, but it no longer feels like the time for customers, so I hang the *Back in five minutes* sign on the door, then head for the children's picture books section, which is at the far end of the shop, and plonk down on the floor. My back presses against the hard shelves, the corners of the books digging into my skin.

'I was just keen to hang, that's all.'

Keen to see a familiar face that isn't Trent's or Mum's or Dad's. Basically anyone who doesn't live at 58 Stone

Street, Durnan, New South Wales, Australia, The World, The Universe.

'I know, I'm sorry. I was too.' I imagine Sal twirling her ponytail as she says this. She always does it when she's freaked about conflict. 'But it's such a whirlwind here. Classes are picking up, there's assignments and there's so much other stuff going on. Ressies is hectic, and for the first time I feel — and this'll make me sound like a loser — that people here like me. They *want* to be my friend.'

'You've always had mates. Heaps.'

'I can't explain it then. Things feel different.'

Tell me about it. Somehow things feel different for me too, even though everything here is still the same. Everything except the people.

'Okay ...' I say.

'You *are* angry.'

'Nah, I'm ... I'm cool.' I force a fake laugh. I don't want to be the guy who wrecks her life just 'cos I stayed. It's my own stupid fault, not hers. 'All good.'

'Oh, thank you, thank you. Thank you, Milo.'

She believes me. Or maybe she hears what she wants to hear. I can't tell the difference over the phone.

'I can't be that girl who everyone stops inviting to stuff 'cos she's bailed so many times. That would be tragic. We'll reschedule, promise. And I'll make it up to you.' She lowers her voice. 'Like, *really* make it up to you.'

I jolt upright. 'Yeah?' Shrieks of laughter flood the phone line. 'Sal?' Rustling. Girls whispering. More laughter. 'You there?'

'I have to go.' She squeaks out the words through a fit of giggles.

'What?'

'Like right now. The boys have water bombs and — ahhh! We're under attack!'

'Okay, wanna Skype soon?'

She's already hung up.

When I finally get up to take the sign off the door, there's someone sitting on the front steps. For a moment, I don't recognise Layla. She's all lanky legs and arms, and her streaked yellow mop is pulled into a knot at the base of her neck. It looks so loose that if she were to grin too hard it might unravel. Not that's she grinning. So much for never seeing her again. Now I'm seeing her on the anniversary of her mum's funeral.

I open the door. 'Hey.'

'Hey.' She jumps to her feet and points to the sign. 'That was more than five minutes.'

'Sorry. Work stuff.' My mind races, trying to decode why she's here. 'Oh! The sunnies, yeah?'

'Yeah.' She passes me a foam cup of hot chocolate. 'This is for you — to say thanks for texting. Sorry I didn't write back. There's two marshmallows in there, by the way.'

'Ah, sweet, thanks,' I say, taking the drink, stunned she remembers how her mum used to make them for me. I used to sneak over to Layla's for dessert after dinner 'cos Mum's queen of the anti-sugar brigade. We were eventually busted, but that didn't stop Layla — she'd just pass me choccie frogs through a hole in our adjoining fence. 'You didn't have to do this.'

'Sure I did,' she says with a soft smile. 'I got it from the café next to the gelato shop on the main street. I forgot how cheap stuff is here. Sidenote: can't believe Durnan's got gelato. 'Bout time.'

'Just think, in another fifty years we might even get decent wi-fi.'

I take a sip and splutter as the hot chocolate scalds my tongue and burns my throat.

Layla steps closer. 'You okay?'

'Holy ... yep ... yep, fine, all fine,' I choke out. 'Come in.'

'Alright.' Layla bends down to tuck her jeans deeper into scuffed boots. 'After you.'

We head inside, Layla dawdling behind me. She's quieter today. Everything about her points downwards.

'How are you anyway?' she asks. 'Living the dream?'

'Always. It's a rock-star life.' I gesture around the empty store. 'More like, I'm killing time before I kill myself.'

It's a bomb of a joke, but the words are already out. I *definitely* didn't plan to bring up death with Layla, especially not today. She doesn't seem upset, but it's been five years and I forget the signs so I can't be sure.

'Sorry,' I add, 'that was kinda messed up.'

She hoists herself up onto the counter, legs dangling above the carpet. 'You *have* been living in Durnan this whole time so I'll forgive you. Besides, I feel about the same. Maybe we could do it together? End the pain now.'

'*Dude,*' I say, as I rifle through the lost-and-found box for her glasses, '*that's* messed up.'

'I'm kidding,' she says with a shrug. 'Relax. So … why *are* you still here? I guess I always imagined you going off to uni or taking on the world somehow. You were such a brain at school.'

'Shut up, you were.' I laugh, before noticing her eyes dart away for a second. The walls are back. 'Just can't decide what's next, I suppose.' I shrug. 'Any ideas?'

'I was going to ask you the same thing. Year 12 wasn't exactly my friend.'

'Serious?'

Layla was always so smart. The type who could get away with barely studying then still kick everyone's bums in the exams. Teachers used to feed her extra homework to try to challenge her, reminding her she could be anything she wanted to be when she grew up, but she'd shrug it off, never wanting to stand out in that way or be seen as different.

'Serious. Anyway, what else, what else?' she asks, shutting down any hope of her elaborating on her final year. 'Going out with anyone, stud muffin? And imaginary girlfriends don't count.'

I laugh. 'Yeah, got myself a real one.'

'No way.'

'I know, right? Ever have a class with Sal — Sally Patterson?'

'I know the name, I think.'

'Well, she's in Canberra now.'

46

'But you're not?'

'Clearly not.'

'Interesting. Maybe you should've gone with her. Shaken the cobwebs off this stale little life.'

Ouch. For weeks I've been telling anyone with an eardrum how much things suck right now, but hearing it from her is brutal. Sometimes you don't want to hear the truth when living it is hard enough.

'Yeah, maybe,' I say. 'Who knows? Not me … and it's not like you really know me. Not any more.'

It sounds harsher out loud than it did in my head. I just meant it as a fact. She doesn't know that I topped chemistry last year, or kissed Leisel Multari under the school jacaranda tree in Year 8 as a dare, or that I eat avocado all the time now even though I used to hate it when we were kids. And I don't know anything about the last five years of her life. But still, I regret letting the words slip out. If only life came with a prepared script.

'I've known you since you were in nappies and that counts for something.' Her mouth curves into a crooked smile. 'Stinky poopy nappies.'

'Would you believe I *don't* need nappies any more?'

'Excellent. Knew you had it in you.'

'Had to happen sometime.' I grin. 'Things change.'

'Sometimes, for sure,' she says, jumping off the counter and landing on the carpet with a thud. 'But sometimes they stay the same.'

My fingers find the sunnies and I hand them over. 'They're pretty smudged, but I can clean —'

'They're fine.' She sits them on her head. 'I should go. You've probably got more work stuff.'

'Yeah. Work stuff.'

'So ... ah ... bye for real this time, I guess.'

'Bye for real.'

Her hand is on the door handle when I say the thing I was too scared to say yesterday, and too surprised to say when I saw her body arched over on the steps today. 'Lay ... about your mum ...'

I'm in it now.

She freezes, fingers still curled around the metal.

'I know what today is and ... well, I wanted you to know I'm ... I'm sorry. I think Mum sent a card to your dad again, she usually does, but ... ah, if you're not staying with him this year, then ... well ... we're thinking of you.'

Layla stares at the ground. Her expression is impossible to read.

'I'm here too, is what I mean. You know, if you need anything. You probably don't ... but if you do.'

I hold my breath, silently berating myself for being such a bumbling idiot. Maybe in the past five years Layla's found a way to forget the anniversary of her mum's death and I've brought it up at the crappiest time on the crappiest day, reminding her of the crappiest parts of it all over again. Jesus.

She looks up, watery chocolate eyes locking with mine, and smiles the smallest of smiles. 'Thanks, MD.'

Layla

I arrived at The Little Bookshop in a daze, glassy-eyed, hot chocolates in hand, not knowing what led me here. It's not just the sunnies, despite what I told Milo, despite them being back in my bag. There was an ache, a feeling tugging at my heart, after I bailed from the cemetery. I needed something to tie me to her again, something other than her gravestone, something other than death. Mum already trickles in and out of my life, but here, today, around him, she almost feels real again. Like I could ride my bike to our old house, wave goodbye to Milo as he dumps his in the driveway, and head inside to find Mum cooking spaghetti in her PJs.

No-one else in my life right now even knows her. Not Kurt. Not Ryan. Not Jay or Mel. Milo is the link, the direct line to the best of the before. Only Milo knows her.

Knew her.

Friggin' hell.

Maybe I shouldn't have come.

Milo's still rambling sweet things so I squeeze out a tiny smile. Then I blurt out that I went to the cemetery and suddenly everything is on fast-forward. Before he can reply, I spin on my heel and walk deep into the store. My lip is shaking a little, but I know if I count to ten I can cap the tears before he sees them. His feet thump behind me as we plait our way through the aisles past wide shelves of books. I end up counting all the way to nineteen and only stop walking when I hit the back wall of the shop.

'Okay, I'm sorry,' I say, turning to face him. 'I'm making this weird. Forget I said anything. Please forget.'

'Lay, I know we haven't seen each other in ages so tell me to disappear, but ... you can still say anything to me.'

I nod. At least he doesn't have the pitying *that-poor-girl* look that I'm so used to seeing from everyone. Still, my chest feels tighter than usual, like someone is stretching the skin around to the back of my body like clingwrap. I want to tell him thank you, but instead I tell him I couldn't do it today. He cocks his head to one side, confused, waiting for me to explain.

'I was there, like two hundred metres away, probably less. My feet couldn't do it. *I* couldn't do it.'

Milo's face softens. His hand edges closer to mine, like he's contemplating whether he should pat me on the back or hold my hand. Whether he should comfort me. He doesn't do either, just tells me he probably couldn't do it either and that I was brave to go to the cemetery. No-one's called me brave in ages.

After that, more words spill out. Kurt pushing me to see her gravestone. The sad little gerberas. The rows of plaques marking death. I stumble over the last part and he notices. This time he wraps an arm around me. It's awkward, like he's learning to use his limbs for the first time, but I appreciate it. Especially the gentle squeeze before he pulls away. I think his breath catches but I'm not sure.

'You did good,' he says. 'I reckon she'd be proud.'

'Doubt that.' I sigh. 'So, that's me. That's my secret.'

'Consider it vaulted.'

I turn to face him. 'This feels uneven.'

He raises an eyebrow. 'I've got nothing.'

'What about your girlfriend? Or your top-secret "work stuff"?'

'Ah, that.' He smirks. 'Oh, it's juicy. *Not*. My girlfriend bailed on a trip to see me.'

'*No.*'

'Have I mentioned long-distance is *awesome*?' I stare at him until he laughs. 'Stop it. I'll live.'

'Fine, I'll say it: people are the worst. It's okay though. One day, dogs will rule the planet and the world will be wonderful.'

'Bring it on.'

Our laughter rings through the shop.

Milo catches me running my fingers over the spines of the autobiographies next to me. 'You really don't read any more? I don't believe you.'

He's staring at me like I have a second set of ears sprouting from my head.

Damn. Never should have said that yesterday.

'Just busy, I guess. It's not that I don't like books, I do. I just … well, look, I love *The Very Hungry Caterpillar*,' I say, as though that'll squash the conversation. Of course it only leads to more questions.

A laugh slips out. 'You mean that kiddie book?'

'Yeah. So?'

I wonder if my eyes look as wild as I suddenly feel.

'It can't be the *one* book you like. It's a classic, but … that's it? The one book you still like?'

'No, but … it was sorta special. Knew it word for word back then.' *Then.* I've said too much. Why do I keep saying so much around him? I pause, considering whether to say the next part. 'Guess 'cos Mum used to read it with me before bed.'

'Oh.' Milo's voice cracks. 'Shit. Sorry, Lay.'

God. Mum's flooded in again, engulfing everything, and I can't seem to stop it. But with Milo, unlike everyone else, I don't seem to want to stop it.

I convince him it's fine, speaking fast in the hope it reassures him. My voice trails off, so I ask if he's ready for a related fact. Anything to steer the conversation in a way that'll make him smile again.

He nods. 'Always.'

'Mum told me I *was* a butterfly once, when I was small … well, that I was almost a butterfly, just like the caterpillar in the book.' I pause, realising I haven't thought of this story in months. Maybe longer. 'Have I told you that before?'

'I don't know … it's kinda familiar. Did you believe her?'

'Well, yeah, 'cos clearly I sucked at science back then. Basically, I came home from school crying one day and she was all, "Wait, baby girl, wait and see. You're amazing but you don't know it yet. One day you're gonna transform into a you that's *so* wonderful that life will never be the same again."'

'Damn.'

'Heavy, right? She always believed I was something. I asked her how she knew, and she whispered in the quietest voice she could — which really wasn't quiet at all, because she was incapable of being quiet — "It's a secret between the butterflies."'

'I can imagine her saying that.' There's a softness to Milo's voice; a whisper on the tip of each word that's so slight it's almost invisible.

'Now all I can think is, stuff that secret woman. When's the metamorphosis coming, you know? Where's this wonderful me?'

'Tell me when you find out,' he says. 'Not that there's a rush for me. Clearly I'm living my best life already.'

'We're *hashtag blessed* or whatever, right?'

He catches himself grinning, then clears his throat. 'I know this is nothing compared to what you're feeling, but, just so you know, I miss her as well. The whole town does, I reckon. She was a real legend.'

'Yeah, she was.' I suck in a breath and check the time on my phone. 'Anyway … I should head. Thanks for the sunnies, and, ah, I hope things get easier with your girlfriend … Sal, right?'

'Yeah. That's her.'

'Visit her, dude. Do it.'

'Yes, boss.' He nods. 'I'll see ya.'

'See ya round.'

Layla

'Layla, someone's here to see you!' Ryan yells.

'Who?' I ask from the couch in our lounge room. No-one knows my new address. Not Milo, not even Dad.

'It's a lady,' he calls out again. 'Shareen someone.'

Shirin. How did she find me? It's not that I'm hiding from her or Dad, not really; I'm just not looking for them. Not yet. Not before I've had a chance to sort a few things out. Mainly my head. And a job. And a new place. And my relationship. Fine, until I've sorted every single part of my life out.

Pizza boxes litter the coffee table. There's a sock lying over the armchair and the room stinks of something indescribably bad. Not that I'm any better. My T-shirt has a toothpaste stain and holes down the side, and Kurt's shorts hang loose on my hips. I'm not even wearing a bra.

I kick a pair of sneakers out of the way before walking to the door, arms crossed over my chest. Shirin scoops me into a hug before 'Hey' even escapes my mouth. She never gives any warning before squashing me against her body. Her hair is as jet-black and frizzy as ever and her hoop earrings seem to have tripled in size. The smell of whichever essential oils she's slathered on clings to the inside of my nostrils.

Out of the corner of my eye, I see Ryan fetching his bong from the kitchen bench, so I block Shirin's view.

'So this is your home.' She tries to peek over my shoulder. 'Sure is an interesting neighbourhood, hon. There was a woman cutting her toenails on the corner of Miller and Doyle.'

'Yeah, it's great,' I lie, relieved she didn't bump into the man who usually frequents that corner. 'So ... how'd you find me? I mean, the place?'

'Kurt, of course.' *Of course.* 'I bumped into him at the bottle shop yesterday after coffee with my reflexology group, and he invited me around. He mentioned you were keen for us to have some time together.'

'He did?'

'It's okay, hon. Everyone grieves in their own way. I found that out when my mum died years ago.'

I freeze, too in shock to reply, but Shirin doesn't notice. She's content filling the air with the sound of her own voice.

'My heart aches for you. It does. Five whole years without that beautiful woman.'

I manage to tilt my head forward, barely a nod but close enough. I'm going to destroy Kurt one limb at a time for dragging Shirin into this.

But Shirin's not done. She clutches her hand to her chest, playing with the long strands of beads draped around her neck. 'I'm just so relieved you felt like you could reach out to me. Finally. I mean, your dad and I are always here for you, always have been, but now ... *you* believe it. I was hoping for a coffee date, something like that, but this ... *this* is such a step forward. And me being a goose, I was just sitting at home doing a puzzle, alone of course 'cos your dad's off again, you know how fly-in-fly-out is, and I thought, bugger it, today's the day. I'm going to see her.' She releases a shaky laugh. 'Listen to me, rabbiting on.'

I can barely take in what she's saying. 'If I knew you were coming I'd have ... ah, dressed up more. Sorry.' I fold my arms tighter to try to hide the stain. 'Maybe we should reschedule to a better time ... for you?'

'Oh poo, I didn't call ahead 'cos I didn't want you to make a fuss. I've got everything. Nail polishes, eye masks, the works.' That's when I notice the esky and the hessian bag of crackers and chips at her feet. 'You hungry? I've got enough food in here to feed the house. Kurt mentioned it's a bit of a zoo now there's five of you under one roof.'

That's one way to put it.

'Reckon I can pop the brie in the fridge?'

Crap. I glance behind me into the house. Ryan's nowhere to be seen. 'Um ...'

'It's fine, hon. A little mess won't bother me. I remember what it's like to be young.'

Before I have a chance to think of an excuse — a headache, unshakeable plans, moving to Mars — Shirin bustles inside, announcing she's putting together her world-famous platter. She's spitting with excitement.

Right on cue Ryan wanders past, cracks open the salt and vinegar chips, takes a handful, and mutters that he'll leave us to it.

Double crap.

* * *

Kurt looks at me from the bedroom doorway in the way he always does when he wants to kiss me. Eyes half-closed, lips curled up. The laziest of smirks.

'Place looks awesome, babe. Did ya tidy up out there?'

I swallow. I've been practising my speech since Shirin left, but I've forgotten every word. 'It's good, isn't it? Shirin helped. When she was here today. *Shirin was here today.*'

There's a silence so wide, so deep, I might sink into it.

'Oh yeah?'

He's playing dumb and I'm having none of it. 'Don't do that. Don't pretend you're innocent.'

He folds his arms across his chest. 'Fine, I saw her, she asked about ya mum. What was I meant to do?'

'Not invite her around?' My voice breaks, giving away that I'm more upset than pissed off. 'I was blindsided. You know Boxing Day was a nightmare! Sunday was just ... and then today ... it's impossible. You keep pushing me.'

Kurt comes over to the bed and sits down next to me. 'You're right. But this is hard for me too.'

I swallow. '*Meaning?*'

'Meaning ... I dunno.' He shrugs. 'Look, let me make ya feel better, babe.'

He kisses my collarbone, moving upwards to my right earlobe. I squirm and he pulls back, rejected. Up close, I can see his eyes are stained red. I can taste smoke on his breath.

'What's wrong? On ya period?'

'What? No. I'm just not feeling it. Today sucked.'

'Yeah, but I'm trying to help ya forget that.' He's barely blinking.

'I know, but ... this is about me, not you.'

'Don't remind me.' He sighs, then grabs his pillow and heads for the door. It's so familiar. 'Bit hot in here. I'm gonna enjoy the lounge room before we mess it up again.'

'You're not going to smoke any more tonight, are you?'

'Nah, babe. I'll be in soon. Promise.'

* * *

The sky burns fairy-floss pink the next morning. I watch the sun hanging low, willing it to move. All I want is to feel a little magic for a second, like I used to as a kid. Mum used to tell me that fairies helped the sun to rise by hoisting it into the sky pull after pull, using nothing but threads of gold and enchanted dust. I believed her. But the sun doesn't budge, of course.

I smile to myself. Maybe the fairies are on strike today.

I pause at the front door to adjust my shorts and pull up the sock that's slipping down the back of my Cons. Kurt is splayed on the couch fully clothed, shoes on, drool on the pillow.

I tiptoe back to our bedroom, flinching at the creaky floorboards. Everything, from the chest of drawers to the carpet, looks like it needs a clean — everything except the whiteboard. It's spotless. Gone are the scribblings, the sweet notes, the dirty jokes. I don't even remember which of us wiped them away.

I scrawl, *Gone out, might be a while. Text me if you need the car, Lx*, in big loopy letters.

It's only when I reach the front door again and steal another look at Kurt that I realise the ashtray on the coffee table is filled with stubs, all within his reach.

I slip out the front door, car keys digging into my palm, and welcome the warmth on my skin.

Milo

The gelato is melting faster than I can eat it. It trickles down my hand, sticky droplets catching in my arm hairs. I stop on the footpath to lick around the dripping edges of the waffle cone. I gurgle with ecstasy as the sweetness spreads over my tongue, then check to make sure no-one's watching. Even though Trent's working at the bookshop today, I can almost hear him telling me to buy the gelato a drink first.

That's when I see her. Layla. She's sitting on a bench nearby, legs pulled up high so her chin rests on bare knees. She's in shorts — the shortest of shorts, the kind where the hem scrapes the skin of her upper thighs. The kind that shows off everything. Jesus.

There're people milling around her with crying babies and bags of groceries, but her attention is stolen by something off in the distance, like she's dreaming while awake. I wonder if I'm dreaming too. It was her casual mention of gelato that led me here after all. If I hadn't seen her four days ago, I wouldn't be here with sugar splattered up to my elbows.

I almost leave without saying hello. We've exhausted all our material, I tell myself. Besides, her back is turned so she'll never know. But for some reason, I walk over.

'Hey, Lay.'

She turns around, face creasing into a smile. 'Oh, hey. Hey, you.'

It's been a while since I've seen someone's face beam like that when they see me.

'Hey, yourself,' I get out. 'Weird, huh? This bumping into each other.'

'It *is* Durnan. There's like three of us in town, remember?'

'I'll pay that.' I hold up my cone stuffed with melting gelato. 'Turns out this stuff is good. Who knew?'

'Me. Tried the boysenberry.'

'Salted caramel here.' I pause, already out of words, realising too late I should've never approached her. Damn my self-fulfilling prophecy. 'So, ah, guess I'll leave you to it … just saw you there and thought I'd say a quick hi.'

She smiles again. 'Well, a quick hi back atcha, MD. See ya.'

I say goodbye and walk off, wondering what the statistical probability is that we run into each other again.

Then I hear her voice call out, 'Hey, Milo. What are you doing now?'

I turn around. 'Right now?'

'Yeah. I'm going for a walk. Gonna leave my car here, look around some more.'

'I'm ninety-nine per cent sure you've unearthed Durnan's one new thing since you left. Not sure you can top this gelato.'

'Probably not … but you can come with, if you want. You know, just in case I discover Durnan's *second* new thing.'

'Well, I wouldn't want to miss that. You're not waiting for someone, though? Your, ah, your boyfriend?'

'Nope. Just me.'

I pause. It's not like I've got anything else going on.

'Sure, lead the way.'

* * *

Thirteen summers have passed since I've swum in the river. I'm not even sure how Layla and I ended up here. Obviously one foot in front of the other on the steaming cement, but there was no prior discussion. No plan to walk towards the water. We simply got lost in conversation, winding past parks and schools and down dingy little streets. Guess we haven't run out of topics after all. By the time the river was in sight, it was too late for me to turn back.

The air's thick with heat, like most summer days in Durnan, so Layla suggests going for a swim to cool off. I can't think of a good enough reason to get out of it, so it's her way, like it always was when we were kids.

From our vantage point high up in the tallest eucalyptus on the riverbank, the water looks murky, far from the Photoshopped sapphire blue on the posters lining the walls of the tourist centre. I stare down and feel a rush of blood to my head. I'm two branches above the tyre swing and six branches above the broken wooden plank that local kids hammered in years ago. I know because I'm counting while trying to stop everything from spinning. My feet are scratched up from the bark, my boxers cling to my thighs.

Layla's still in her singlet and shorts. 'No hands!' she sings out from the branch above mine. Her body sways and she squeals, lunging for the trunk. 'Oh my God. Oh God.'

My knuckles harden as she cackles with laughter.

'You okay down there?' she asks. 'You look kinda pale.'

'Not all of us tan like you.'

I glance at the water below again. Huge mistake.

'Damn, this is high,' she says. 'We must've been brave doing this as kids.'

'Yeah, we were basically Bear Grylls.' I don't remind her I've never jumped before.

'I reckon we head down to the swing,' she says. 'But I'm going to need that branch you're on so move your bum.'

'Still a wallflower, I see.'

I tighten my grip on the trunk and lower myself onto the next branch, scraping my palms and shins. Layla stays close, swinging her wiry legs down with the ease of an aerialist.

'One more, then you're there,' she says.

I'm flooded with images of me either hitting every branch before head-planting into the water, or having a panic attack and needing to be thrown over the shoulder of a fireman and carried down. Either way I'd be on the local news. Perfect.

I edge my way down to the tyre swing, fighting shaking legs and burning arm muscles. The branch sags under my weight.

'Just grab on, swing out and let go!' she calls.

'Gimme a sec.'

I drag my hand off the trunk and fumble for the tyre. It's worn and the rope doesn't look much better. I give it a tug. It seems fine, but I steal another glance at the river anyway. The water is muddy, the current strong.

Layla's eyes burn into my back. 'What's the hold-up?'

'Nothing.' I pause. 'Didn't Cliff Shepherd break his back doing this?'

'I heard he broke his legs and four ribs.'

'Serious?'

'Yeah, there was a shopping trolley floating under the surface.' She releases an exasperated sigh. 'Move over to that branch. I'll go first.'

We may as well be four years old again and yabbying at a family friend's farm. Layla was splashing around, covered in muck, ferrying yabbies back and forth from the water to a row of buckets. I hesitated next to them, kicking my gumboots against the grass. She ran over, dumped her latest catch in a bucket, smeared mud on my nose, then darted off, announcing to the grown-ups she was calling the biggest yabby 'Milo' and was going to eat it for dinner. I ended up chasing her into the dam, gumboots and all, and we didn't leave the water for another hour. Layla never looked before leaping. I looked too much.

'It's fine, I'll jump.'

I've said it now and I'm not unsaying it, no matter how much my legs tremble.

'You're peeing your pants, Milo Dark. Let me go.'

I wobble up into a standing position, right hand pressed against the trunk, left hand feeling the rope burn against my palm. I try to ignore its frayed ends. Another jerk, just to be sure. It holds.

'Jump before you fall. You're shaking heaps.'

'Dude! I'm not.' *Liar.* 'I'm thinking.'

'That's your problem.'

I strain my neck to look down one last time. Seizing the rope with both hands, I leap forward and pray to all the gods that my feet connect with the tyre. I swing out above the river, whooshing past blurry greens and browns and blues. For a moment, time freezes and I see Layla waving from the tree.

I let go, screaming, mouth locked open, as I hurtle downwards. My body slices through the water and I thrash around, struggling for the surface. I find it. In between spluttering and gasping for air, I paddle towards the bank, which is overgrown with long, slimy reeds.

I did it. I freakin' did it!

'That was awesome!' Layla hollers. 'You crazy monkey — I could kiss you!'

I barely take in what she's saying as I suck in breath after breath, each gulp feeling like a triumph.

* * *

We lie on the grass, listening to the galahs chatter.

'Your nose is getting kinda red,' Layla says. 'We better be quick before you turn into a tomato.'

She peels off her singlet to reveal a black bra. A black bra with lacy bits on the sides.

I sit up. 'What are you doing?'

'Drying off,' she says, before shimmying out of her shorts, swearing as they catch on her hips, and bouncing around until they're finally off.

She plants down next to me on the grass, barely thirty centimetres away. I don't know where to look, so I look anywhere but at her. In my peripheral vision, I see her unclipping her bra. *Jesus.* Covering herself, she wriggles out of it, then rolls down, chest to the grass. She's in nothing but black undies — black undies with lacy bits on the sides. A misjudged turn of the head and our eyes meet. This time, I forget to look away.

'What?' she says, as though it's normal she's lying next to me like this. 'I don't want tan lines.'

'Cool.' Smooth.

Layla lets out a long sigh tinted with bliss. 'Man, I don't remember it being this quiet here. Have you even seen anyone else around in the last hour?'

'Nah. You?'

'Nope.' She readjusts herself on the grass, edging slightly closer to me. Maybe deliberately, probably accidentally. I try not to notice her undies slipping. Her hand reaches around and pulls everything into place. 'It's all ours then.' She tugs at a blade of grass. 'This is pretty nice, right? Bumming around together again, I mean. Random … but nice.'

'For sure.'

Looks like I've left my vocabulary in the river. I reach for a clover and tear at the leaves; anything to stop me catching a glimpse of the curve of her hip or the fleshiness of her mouth. And that black lace.

Anything but the black lace.

'Hey, MD, my stuff's still wet — can I borrow your T-shirt for a bit? I'm kinda cold.'

I pass it over, relieved I don't have to avert my eyes any more. It hangs off her like a garbage bag.

My stomach churns as she wriggles closer to rest her head across my legs, her long limbs stretching across the grass. Over the years we've sat or laid in various positions like this a hundred times, in rumpus rooms, in campsites, on trampolines, but it feels different now. Or she's different. Or maybe I'm different.

Layla nibbles on a fingernail, not seeming fussed at all. We're still like this for a while, letting the cicadas fill in the quiet.

She looks up at me, black smudged around her eyes from the water. 'Hey …'

I look down at her. 'Hey …?'

'Race you to the river?'

'Now?'

She nods.

Without warning, I pull my legs out from under her and sprint across the grass, bellyflopping into the shallow water with a splash. She charges after me, clambering up my back until she's perched on my shoulders. She raises her arms high and pumps her right fist.

'I've seen Milo Dark naked!'

Her call hangs in the air, before she cracks up laughing so much she falls backwards into the water.

As we're splashing, and screaming, and laughing, I notice there really is no-one else here. The river is ours.

Later, when we're back in her car, our bodies dampening the seats, I think of Sal. Or the fact I haven't thought of Sal. Not for hours. Not once.

Layla

Milo's mum, Jen, has always been kind but firm — a potent combination. Somewhere along the way I realised it's easier to say, 'Sure, I'd love to come in for some mushroom risotto,' rather than making up polite excuses. During primary school, she was the kind of mum the other mums envied for seeming so perfect. Every day, she flitted between canteen duty, working for The Little Bookshop and packing nutritious lunchboxes. My mum never tried to compete with her friend, just watched in glee as everyone else did. 'We all have our ways,' Mum'd say as she supervised me spreading Vegemite onto my bread before school, and a little on the kitchen bench. I wonder if Milo's ever made his own lunch.

From the driveway, Jen looks the same as always — flawless make-up, hairdo and pearl earrings — but up close I can see fresh crinkles on her forehead and neck. My mind moves so fast — faster than I can handle mostly — that for a moment I wonder if Mum would've had new folds and creases on her face if time had let her. She used to squeal when she spotted a wrinkle in the mirror, then when she noticed me hovering behind her, she'd tell me it's a gift that only comes with age, and age isn't a gift that everyone is given so it's important to treasure it. I didn't get what she meant until now.

When Jen drags me in for a hug, it's like she's breathing me in. Milo watches on, as awkward as ever, before shuffling to his bedroom to call Sal.

Suddenly Jen and I are sitting in the Darks' living room, alone for the first time in five years. I consider storming into Milo's room and dragging him back out to join us. Anything to stop me being in the interrogation chair. Instead, I stay, and we cover school, family and friends, with me tiptoeing around the edges of the truth where I need to soften it. I can feel Jen trying to connect the dots, even ones that aren't there, struggling to solve the riddle of how I ended up in her living room again.

It's not until she takes my hand in hers that I notice the bracelet hanging from her wrist. It's loose on her, just like Mum's was. Gold chain, fine, elegant — the style suited Jen more, but Mum wore hers every day, only taking it off to shower or wash the dishes. She loved it, said it was the nicest thing she owned. But in the chaos after she died, it went missing so we couldn't bury her with it.

'It's been a while since I've seen your father,' Jen says, topping up my tea and pulling me out of my daydream.

I cram a biscuit in my mouth and stammer something about him being busy with work and he doesn't mean anything by it. My throat is tight as I say it; it's like stretching a muscle that hasn't been used for a while. It used to get regular exercise whenever he missed parent–teacher nights, or I was forced to show up to school excursions without the obligatory signed permission slip. I don't tell Jen I haven't seen him since Boxing Day.

I'm now glad Milo isn't in the room. My jaw is already aching from clenching it, and I'm supposed to be the strong one. The one who raided Mrs Landry's rubbish bin when we thought she was collecting children, hiding them in her back shed and disposing of them when she was done sucking their blood. The one who told Mum that Trent was picking on Milo when we were away at Easter one year and he wouldn't explain where the bruises on his arms were coming from. The one who did a ten-minute presentation to Jen on Milo's behalf, complete with props and a scribbled handout, on why he deserved a ten per cent pocket-money increase. I was the lighthouse. The anchor. At least for a moment in time.

'I know you have a lot of people who love you,' Jen says, 'but please know you've been in my thoughts.'

I take a sip of tea, unsure what to say to that.

'I still think of that day often,' she goes on. 'It was a beautiful service.'

Tulips are beautiful. A sunset is beautiful. I can never understand why adults say Mum's service was beautiful.

All this talk takes me back: to sobbing in the church bathroom's toilet 'cos bright red blood stained my favourite sunflower undies. I couldn't tell Dad; he was so weighed down with grief he could barely put on his suit. Besides, I was worried. What sort of girl gets her first period on the day of her mum's funeral? I would've thought I was dying too if Mum hadn't told me it was natural months earlier. With no-one to ask for advice, I stuffed toilet paper in my undies and hoped it would finish as quickly as it started. That was the day I learnt the unbearable thing: that every decision I was going to make from then on, every moment I was going to experience, would be without her.

I was alone. Until Jen came into the bathroom.

She heard me sniffing, but her voice stayed calm as we spoke through the door. She wasn't going anywhere, she told me, she was going to wait there for as long as I needed her to. When I eventually told her the truth, she passed pads — a thick one and a thin one — under the door for me and checked I knew what to do. Mum had shown me months earlier but I'd forgotten. Her words sang in my ear as I stumbled through it: *Periods aren't that bad. It's just our amazing bodies doing what they're designed to do.* She'd made me feel like a superhero or a powerful machine. Like my body — *me* — had been created by the greatest inventor in the universe.

When we left the bathroom together, Jen's hand touched the small of my back. All I wanted was to splinter into pieces, but she steered me forward and I made it to my seat without buckling at the knees.

'Layla,' I hear her saying. 'Are you okay? We don't have to talk about it.'

My head is foggy. 'Sorry … yeah, yeah, I am … but thanks.'

I feel her squeeze my hand. 'Milo mentioned you're here for a little while?'

'Maybe. Probably not.' I hope not.

'Oh. Well, maybe's a good start,' she says. 'And what did you two get up to this afternoon? Milo's lobster-red. I always tell him he needs to reapply sunscreen every two hours or he'll burn to a crisp.'

'We didn't do much, just went to the river. Jumped from the old swing — remember it?'

'Milo too?' Jen's eyes are wide, like I've just told her we hitchhiked to Queensland to hit up the casino.

'He went first.'

Jen almost chokes on her tea. 'But he hasn't been swimming there since …' Her voice trails offs.

Behind me, the kitchen door creaks, but I don't turn around in time to make eye contact with him. By the time I thank Jen for my tea and charge into Milo's bedroom, he's sprawled on the bed checking his phone.

'All good out there?' he asks, pretending he didn't just sneak away.

'Peachy.' I shut the door, then collapse next to him. 'Hear anything juicy?'

He shakes his head. 'Arrived too late for the goss. I just got off the phone. Well, sorta. There was no answer so … looks like I'm in a relationship with Sal's voicemail. I don't want to jinx it, but I think it's getting serious.'

He laughs. I can tell he's faking it.

'You little cheater, you.'

'Oh yeah, you know me. Player.'

I snort out loud at the thought.

'So, ladies' man, your mum said some stuff to me out there.'

'I knew it! Ignore it all. Unless it was good stuff.'

'She sorta flipped when I told her we'd been at the river.'

He pauses. 'What'd she say?'

'Nothing really — you tell me. Or I might have to tickle you like that time in Bendigo when you wet your sleeping bag.'

'You're gross.'

'Your face is.'

He grins. 'Whatever, I'm not even ticklish any more.'

'What happened at the river? Did you spy on Trenticles hooking up with someone there?'

'What? *No.*'

'Your folks hook up there?'

'Jesus.'

'Well?' I hover my hand over his chest, prepared to tickle. 'That's not a no.'

'You serious?' he says, edging away from me. 'You've committed the sleeping bag saga to memory but *this* you forget? Damn Mum and her freakin' mouth.' He pauses, then mutters, 'I almost drowned there. When I was a kid.'

I trace over the words before I can stop myself. 'You almost ...'

'Drowned.' He rolls his eyes. 'Just hit me with your jokes about me needing floaties. Get them over with.'

'Shut up, I'm processing … God, it was … oh, it was the teddy bears' picnic day … wasn't it?'

The memory from years ago seeps in, slowly at first, then all at once. I can't believe I almost forgot. It was the top story on the news. A living nightmare for the Darks. The whole town was on pause to see if Milo had survived.

'You'd already left the river when it happened, Lay. It's no big deal.'

At first it had seemed like an adventure the rest of us kids didn't get invited to join. One boy told me about watching all the flashing lights and how cool it was to see Milo going really, really fast in the ambulance. Apparently all the kids wanted a turn after that, begging their parents for a ride. I also remembered the daughter of one of Mum's friends telling a group of us, wide-eyed and hanging on every detail, that she'd seen Milo sleeping on the riverbank, and no matter how much she yelled or poked or tickled him, he wouldn't wake up. When I first heard that I thought it was a miracle, like mermaids in the river had cast a sleeping spell on him. I think I even asked Dad if I could try it on my birthday. Oh God.

The story of what really happened got twisted and turned over the years, especially once the kids at school heard about it. The biggest rumour of all was that Trent had thrown Milo's teddy bear into the river as a dare, and when the parents' backs were turned Milo waded out to try to save it, but the river's current was strong and swept him away. None of the kids, not even Trent, raised the alarm for a while. They didn't get that his toes couldn't graze the dirt below.

Despite our lives overlapping for years, Milo and I have somehow never spoken about it so I still don't know if that's true. Either way, I should have remembered. I thought I knew everything about this town, about Milo and his family. Maybe things have moved on more than I realised.

'Dude, we didn't have to go to the river today,' I say.

He shrugs. 'I only know what I've been told. And it was ages ago. I can swim — you saw me. It's fine, Lay, really.'

I raise an eyebrow. *Come on.*

He waves me away. 'Relax, I'm not a boy in a bubble. Even if Mum thinks I am.'

'What you did today is kinda huge when you think about it.'

'Don't start.'

'Okay.' I cross my legs and take his hands in mine. His palms are sweaty but I don't let go. 'Just let me finish then. I want to say something quickly, because today *wasn't* nothing, and you can hate me for saying it, but I kind of feel like you hate me anyway, so I'm saying it, even if it makes you hate me more. I'm saying it.'

'*Just say it.* And yeah, I hate you.'

'Good, hate you too. Now, don't interrupt before I'm finished. I think if you can survive that crappy, crappy thing that happened all those years ago, then you can survive anything.'

'Lay ...'

'Anything. I mean it. The end.'

Milo chuckles as he looks at his hands in mine. 'That was so freakin' cheesy, dude.'

I pounce. He's stronger than he used to be, obviously, making it harder for me to pin him down. I lean all my weight into it, but it's not enough. Limbs are everywhere, so I swing one leg over his body until I'm sitting on his stomach.

He chokes with laughter as I tickle his armpits. 'Ow! Stop!' he manages between cackles.

His face is flushed pink, his hair ruffled against the pillow. I stop and pull away, suddenly aware I'm alone with Milo in his bedroom, on his bed, where we used to play with our Teenage Mutant Ninja Turtles action figures into the night. Yet this time our faces are barely a ruler's length apart.

'Anyway,' I murmur, clambering off him, 'dinner's probably ready soon.'

He nods. 'Yeah.'

I stand up, desperate to widen the space between us, and wander over to the window. You can't see much. Milo's view consists of a rusty shed with hints of a rotting wooden fence and a slight glimpse of the neighbours' backyard.

My old backyard.

When I stand on my tippy-toes, I can see the treehouse, the yellowed lawn in need of a mow, the overgrown pergola. The vines hang over so much I almost expect

Mum to rush out yelling, 'Bring out some secateurs so we can give this beast a haircut!' The treehouse, like many things in Durnan now, is unkempt and dated. I blink. For a second I don't see the faded blue splitting wood and the ladder with broken rungs; it's as fresh as the day Dad painted it into the early hours of Christmas morning.

I catch Milo watching me.

'It's gotta be breaking a stack of health and safety rules, right?' he asks with a glint in his eye.

'I've got a splinter just from looking at it.'

'The neighbours are away for a fair while, caravanning around Australia, I think.' He says it slowly, deliberately, like he's leaving a trail for me to follow.

'Interesting ...'

The door swings open to reveal Jen standing there holding a wooden spoon. 'Open-door policy, please, you two,' she says. 'I'm not ready to be a grandmother.'

'Jesus, Mum.'

Despite the sunburn, Milo's face darkens to cherry-red. Even my cheeks feel warm. It's like I've stepped into an alternate universe where everything is backwards and upside-down.

Because this is Milo. *Milo.*

I pull my phone from my shorts pocket to distract myself. Anything to stop the strange thoughts burrowing into my brain.

No missed calls. No text messages. Guess Kurt's busy again.

'Ah, sorry to do this, but I have to go,' I announce anyway, feigning disappointment. 'I've got a ton of missed calls and messages. I'm such a flake — I forgot I have a thing tonight.'

'Yeah?' Milo sounds relieved.

'Yeah, and I'm already late so ... thanks for the chat and stuff, Jen.'

'You're welcome, Layla. Sure you can't stay?'

'Run before she gets out the baby pics,' Milo says.

Jen claps her hands together. 'We do have an adorable video somewhere of you all running under the sprinkler.'

'Go,' he says. 'It's too late for me, but save yourself.'

'Risotto smells great,' I say, and kiss Jen goodbye on the cheek.

Out of momentum, I do the same to Milo, but realise two seconds too late that we don't do that. My lips press against the apple of his cheek and I feel him flinch, yet there's a crackle — an underlying fizz. I pull away, noticing a soft dusting of freckles across his nose and his trademark crimson spreading down his neck and colouring his collarbone.

I'm still in the hallway when I hear Jen whisper to Milo, 'What on earth is going on between you two? Have I missed something?'

'She has a boyfriend, Mum. It's just Layla.'

I don't wait to hear the rest of the conversation.

* * *

Mosquitoes nip at my ankles as I walk across the front lawn of the house, my skin already painted a few tones darker. Milo used to say I could tan under a light bulb. A swirling mess of purples and oranges sweeps across the sky — Durnan's one redeeming quality: perfect sunsets — but I don't have long to enjoy it. The front door opens and a barefoot Kurt comes out. He doesn't say hello or meet me halfway, just plants himself down on the top step of the veranda. Before the move here, he would've run at me like a bull, reaching his arms out wide before picking me up and throwing me over his shoulder. I would've bobbed along upside-down, hair swinging, pretending I hated it when really I loved every second. But now we're in the after.

My heart pounds as I climb the veranda stairs. When I reach the top, I'm looking down at him, but he's looking down at his feet.

'Hi,' I say.

'Hey.'

'Good day?'

He shrugs, rubbing his right thumb over his left, his eyes still focused on anything but mine.

'Did you see my whiteboard message?'

'Yeah, babe — I saw it?'

He looks up at last. His eyes are red again, but I know he hasn't been crying.

'I figured you wanted space, so I went for a drive. Then I went walking.'

I don't tell Kurt that I made it to the corner of Butcher Street, my eyes avoiding the sight of Durnan Hospital looming behind it, before bailing back to the main street to soothe myself with gelato. I don't know what I was expecting to see on Butcher Street. There were no flowers heaped in a pile like there were five years ago. If anything, the corner's been done up. The garden looks landscaped, maybe even a new signpost. It looks like any normal Durnan street.

'Anyway, that turned into more walking, and then … and then I ran into a friend.'

'A friend? Who?'

I guess I'm doing it … I'm telling him. Anything to cut through the weirdness of whatever happened in Milo's room earlier. I sit down on the step next to him.

'Milo,' I say, before adding, 'You've met him … the guy from the bookshop.'

'That quiet dude? Didn't realise ya were tight with another guy here.'

I tell him in a rush that Milo has a girlfriend, that his mum was close with mine, that there's a whole history I'll bore him with one day.

Kurt doesn't say anything, but I'm not sure if it's because he's okay with it or because he's stewing. It's moments like this I wish I could tap into his brain to read his mind.

'But,' I add, trying to use a more upbeat voice, 'I did see my old backyard.'

'Yeah? Didn't think ya wanted to see it again.'

'It was pretty rundown, but the treehouse is still there.' My chest pangs as I remember the paint peeling off it.

'Treehouse?'

I nod. 'Saw the river too.' I hadn't planned on telling him any of this, but now I'm talking, I can't seem to stop myself. 'It's sorta nice down there. More peaceful than it used to be. I guess everyone only goes to the pool now.'

I'm still struck by the eucalyptus trees ruling over everything, and the weeping willows where I could've lost myself for hours. Even the caravan park by the river has a certain charm I hadn't realised I'd missed.

'Sounds alright. Maybe we could go sometime?'

I pause. 'Maybe.'

Kurt reaches out, so slowly it's like he's forcing himself to drag his hand through the air to connect with mine.

'Lay,' he says. 'You haven't kissed me properly in ages.'

Before, Kurt's words wouldn't have hung in the air in anticipation. His hands would've found the turns of my waist and his mouth would've found mine. But now, next to me, he's nervy. It's like he's worried he'll hurt me even more, like all my pieces already need gluing back together and he doesn't want to do any more damage. He's seen the real me, I guess — the shadowy dark corners that most don't even know exist. But he wants me fixed. And I want to feel something other than this for a second or a lifetime, whatever I can get.

I lean in, brushing my lips against his to remind him I'm not broken. His hand quickly gets lost in my hair, then he traces the edge of my eyebrow, my chin, my collarbone. Eventually he pulls away and it's like he's been injected with bliss.

But, despite the taste of his mouth against mine, the after is already seeping back into me. I don't want to give in so I curl against him, fighting it back down, trying to fill myself with as much of this moment as possible.

Before it disappears and the darkness in me rises again.

Before I remember I'm broken.

Milo

Mum says I need to be careful. 'Layla isn't the same any more,' she whispers, like Layla might tap her on the shoulder. 'She's going through a lot, and you should focus on your future instead of complicating things with a girl who's got a boyfriend.'

I mutter, 'There's nothing going on, it's *Layla*, she's doing fine. I *am* focusing on my future and *I* have a girlfriend.'

That's when Mum serves up the raised eyebrow. Her knowing look. Mother's intuition, she calls it. I reckon it's an excuse to stick her beak where it's not wanted.

'I saw something,' she says. 'A spark.'

This woman needs a new hobby.

'You're way off, Mum. She thinks of me like a brother.'

'I saw what I saw. You stayed in Durnan for a reason, Milo — to work out your life. It's the only reason your father and I aren't pushing you more, and I don't want you to blow it. Do you know how shocked people are when they realise you're not studying yet? With those marks, I barely understand it myself.'

'I'll get there. And my marks weren't *that* good.'

'They were good enough to do something great with.' Mum sighs. 'It's a waste, that's what it is. Layla's rebuilding her life, while you have to start a brand-new one. I'm not sure if those goals mix well. I love her, you know that, and you two have always been close, but —'

'We're mates,' I say, cutting her off. 'That's why it's easy. Stop seeing things that aren't there.'

My phone rattles on the chest of drawers. I check it. A message from Sal. She's free if I want to talk.

I hold the phone up in front of Mum's face and nudge her towards the bedroom door. 'Anyway, that concludes our session, Dr Phil. I'm talking to my girlfriend now — because I have one. Shall we do this again at the same time next week? Or not?'

I close the door before calling Sal back.

'Hey, stranger,' she chirps. 'Sorry I missed your call. We've got about five minutes before I head out with everyone.'

Five whole minutes. Everything about Sal's life is scheduled right now, even the phone calls.

'Okay, so you know what I've been doing,' she says. 'Uni, party, repeat. Now talk me through yours. I want to know everything.'

'It is an exciting life I lead,' I say dryly. 'Had a day off so I slept in. Mum's on my case, again.'

'Of course. Then what?'

There's no point in lying. It'll only give power to Mum's stupid theory about me and Layla.

'Then I went to the river.'

Sal gasps. I knew she would so I almost didn't tell her.

'Did you swim?' she asks.

'I swam.'

'But, like, where you couldn't touch the bottom?'

'Yep. Jumped out of a tree into the water too.'

'Milo, that's huge!'

'So everyone keeps telling me.' I pause, thinking back to Mum's lecture about Layla. She couldn't be more wrong. 'Anyway, a family friend — well, an old next-door neighbour actually — is back in town and that's who I went to the river with.'

'No way! You've got a mate to spend time with. Sweet. What's his name?'

His name? Wasn't expecting that. 'Oh, the thing is, *he* is actually a —'

'Go away, you devil!' she squeals.

'Sal? You there?'

'Sorry, it's Woody,' she laughs. 'It's impossible to have a private conversation in this place.'

'He's there? Right now?'

'Him and about half of uni. They say hi — *hang on, Woods!* — we're all going to dinner. Anyway, what were we talking about? Oh yeah, the river. I'm proud.'

We chat for another minute before our time's dried up. For some reason, I don't clear up the miscommunication. It would've been simple to explain — 'The thing is, my family friend is actually a girl called Layla who I've known since we were kids. But don't worry, she's a bit of

87

a pain and there's nothing going on' — but I don't. I'm not sure why. I wonder if Sal's ever done the same to me. Lied by omission.

As we say goodbye, Sal tells me she misses me. For the first time in a few days, despite Woody sounding like a jackass in the background, I believe her. Which is why it's so screwed up when I hear myself telling her I've thought about her all day.

I hang up and all of a sudden I want to press rewind on the week. Go back to missing Sal, my mates and my old life, even if it makes me feel like I'm sinking in quicksand.

Go back to Layla being nothing but a memory.

* * *

Layla: *Hi*
Layla: *It's Lay, btw (not sure if you saved my number)*
Milo: *Hey, stalker*
Layla: *Ha!*
Layla: *So, I've been thinking …*
Milo: *Dangerous*
Layla: *If I want to survive in Durnan, I need a plan*
Milo: *Go on …*
Layla: *#1 Bag out people lapping the main street. Snacks compulsory*
Layla: *#2 Eat body weight in gelato. Choc-chip, peanut butter, salted caramel, repeat*
Layla: *#3 Have a treehouse party*
Milo: *GO ON …*

Layla: #4 *Do whatever it takes to forget my sad little life. PS: Your shout 'cos I'm broke. The clucking A-holes at Joe's still haven't called*

Layla: #5 *Skinny-dip at the river*

Layla: *Kidding. (Or am I?)*

Milo: *You've seen me naked anyway*

Milo: *Perve*

Layla: *Once was enough, ha ha*

Layla: *PS: I bumped into Trenticles down the street. Swear he talked about his calf muscles for 10 mins*

Milo: *It's official: I'm the better Dark brother*

Layla: *Time will tell. Night, MD*

* * *

Layla: *Hey! Me again. Hope your week's good. Clucking great/scary news: got an interview at Joe's!*

Milo: *Eggcellent*

Layla: *Should I tell them raw chicken grosses me out? So foul*

Milo: *Fowl ...*

Layla: *You cluckhead*

Milo: *Nah, I'm a chick magnet*

Layla: *Go lay an egg*

Milo: *Still hate you*

Layla: *Hate you more*

* * *

Layla: *Morning! Miss me?*

Milo: *Cluck off*

Milo: *Hope the interview goes eggs-traordinarily well*

* * *

Layla: *Dying, dying, dead. Layla's time and place of death: Monday, 10 am, job interview, Joe's Charcoal Chicken Shop*

Milo: *Bet you smashed it. (Like an egg. I'm the worst)*

Layla: *His wife hated me. Said my hair was pink. (You really are)*

Milo: *Your hair is pink*

Layla: *Didn't sound like she enjoyed my pink hair*

* * *

Layla: *Argh! I got the job! WTF?!*

Milo: *Of course you did! We should celebrate*

Layla: *Yeah? Free on Sat?*

Milo: *I'm in*

Layla

Milo is drawing circles in the dirt when I get to the river, tubs of gelato in hand.

'Chocolate brownie for you, sir.'

'More gelato? Well, cheers to your clucking new job.'

I scoop out a chunk of salted-caramel gelato and plant myself down next to him, keeping a decent enough space that our shoulders and hips and toes aren't touching, without being too far away that it seems like I'm avoiding being close. It's all so coordinated, but I'm conscious of keeping things safe. I figure enough days have passed for whatever the weirdness zapping between us for a microsecond was to dissolve and float off like a dandelion clock in the wind, but I don't want to take any risks.

Milo swaps sweeping circles in the dirt for shovelling gelato into his mouth while scrolling through his phone, his thumb flicking to its own beat.

'*Dude*. You're being that guy.'

'Huh?'

I point at his phone, then at me. 'Hello? Rude. How are you?'

'My bad. Sorry. Cool news about the job. Very cool.'

'Yeah, I guess. Really need the money so …' I watch him steal another glance at his phone. 'Okay, what's up?'

'What?'

I raise an eyebrow.

'Bad habit,' he says, tucking his phone into his pocket. 'So when's your first day?'

I'm about to launch into an explanation, but pause. 'You're dying to check it again, aren't you?'

'Nah, I'm good.'

'*Please*. Show me what's going on.'

'Bossy.' Shaking his head, he passes me the phone.

On the screen is a pretty girl in a bikini with her arm wrapped around a guy in board shorts. Their mouths are frozen into two mammoth grins. I zoom in on the shot. The sides of their faces are pressed together and his hand is grazing her hip. They look like a Diet Coke ad, all fresh and light and giddy with laughter on a scorching summer's day.

'Who are they?' I ask. 'And why are we ogling them? Context, please.'

'That's Woody — he studies law and has already kissed more than thirteen girls since Orientation Week.'

I snort. 'Interesting bio.' I zoom in closer. 'Cute. Bit jocky.' More zoom. 'Whoa, he has a nipple piercing!'

'*What*?' Milo clambers in for a better look. 'Jesus. So … that's Sal next to the walking nipples.'

'Really? I wouldn't have recognised her.' I zoom in again. 'She's such a babe now. You never told me that.'

He shrugs, snatching the phone back to keep scrolling. 'They're kinda close, right? This guy is all over *everyone* in the photos, but she's always with him.'

'They're friends.'

'That's what she says.' He doesn't sound convinced.

'Let's buy you some time while we sort this out. How are you on the texts?'

He shrugs. 'Alright.'

'No … *the* texts. Alright's not gonna cut it, MD.'

I take the phone back, open up his messages and start typing. He grabs at it, but I wriggle out of his grasp and finish writing my masterpiece.

I show him the message. 'Hot, right?'

'You came up with that? Just then?'

'Some of my finest work.' I press send. 'Sal won't give that guy another thought.'

'Did you just …' Milo's jaw nearly hits his knees. 'You sent *that* to my girlfriend?'

'Yeah, but you get to take all the credit. But if you ask me —'

'I'm not asking for anything!'

'— it's still not enough. You have to visit her. Make a scene. Long-distance sounds hard, but you're focusing on this random nipple guy too much. She couldn't come to you, right? So go to her.'

'I have a little something called work.'

'Get Trenticles to cover your shifts.'

Milo scoffs.

'Go up for one night then! There's the bus, although they only have like one stupid time a day, or you could road-trip it. I'd loan you my car, but Kurt'll probably need it for stuff. Any other ideas?'

'Not really. There *is* the family work car ... it's sort of mine and Trent's, but —'

'Perfect! Ask him.'

'Nah.' His brow furrows; he's pissed off at himself for letting me find out about the car. 'He'd never let me borrow it.'

'In that case you'll need an alibi for when it goes MIA.'

'Familiar with the phrase "grand theft auto"?'

'Think of it more as a little white lie.'

'I can't drive.'

'Come on, there are toddlers in this town who can drive. Who in Durnan *can't* drive?'

He bounces his thumbs on his chest.

I fail to hide my smirk. 'Wow. Just ... wow. Okay, Romeo, I'm sure a driver can be arranged for you. But just for the record, I will be paying you out for quite some time about this.' I pause, unsure whether to say the next words on my tongue, but they blurt out before I'm sure whether I'm doing the right or wrong thing. 'I can probably drive you there if you're stuck, like do a road trip sort of thing.'

Milo's eyes widen.

'As a favour,' I add. 'You and Sal will owe me forever when you're married with triplets and I'm living alone in a basement with a pet ferret. But if you're worried about me being a third wheel … I mean, if it'd be weird to have me tagging along …'

'Nah, course not.' Milo runs his hands through his hair. 'I'll think about it. I reckon it might be better to plan something for later, you know? Do it properly.'

I poke at my gelato. 'Up to you. But sometimes you've gotta paint outside the lines, dude.'

I hear a crack as he breaks a stick in half.

'Like, if you were my boyfriend and you pulled off a romantic gesture like that …' My voice trails off.

'What?'

'What?' It takes me a second to catch up with what I've said: *if you were my boyfriend*. 'I mean, if my boyfriend did this for me … I'd be blown away.'

'Right … yeah, cool.'

Milo's phone buzzes. He scans it once, twice, then grunts with surprise.

'What is it?' I ask, trying to peep over his shoulder. 'Sal again?'

He hesitates, then passes me the phone.

'Dude.' I whistle. 'You owe me *so* bad.'

Saved by the text message.

Milo

My mind hasn't stopped racing all week, but for once it's all good stuff. I'd say things are back to normal with Sal, but they're not. They're better than normal. We've been texting non-stop ever since *the* message. My phone is pasted to my hand; I'm addicted.

After turning off my bedside lamp, I scroll through my phone to reread Sal's texts. Damn. Layla knows how to get a girl's attention. She could run courses for guys like me.

Last time we spoke, Sal told me she's going to have a quiet one this coming weekend so she can catch up on all the things she's let slide during the first six weeks of uni. I've never pulled off a surprise before. I'm not that guy, the one who orchestrates big gestures. Even Sal's birthday presents have involved her input — a clue, a hint, a straight-up request.

Her voice softened when she said she was happy that I'm taking the time to work out what I want to do, but she misses me, apparently, and wants us to Skype more. My stomach wobbled — guilt maybe? — when she said I seemed more like myself again, and whatever I was doing I should keep doing it.

I still haven't corrected her on the 'family friend' issue, mainly because I don't want it to sound like something it's not. If there was any weirdness with Layla — and I'm still not sure there was — then it's disappearing … no, it's gone, and I don't want to do anything to throw things out again. Not over nothing. Not when everything is going well.

I should've gone to sleep an hour ago, but my brain isn't cooperating. I'm back online and lost in everyone else's lives. Halfway between sniggering at the comments on BuzzFeed and rolling my eyes at a long-winded status update from Murph, the master of online slacktivism, I notice Woody has been tagged in more photos on Sal's page again.

I tell myself to stop being jealous. It's nothing.

Don't click, don't click, don't click.

I rarely take my own advice.

Woody's profile has exploded with new photos since Layla and I pored over it. He's updated his main picture three times since then; in all of them, his nose is just as burnt, his hair just as messy. Sal has liked the photo, but so have one hundred and seventeen other sheep.

I stare at the endless stream of partying, mates and girls until all the images blur into one ginormous mess.

Shouldn't have clicked.

* * *

Milo: *You up?*
Layla: *Yeah. Hi*

Milo: *Hi. I'm in*

Layla: *?*

Milo: *For the road trip*

Layla: OH MY GOD! Yes!

Milo: *Tomorrow after I finish work? It's last minute, but Trent's away — we can take his work car*

Layla: *Sweet! TGIF road trip! I have work training at Joe's on Sat arvo so need to be back by 2, OK?*

Milo: *Done. Get some sleep, driver*

Layla: *Forgot it's past your bedtime, grandpa*

Layla

We jolt to a stop outside my house, straining against our seatbelts. I'm still adjusting to driving Trent's work car.

'There's just someone I've got to see real quick before we leave,' I tell him. 'Don't talk to anyone, okay? Or do anything. Just wait here.'

Milo raises his arms above his head like he's about to be arrested. 'But I was planning on having tea and scones with your dodgy drug-dealing neighbours. *Joking.*'

'You're such a snob.'

This is why I can't tell people I live here. Not that he's wrong.

I snake my way up the driveway, passing the tangle of garden that's so overgrown it's creeping onto the concrete. The lawn is dry as straw and almost as yellow. None of us have been keeping up with Mel's chore roster.

'Hello?' I call out as I open the front door. Only the whirr of the fridge replies. 'Kurt, you home, babe? Anyone?'

When no-one answers, I head for the bedroom. Kurt's clothes are strewn on the floor next to our unmade bed, and my make-up is scattered all over the chest of drawers.

There's a dog wearing a bow tie waiting for me on the whiteboard. I add a speech bubble: *Woof!* My nose scrunches up as I stand on my tippy-toes and scrawl love hearts in the top right-hand corner for Kurt, then write: *See you tomorrow night. PS: If you don't know what I'm talking about, check your phone!*

I squiggle in an extra heart, then look at my phone, willing it to ring or buzz. Still no missed calls or messages. Dammit, Kurt. Get back to me.

He left the house early this morning — apparently he's helping Ryan with something — so we didn't have a chance to talk in person about the last-minute road trip, but I've left him four missed calls and a text message: *Something's come up so I won't be home until tomoz night. Call so I can explain. Lx*

All Kurt wants is honesty, and all I want is to give it to him. Every last drop of detail. Milo. Sal. Woody. The grand gesture. All of it. But he doesn't seem to want to hear about it.

I call him again. No answer. *Again.*

I scan the room for anything I might have forgotten for the trip. Jelly snakes hidden in a stack of Kurt's stuff on his bedside table. Perfect. Furry tartan cat ears hanging off the hook behind the door. Hilarious. Red lipstick on my chest of drawers.

In the middle of the chaos, I notice a bag of pot and papers spilling onto a framed photo that's fallen down.

Swallowing hard, I sweep the loose pot into the bag and wipe down the photo with the back of my hand. My heart pangs. It's the shot of me and Mum at Dubbo Zoo. I'm about six, missing my two front teeth and have a butterfly painted on my cheek. Mum's tiny butterfly. She beams up at me from the frame.

I stand the photo back up and clear everything else out of the way. When I look closer, I notice a small scratch on the glass. My jaw tightens and I glare at the bag of pot, as though that will somehow make it disappear. Despite what I'd told Kurt at the cemetery, no amount of 'easy money' is worth feeling like this.

Mum would know what to do. She'd know what to say too. She always did. I stare at the photo again, willing the answers to come to me. Wondering whether I should call Dad, even though he's as useful as a cactus; whether I should admit what's going on to Milo; whether I should tell Kurt it has to stop or else. Because it has to stop or else. I can't try to convince myself any longer.

There's no response from Mum to any of this. No magical, enlightened moment of knowing what to do. Of course there's not. She just keeps smiling at me.

My bottom lip quivers.

Milo

An hour into the trip and Layla hasn't stopped screeching along with the radio. She doesn't know most of the words, just jolts between lead and backing vocals, filling the gaps with nonsense. Usually it'd annoy me, but with the wind blowing in my face, my bare feet on the dashboard and Durnan a hundred kilometres behind us, nothing's touching me. Not even the fact I got a last-minute text from Murph and he's back in Durnan for the night, crashing at his dad's townhouse. Of all the weekends in the calendar, he has to pick the one when I'm out of town. Timing, huh.

Everything else has gone to plan. Layla and I took the work car without a hitch — no alarms, no wild police chase, nothing. For my alibi, I told Mum and Dad I was staying at Murph's so they won't wait up. Trent is camping with mates 'off the grid', according to his not-off-the-grid status update, so no-one will even realise the car is gone.

With every loose end sewn up, I'm free to fantasise about the grand gesture.

How happy Sal will be when she sees me running in slow-mo towards her across the uni car park.

How I'll finally be the guy who did big things.

How sweet it is to road-trip to Canberra with Layla.

No, brain. *No.*

'Hey, is there any gum?' Layla asks, pinching my arm. 'Trenticles has gotta have something in here.'

I rummage through the glovebox. Scrunched-up cheeseburger wrapper. Trent's boxers. No sign of gum.

Wait. *Trent's boxers.*

I drop them on the mat. 'Jesus!'

'What? What is it?' she asks. 'A spider? They're harmless, dude.'

I reach down, grab the elastic between my thumb and forefinger, and wave the boxers next to her.

She cackles. 'Oh my God, get them away from me!'

I fling them out the window, watching them flap in the wind before being sucked away out of view. 'I need to sterilise my hands.'

'What was he thinking? What's happened in this car? I have so many unanswered questions.'

'This is Trent, Lay. We don't wanna know.'

She laughs again before something catches her eye in the rear-view mirror. I steal a look. A red station wagon is speeding up in the lane next to us, creeping closer as it attempts to overtake our car.

'What a douche-mobile,' she says, as the station wagon suddenly swerves back behind us. Keeping her eyes ahead, she points at the plastic bag filled with her stuff at my feet. 'Chuck on the cat ears. It'll calm me down.'

'No way.'

'I'm your personal driver and I say, "Yes way".'

'Five minutes, that's it, then they're off.'

I follow orders.

She side-eyes me and a cackle hurtles out of her mouth. 'Good kitty.'

I let her have this one — even look in the mirror to straighten the ears — then return to watching endless kilometres of empty paddocks and rolling hills pass us by. My left arm is already pink from an hour of leaning on the open window. Dusk is coming. The sun edges down through the sky, bright and warm, eager to call it a day. I shut my eyes.

Layla slaps my thigh. 'Nope, wake up! Have a snack to refuel. Passengers need to entertain the driver, that's the rule.'

'I put the cat ears on, didn't I?' I take them off and twirl them around my finger.

'Talk to me, MD. I don't want to fall asleep.'

'Fine.' I give in, cracking open a bottle of water. 'Tell me something. Tell me about ... tell me about your boyfriend. I don't know anything about this guy. How long have you been going out?'

Layla's hands tighten on the wheel. 'I don't know.'

'How can you *not* know?'

She shrugs. 'Never really paid attention to a calendar ... I don't know! One day we weren't going out, one day we were.'

'You must know.'

'We've been on and off, and ... when does it even count as being official? If I had to guess —'

'You have to *guess*?'

'Maybe like a year and a bit. Or just under a year? I'm probably making that up.'

Sal counts our relationship to the month. Seven months. One year and four months. Two years and two months. There was a point early on when she was even counting the weeks. Seventeen weeks. Forty-three weeks. That sort of thing.

'Did you meet him at school?'

She laughs. 'What, like you lovers? Nah, I wasn't like head of the debate team and he wasn't like captain of the footy team. We met through a friend of a friend, I guess you'd say.'

'Okay. And what's he like?'

She bites her bottom lip.

'Come on. You're the one who wanted to talk.'

'He's ... he's a guy. He likes ... stuff. I dunno, how do you describe anyone really?'

'Milo: handsome, intelligent, brilliant, genius. See? Easy.' I raise an eyebrow to see if she bites. Nothing. 'Geez. You could be a politician.'

''Cos I'm full of crap?'

''Cos you evade questions like a boss.'

'Maybe it's my turn to question you. Can Sal drive?'

'Yes.'

'Then she's already a million times cooler than you.'

She looks in the rear-view mirror, pausing for an extra-long second so I glance out the back window. The station wagon is kicking up dust as it closes in, trying to overtake again.

'Maybe let it pass, Lay.'

'Nah, they can learn some patience. So, how did you meet Sal then?'

'The debate team.'

Layla snorts. 'Of course. You master debater with your — whoa! Stop speeding, you moron!'

I'm thrown forward in my seat as we swerve to the left to allow the station wagon to overtake us. My water has sprayed all over my jeans.

'Damn,' I mutter, shaking my head.

'I can't believe that car! What a steaming pile of —'

SMASH!

Something's slammed onto the front of our car, hitting the bonnet. I'm thrown forward, my hands pressed against the glovebox, while Layla struggles with the wheel. A maze of cracks spreads down the bottom left of the windscreen. Above it, a thick wet smear of red.

Layla has lost control of the car — I know it before she even starts shrieking. Fear is trapped at the base of my throat. I can't find my voice, not even to yell. Layla's deep, unbroken screams pierce the air.

We barrel off the highway, crunching down on gravel before whipping through knee-level grass. Despite the fading pink light, I can see we're hurtling towards a stand of trees.

'The brakes!' I manage. 'Hit the brakes!'

This is it. This is how we're going to die.

I wait for my life to flash before me but nothing comes.

Now we're spinning like we're on a ride at Disneyland.

And now I'm screaming.

My head whips forward then snaps backwards, whacking the top of my seat.

We've stopped. At least I think we've stopped.

I lean back against my seat, cringing at the ache at the base of my neck. There's glass sprinkled across my feet, scratching my skin, but all I can focus on is the sound of Layla crying next to me. I haven't heard her cry since her mum's funeral.

Layla

Milo uses the light on his phone to inspect the damage to the front of the car. Cracked windscreen, bloodstains, dented bonnet, shattered glass. I linger a metre behind him, wiping away evidence of wet cheeks with my T-shirt, but I don't bother pointing out that a windscreen wiper has been torn off in the crash. There's enough to worry about.

The sun has set now. Our car is off the highway, wedged in a cluster of trees. I can make out the purring drone of traffic, but can't see anything other than long grass, shrubs and a glint of moonlight squeezing through the tree branches. Milo and I are hidden away in the dark. Based on the circumstances, I'm not sure if that's a good thing or a bad thing.

'Do you think we killed it?' I ask.

I'm not even positive what 'it' might be. Probably a roo. Hopefully not a roo. Although I don't know what else I'd want it to be either. All I can think about is the crimson blood splattered on the car. I need Milo to hug me, to break through the air separating us, but he stays still as always, arms straight, hands heavy. I can't seem to go to him either.

'It came out of nowhere, I couldn't see properly and —'

'Don't worry, Lay, it'll be …' He can't finish his sentence. '*You're* okay, right?'

'I'm okay.' I'm lying. 'You?'

'I'm okay.' He's lying too.

We're silent, both staring at the car again. The air is dry, but my T-shirt is sticky. I'm hoping it's just sweat. Milo is flushed, his hair is damp. He can't stop shaking his head; can't stop swearing in a low, deep whisper. It's like he's on repeat.

I can't stop thinking what it must've been like the day Mum died.

Dried blood in matted hair.

Her lifeless body.

Twisted metal.

I dry-retch at the thought, crossing my arms as I try not to gag again. I exhale.

Milo's gaze is on me. The corner of my mouth quivers in an attempted half-smile — a weak effort to reassure him I'm fine — before he breaks eye contact, like he's intruding.

A moment later, or maybe a collection of moments — time suddenly means nothing — he reaches over and takes my right hand in his left. I don't say a word, just let his touch warm my fingers and spread through my body.

I inch closer. It's my turn to look at him, straining to see how he *really* is, but he's too fast for me to catch his eye and his long lashes hide the truth. His shoulders are broader than I remember, and he's taller too, or maybe I'm slouching, trying to disappear within myself, trying to disappear into him.

His fingertip traces semicircles over where the tears have stained my cheeks, before linking his fingers with mine to stop my hand trembling. Then, without warning or hesitation, he pulls me in so tight it's like our bodies are melding together.

Milo

Layla's nose is pressed against my chest, while her fingers dance against the small of my back. They're there, then they're not, like she can't make up her mind whether to hold me or not. When she first curled into me, my heart was hammering — I bet she heard every thump through my T-shirt — but we've been standing like this, almost burying ourselves in each other, for so long my anxiety has thawed.

'I'm a dead man,' I say.

She pulls away, her arms loosening from around my waist. '*Almost.* You were almost a dead man. There's a difference.'

I tell her Trent is going to kill me for stuffing up the work car, then bring me back to life so he can kill me again. I can't even imagine what Mum and Dad will do if they find out. It's simple. They can't find out. *They can't.*

She snuggles back into me so suddenly I'm caught off guard. There's that familiar smell of coconut again. Jesus. It feels wrong to notice that now.

The battered car is still sitting where it landed. Layla hasn't dared move it yet, and I'm not making my driving debut at the scene of an accident. I look over her head at the trees lined up in a cluttered row in the spreading dark. One tree, with its craggy trunk and branches spiralling into the sky, is within arm's reach of the car. I try not to let my mind go there; the place where I think about what might've happened if Layla hit the brakes one second later. It's taken this long to stop my heart from thrashing inside my chest.

'Should we keep driving, or call someone?' Layla mumbles.

I shake my head. Neither option sounds good when we're two hours from Durnan and an hour from Canberra. I rule out my parents and Trent for obvious reasons. She rules out Kurt 'just because' and refuses to say much else about it. I rule out Dad's insurance company 'cos I have no idea how that works. She rules out her dad's girlfriend because she doesn't want to upset her.

Looks like Sal's it for now. My grand gesture's in the toilet.

'Hey, you've reached Sal,' her voicemail chimes. 'I'm probably doing something way more fun right now so please leave a message and I'll try to remember to check it. If that's you, Mum, yes, I'm looking after myself.'

I leave a voicemail and send her a few texts as back-up.

Half an hour passes and she still hasn't replied. I scowl at my phone, which is rapidly losing battery, then try her number again.

Layla tries to talk herself into reversing the car out of the thicket. Her hands shake on the steering wheel, while mine shake in my lap as I try to ignore the jagged hole in the windscreen.

'You've got this, Lay. Let's take it slow, yeah?'

'Yeah.' She's chewing on the inside of her cheek so hard I'm worried there'll be blood.

'Sure you're alright?'

'Yep. Fine.' Her bottom lip trembles. 'Stop staring at me like that, Milo. I can feel you staring. Just gimme a sec.'

I watch as she sucks in short, sharp breaths, her hands tightening around the wheel, knuckles clenched.

Jesus.

Her eyes fill with tears again. We can't drive anywhere tonight. I can't put her through it, no matter how much I want to get home and deal with the fallout before we risk getting in even more shit.

I tell her to turn off the car and we'll leave in the morning, then she grabs a bottle of water out of her plastic bag, leaps out of the front seat and clambers onto the boot with the cat ears on her head. I don't blame her. Not after what happened to us. Not after everything with her mum.

Not that she's brought that up. And I don't know if I should bring it up.

Yep, just another day with Layla Montgomery where I wish I had someone whispering lines to me from the wings.

I lift myself onto the boot next to her. Our legs hang side by side and, for a second, as I lie against the back window, everything feels calm. Somehow the accident already seems blurry in my mind, like it's a dream from a few nights ago and I'm struggling to recall it in full detail.

'Kinda wish we had something stronger to drink,' Layla mutters. She sighs. 'We need to do something about that blood.'

And the dream's a reality again.

'We'll sort it. Promise.'

'Thanks, dude.'

'Anytime. Well, hopefully not ever again ... you know what I mean.'

'I do. Hey, I was thinking ... if we're stuck here for the night, can we hold a memorial service? For Skippy?'

'Serious?'

'I don't joke.' Pause. 'Fine, I always joke, but not about this.'

'Not about roadkill?'

'Don't call him that. Or her. It might've been a her.'

'You really want to do a funeral?'

'I do.'

We lie in silence for a while before Lay repositions herself on the boot.

'Hey, so we seriously could've died today, huh?'

'Don't say that.' Hypocrite. I've been haunted by the same thought.

'Hear me out,' she says. 'We nearly died, our phones are running out of batteries, we're stuck in Trent's dirty-jocks wagon, and you don't get to see your girlfriend. Tonight blows. It blows hard. We need a little party for two to cheer us up, don't you reckon?'

'Here? In the middle of nowhere?'

'Yes! Okay, there's no cider or beer, but what good is sitting here doing nothing?'

I gulp down the rest of my water. I can't tell if she's serious or trying to distract us, but without a script I'm following her lead and side-stepping any triggers that might upset her. Anything to stop me saying or doing the wrong thing.

'Alright,' I say. 'But we're leaving by eight in the morning.'

'Eleven.'

'No way. Nine.'

'Ten.'

'Nine fifteen. We've gotta get back for your training in the arvo.'

She swears at herself. 'At least *you* remembered that. Hey, any word from Sal?'

I glance at my phone out of habit, but know there's still nothing. I shake my head. The only thing that's changed is the battery has dropped down even further. As I turn off my phone to try to save it, I resist the urge to ask Layla why she didn't call Kurt.

* * *

I lie on my stomach on the car roof and watch Layla rifling through the boot.

'Boring,' her muffled voice says. 'There's just boxes of books.'

'Funny that, in a car owned by a bookstore.'

I hear laughing, then, 'Jackpot!' She pokes her head out of the boot and waves around a Little Bookshop shirt. 'There's a whole carton of them in here. All sizes and everything.'

She passes me her water to hold, then unzips her jeans.

'Er, whatcha doing?'

'Dress-ups.'

She rolls up her top, baring her stomach, then tugs at her jeans until they're over her hips. I look away. I'm still recovering from the first time black lace made a surprise appearance.

'Dude, chuck me your belt.'

'Huh?' I'm still not letting myself look.

'Just face me, dorkatron. You're safe.'

Her boots are off. Her jeans are in a heap in the dirt. The top swims on her frame, touching the top of her knees.

'Your belt?' she says, holding out her hand.

I roll up to a sitting position, unhook it, then pass it down to her.

'Nearly there.' She wrestles my belt around her waist, fashioning the top into a dress. A very tiny dress. She leans against the car as she yanks on her boots, then swipes more red onto her lips. 'Ta da!' She puckers her mouth and flings her hands into the air, causing everything to ride up. 'Friggin' hell. I guess sudden movements are out.' She readjusts her outfit, then notices the nametag pinned to the pocket. 'Veronica?'

'Our old weekend manager. She's in Wollongong now.'

'*Veronicaaaa*,' she rolls the word off her tongue. 'I can be a Veronica.'

'Veronica would never do this. Any of this.'

Layla ruffles her hair, making it as frizzy as she can. 'Sure she would. This is such a Veronica thing to do. Now, let me get into character: I'm Veronica, a busy mum with three kids. I'm into scrapbooking, baking wedding cakes for bridezillas, and, when my husband Enrique is at work, knitting sweaters for our sixteen Scottish terriers.'

'Your imagination terrifies me.'

She grins. 'Or how about this: I'm Rach, a perky straight-A student who falls for the biggest jock at school, but one day — one seemingly ordinary day — when I'm tutoring him in maths — no, wait, in modern history — at the library, I take off my —'

'Perve.'

'I was going to say glasses, *perve*. Anyway, I take off my glasses, and then we have an epic pash-off in the history section in front of everyone.'

Maybe it's because she looks ridiculous with her puffed-up hair and smudged lips, maybe it's because she said 'we have an epic pash-off', that my brain almost explodes, or maybe it's a little of both. Whatever it is, my mouth slides into a smirk. I try to hide it before she sees.

'Just be you,' I say.

'Fine. I'm Layla and I remember when you weren't so afraid of having fun.'

I gesture at the trees and the twinkling sky. 'This isn't fun? Well, considering the circumstances …'

'It's getting there,' she says, kicking at the dirt before closing the boot and climbing up next to me. 'But remember when you stole your nanna's false teeth and put them in your mouth? *That* was fun.'

I cringe. 'I'd blocked that out. Don't you have any good memories of me?'

'All of it's good,' she says, squeezing my knee. 'I shouldn't tell you this 'cos your ego will grow to the size of the sun, but Mum *kinda* wanted us to get together one day.'

My guts somersault.

'Not your dad, though?' I joke, letting out an awkward snort. 'It was probably 'cos your mum thought I was boring — a safe option.'

'*Please.* I wouldn't be in the middle of friggin' whoopdee-knows-where if it wasn't for you. This isn't like a normal Friday night for me. You're not as boring as you think you are, MD.'

'Ah, thanks. I think.'

'I never agreed with her, you know? With Mum. About ending up with you.'

'Yeah. Imagine that.'

'Oh, I have.'

That's new information.

'Kinda anyway. But back then, I'm pretty sure I imagined marrying every boy I met.'

'Picky, much?'

'The pickiest.' She laughs, suddenly interested in the scuffs on her boots. 'I guess I wondered back then if a Dark would be my first one day.'

'First what?' Then it hits me. '*That*? You did?'

She bumps her shoulder against mine. 'Maybe. Too late now though.' She mouths *oops*. 'Don't tell Dad. He'll murder Kurt in his sleep.'

'Too late, I'm Snapchatting this conversation.'

'Quiet, you. So have you and Sal ...?'

I nod. Barely enough times to fill a hand, but enough for that answer to be the truth.

'Well. There you go.'

'There *you* go.'

Layla scuttles down from the roof and onto the car boot. 'You were always too scared to kiss me.'

'No way. I mean ...' Jesus. What do I mean? 'That came out wrong —'

'Hello, spin the bottle six years ago,' Layla says, coming to my rescue. 'I ended up making out with Toby that night, remember him? He went in with the tongue and everything. Ballsy move, but I guess it made up for your *very public* knockback.'

Okay, she's not saving me after all.

But then she smiles. 'Yep, you were in my museum of hurt or whatever after that. And don't look so surprised, MD. People always remember the ones who turned them down.'

Shit. How much longer are we stuck here alone together?

Layla

The night has cooled off so we venture into the back seat and push the front seats forward for space.

'Your turn,' Milo says with a mouth full of Cheezels. 'Truth or dare?'

I take the Cheezel looped over his left thumb and pop it in my mouth. 'Truth.'

'Again? I'm running out of questions.'

'Can't be bothered moving.'

'Fine. Truth … truth …' There's a pause then he clears his throat, building up to asking me another question. 'So … truth: why'd you *really* come back? When you left, you were just gone and … I guess I never thought I'd see you again.'

Just gone. He says the words like I vanished out of existence, and in a way I guess I did. The old me did anyway.

I can still remember Dad's fingers digging into my shoulder, shaking me awake. His voice croaked, 'We're leaving — not in the morning, right now', then he told me to get up, move it, get my stuff, stop crying. I was still wrapped in my bedsheet as I screamed for him to let me stay in Durnan, but he continued to tear through the wardrobe, ripping my clothes off hangers and tossing them into suitcases laid open on the carpet. Kneeling on the doona, tears streaking my cheeks, I threatened to run away to my friends, to get Jen, to call the police, but Dad didn't stop. He was like a machine as he grabbed and threw my belongings into the cases.

I stopped shrieking when I realised he was crying too, but I refused to help him pack up our stuff. I clung to every extra minute in Durnan I could. We left most of our belongings behind for removalists to move into storage later, only taking what fitted in the car. Turns out there's only so much of a life you can fit in a car. As we left town, Dad told me he couldn't stand one more night in the house where she'd lived. There were too many memories trapped within those walls. He didn't understand that I needed to spend *every second of every minute of every hour of every night* in the house where she'd lived. But what I wanted didn't matter any more.

Milo clears his throat again. I remember I'm supposed to be answering his question. 'Sorry,' he mumbles. 'Not my business.'

'It's fine … I'm here 'cos … 'cos I have to be. Until I work out what's next anyway.'

He nods.

'And yeah, Dad and I left in a rush, but you wouldn't have wanted to hear from me. Not how I was.'

'Whaddya mean?'

'One truth at a time, dude.' I bite my lip, suddenly feeling like I'm playing with my old best friend in the treehouse again, like I can tell him anything. 'Okay, you want to know why you wouldn't have wanted to hear from me?'

He nods. 'Yeah, 'cos I can't think of a single reason.'

Oh, Milo.

'Well ...' I hesitate, realising I'm not sure if I can explain this without sounding bonkers. 'I ... I kinda stopped being me five years ago ... and turned into someone else. That must sound weird.'

I wait for him to scoff or laugh or shift uncomfortably in his seat, but he only waits for the rest to be filled in.

When I don't, he clears his throat once again. 'Who did you become, Lay?'

I shrug off the sudden thumping in my chest. 'The girl with the dead mum.'

His hand edges closer to mine but he doesn't link our fingers.

'Believe me, no-one knew how to talk to or be around that girl — me — whatever.' I shrug. 'And Dad ... wow. For him, *not* being here in Mum's places and with her people ... that was the only thing that worked. So we stayed away and we stopped remembering. Then, years later, he met Shirin.'

'And he came back,' Milo says, his voice almost a murmur. 'And so did you.'

'Don't remind me.'

'Couldn't resist Durnan's charms, huh?'

'Oh, it's *very* charming and almost impossible to resist.'

I pluck a Cheezel from his hand, then quickly look away. Are we being weird again? Is this flirting? Or have I simply forgotten how to be a normal functioning human and I'm reading way too much into a situation? The latter, I tell myself, always the latter.

'Anyway,' I add in a rush, 'you cheated in this game by asking me too many questions and now you have too many answers. So here's a question for you: is there chocolate somewhere in this car?'

Milo holds up a block of caramel chocolate, and tears it open to snap off a row before passing it to me.

'Hey, remember that slice we always had at barbecues?' he says. 'So good. Caramel, wasn't it?'

'Cherry.'

Slice was always Mum's speciality at those gatherings.

'Right, cherry ... so good,' he repeats as he climbs out of the car. I hear him release a long whistle, then he pokes his head through the window. 'Hey, come out here for a sec. You've gotta see this.'

I follow him around to the boot. The white moon carves a perfect arc in a sky sprinkled with stars. It's crisp, tranquil and almost spectacular enough to make me forget we're stranded off the highway and hundreds of kilometres from a warm bed.

'Here.' Milo raises a half-eaten row of chocolate to the sky and elbows me to do the same. 'As promised ... to our little mate Skippy, wherever you are. Hope you're

having, or have had, a life packed with great times …
and, ah, fingers crossed you're at peace out there in the
bush again. Cheers, champ.'

'You did good.' I shuffle towards him, closing the gap.
I rest my head on his shoulder. He doesn't move away.
We watch the moon.

* * *

Milo's knee digs into mine. 'Oi, MD. That hurts.'

'Sorry. Why aren't you sleeping?'

'Can't.'

'Same.'

I sit up and gaze out the window. The moon is
still burning a white hole in the night. I don't want to
bring up the crash, but the words are building up inside
me.

Milo uncoils himself until he's sitting next to me, legs
stretched out wide. I notice he has chocolate crumbs on
his chin, so I lean forward to wipe them off, but he pulls
away, the skin near his eyes crinkling with confusion
before I even touch him.

'You've got stuff on your … doesn't matter.'

He clears his throat. 'Hey, Lay?'

I sit up a little straighter. 'Hey, MD?'

'I'm so freakin' sorry about this — the drive, the
car … getting stuck here. We wouldn't be on the side of a
highway if it wasn't for me. You can't deny that so don't
even try.'

I'm so stunned by his vehement apology that I almost laugh. 'Dude, I'm the one who drove us off the road and towards a tree.'

'But I made us do this … you've been through enough.'

Knew I shouldn't have told him about me and Dad.

'*I* was driving us. Chill.'

'I just … everything can fall apart, like in the worst possible way, so fast.' He hangs his head. 'Like, when *your* life changed overnight, in seconds really, I don't think I got it. I had no idea.'

'MD, we were kids.'

'I thought we'd go back to hanging out normally after a while, you know? Like I hadn't realised everything was different, even though *everything* was different. It is so obvious now. What an idiot.'

I nod, not 'cos I think he's an idiot, but 'cos I've been there too. It took me ages to admit Mum wasn't paying bills on her laptop in the home office, or outside in the backyard weeding the garden behind the treehouse. Even now I sometimes expect to see her face peeking around the door to my room, especially on birthdays. She always greeted me on my birthday with cupcakes in bed. Cupcakes with rainbow icing.

'I shoulda been there more,' Milo continues. 'Maybe you could've stayed in Durnan with us, at least for a bit longer. Not that I think you needed rescuing or anything! You're strong — stronger than anyone I know.'

That makes me smile. 'Even more than your boy Murph? Those guns of his are strong.'

He laughs. I've got him.

'I'm being serious! And you know what I mean … or maybe you don't realise how tough you are. It's pretty amazing. You're amazing.'

Nightfall hides whether he's managed to say it without blushing. I bet he hasn't.

'Now who's being cheesy? Well, if it is amazing then I guess I learnt from someone amazing. Mum *was* super-cool when she caught us digging that tunnel to the North Pole, remember?'

'Yeah, she didn't tell your dad, even though we'd stuffed up the lawn around the lemon tree.'

I'd forgotten that part. 'Did she blame it on the neighbours' dog? I dunno … but Santa got me an extra present that year for being enthusiastic about Christmas.'

'He didn't get me one.' Milo elbows me. 'Suck-up.'

'Always.'

I don't know if it's the stolen hours in the night, or the feeling that this strange moment in time between Durnan and Canberra is barely real life, but I suddenly don't want to forget anything. I'm drawn in. I *want* to remember.

'Hey, MD?'

'Yeah, Lay?'

I curl up a little closer to him. 'Tell me something else about Mum.'

Milo

Her head is on my shoulder when she asks me again for a story. I heard her the first time, I'm just light on stuff to say.

Well, the right stuff to say.

'I'm thinking.'

She smiles. 'Think faster.'

It's hard to think fast when she's close enough to hear my heart thumping in my chest.

'Alright. Got one.' I clear my throat. 'Remember when your mum came to parent–teacher interview night dressed as Wonder Woman?'

Her mouth opens. 'Do I? How could I forget? She wore Dad's blue Speedos over her stockings. She had a wedgie … *in public*.'

I crack up. 'I remember.'

'And they were all baggy and saggy from the wash,' she shakes her head. 'Oh my God, that's why we never should've dared her to do anything! Shameless. She'd do anything for a laugh.'

'Sounds like you.'

'You didn't see me strutting around Durnan High in budgie-smugglers.'

I tug at the uniform clinging to her body. 'True. But you've got potential. Genetics.'

'Maybe.' She smirks. 'I liked the time she filled your family's mailbox with chocolates.'

'Ah, the *melted chocolate incident*.'

Layla snorts. 'She didn't realise you'd all gone away for the weekend! She wanted to surprise you guys.'

'She did. And they still tasted good.'

'She knew you loved them.'

I nod, transported back to the day of discovering the soft, squishy bars of chocolate stacked high in our mailbox.

This is the problem with peeling back the lid on old memories — everything spills out in all directions. Because now when I remember our mailbox, I also remember the Montgomery's mailbox.

They sat side by side. They were matching.

Mum was the first to notice the Montgomerys' mailbox was heaving over with junk mail. It could've been days after the funeral. Maybe weeks. All I know is Dad realised their sedan was missing, too.

The warning signs were wasted on me and Trent — Layla had become a ghost since the funeral. One minute she was stretched out on the strip of grass between our driveways with her friends, flipping through magazines and listening to music on a portable speaker; the next, she'd disappeared into her house and shut the curtains around her and her dad. I rarely saw her come and go any more, and I never saw him. When she stopped showing up at school, I didn't question it; just figured I'd skip class too if the same thing happened to me.

Everyone thought that.

We never imagined what else might be going down.

Jesus. We had no idea.

I heard Mum and Dad whispering in the dark of the kitchen one night — quiet enough that I couldn't hear all the details, but loud enough to know something big was up. While their voices rose and fell — Mum's shook the louder she spoke — I snuck out through the laundry door to check for myself.

My hand pressed against the splintery wood of the fence that separated our backyards as I strained to look through one of the holes. The grass was clipped. The garden was tidy. The treehouse loomed large. There was nothing out of place — a few teachers from Durnan High had been cleaning up the backyard once a week.

I tiptoed along the fence, swearing as my arm scraped against the wood, then eased open the side gate. I sprinted up the steps to Layla's veranda and, sucking in a breath, peered through the window into their kitchen. It looked normal to me, other than a few cupboard doors were open and there were bowls and plates stacked on the sink.

I didn't know that it meant something.

When I woke up the next day, Mum and Dad called Trent and me to sit down and they told us: the

Montgomerys had left town. They didn't know why. They didn't know where they were. They didn't know if they were coming back.

They were just gone.

But now, with Layla's head resting on my shoulder again, I don't tell her any of that. She's already carrying scars that sit just below the surface.

I stretch out on the back seat and try to ignore the touch of her fingertips on the back of my hand as she whispers that she hasn't let herself think of all that for years.

Layla

Bright light rips through the window. I rub at my eyes, which have shrivelled to slits, and wince at the thumping cacophony in my head. Morning has caught up to me. I have to suck it up and drive home whether I'm up for it or not — and I'm definitely not up for it.

There's no sign of Milo. Propping myself up on one elbow, I cringe at the cracked windscreen and dented bonnet. I'd almost blocked out that part. I strain to see him lying on the grass in the shade, arms crossed over his face. My boots crunch down on a half-eaten packet of chips, which have spilled across the car floor. I fiddle with the handle until the door struggles open.

'Hey,' I croak, peering down at him. 'You alive?'

'Maybe,' his muffled voice replies. 'Unless this is hell?'

'Possibly. Why does it feel like I haven't slept?'

'No idea. Especially 'cos you snored for like an hour.'

'Damn Veronica, this is all her fault.' I pull at the nametag still pinned to my T-shirt. 'Tell everybody: Veronica made us do it.'

Milo groans. He still hasn't removed his arms from his face.

'MD, I want eight thousand McMuffins.'

'You're a McMuffin.'

'I wish. Hey, what time are we leaving again?'

'Nine fifteen. Why? What time is it?'

'No idea. I'm outta battery. Reckon I can go back to sleep for a bit?'

'Probably.' Without getting up, he turns on his phone.

When he springs to his feet, I know we're screwed. And boy, are we.

Because it's 12.23 pm, and it takes about two hours to get back to Durnan. My training at Joe's Charcoal Chicken Shop starts at 2 pm, I stink like someone on day five of schoolies' week, and I feel like I've spent ten hours trapped in a tumble dryer. I'd be furious at my terrible life choices, but I'm too busy wondering whether I can curl up under the nearest tree and wait for a truck driver to throw me a double cheeseburger.

With bacon.

And maybe large fries.

Definitely large fries.

Milo passes me his phone, which beeps in my hand. The battery is close to quitting. I dial the chicken shop's number while Milo watches on, his hand buried in a packet of pretzels. It rings out, then the phone beeps again.

'Just say you're sick,' Milo says. 'It's kind of true. Like a half-lie.'

'It's not enough. Joe's a tough old dude from the city. Like, if I actually was sick, I'd have to show up

133

and prove it by, I don't know, coughing up a lung or bleeding from my nose, then hang on until he sent me home. He might be new around town but I know his deal. If I say I'm sick, he's either going to think I'm a wimp or I'm lying.'

'Which you are.'

I scrunch up my nose at him — *not helping* — and try again.

This time Joe grunts hello down the line after two rings. I'm on.

I'm on and I'm not ready.

Joe puts me on hold while he swaps to the phone in his back office. My mind kicks into overdrive. Panic at the thought of losing this job rattles my brain. I need to be able to pay my way. I need to prove to Kurt that he doesn't have to get messed up in whatever he's getting messed up in. I need to get my life started again, even if I'm elbow-deep in chicken fat while doing it. All of that depends on the next second, the next words out of my mouth, on telling a lie so detailed, so creative, that it can't possibly be made up.

I'm not proud of lying, but as I hear Joe's voice asking me what's going on, there's no time to back out. Thirty seconds in and I know he believes every word I'm feeding him: that I can't come in today because my mum has dislocated her shoulder while hanging out the washing and I've taken her to emergency.

Joe tells me he understands and we'll reschedule, adding, 'You're a good daughter.'

I thank him for his kindness. Despite my heart pounding, somehow my voice hasn't wobbled over the word 'mum'. Not once. For a few small minutes, the real me no longer exists. I'm lost in my lie, believing it so much it almost feels true. I'm 'Layla the girl who'd do anything to help her family in a time of need', not 'Layla the screw-up with a sorry state of a bank account, a boyfriend who's dealing pot and a dead mum'. I'm transformed.

I'm midway through explaining that Dad is away for work, which is why it's up to *me* to drive Mum to the hospital, when I catch Milo gaping at me. I've been so caught up in orchestrating my performance of a lifetime that I'd forgotten he was watching.

I'm not sure how I feel about it myself — it wasn't planned, or something I've ever done before. But as shame rises through me, from my toes to the top of my head, dusting my cheeks with a cherry glow, I know I never want him to look at me that way again.

When I hang up, he doesn't ask me why I said what I did.

Maybe he doesn't want to risk upsetting me.

Or maybe he's scared of the answer.

* * *

The staff at Macca's let Milo charge his phone while we scrub the car at the petrol station next door. I don't bother charging mine. Kurt had his chance yesterday but went MIA. Another hour or so without hearing from me won't bother him.

'I should go get my phone before Ronald McDonald nicks it,' Milo announces, hosing down the bonnet. Everything still bends in the wrong places, but at least the blood and dust is gone. I spare another thought for Skippy. 'Want anything while I'm in there, Lay? Coke? Sneaky cheesie?'

He still hasn't mentioned my phone call with Joe.

'Nah, I feel a bit off,' I say as he hangs up the hose. 'Actually who am I kidding … nuggets! And don't forget the sweet and sour. Thanks.'

'On it.'

He lopes over to Macca's, and I can see him through the glass, standing in line, phone pressed to his ear. A few minutes pass. His head is down, he's shaking it. Something's up.

When he returns, shoulders hunched, he's carrying two bottles of Coke and a cheeseburger.

I lean on the car, peering across the roof at him. 'No nuggets?'

'Crap. Sal rang and I flaked. I'll go back.'

'All good, we'll split the cheesie. And by split, I mean I'll eat most of it.' I pause. 'Hey, MD?'

'Hey, Lay?'

He climbs into the car so I follow suit. I rev the engine.

'You're kinda quiet. You mad at me?'

''Cos of the nuggets? Nah, just forgot.'

'No, 'cos of before … with Joe?'

Milo stares through the splintered screen. 'What? I haven't said anything.'

'Exactly,' I say, driving us out of the petrol station and onto the highway.

'Wait, you want me to?'

His eyes are on my hands now. I readjust my grip on the wheel, almost to prove I'm still capable of driving.

'No ... well, kind of. You *not* saying something is worse. I'd rather you be angry at me than *nothing* at me.'

'I'm not angry, I'm ...' He pauses, probably realising he's got himself in it now. 'Bit worried, I suppose.'

I turn to face him. 'That's even worse.'

'Can you watch the road?' He opens the packet of jelly snakes and coils one around his finger. 'I vote we talk about this later. Let's get home, get to a mechanic, get some sleep. In that order.'

His phone buzzes. A message.

'Is that Sal again?' I can't help myself, so I pop a snake in my mouth in the hope it shuts me up. 'How is she?' Nope. Didn't work.

'Great.' There's a bite to his tone that I haven't heard before. 'Apparently she ended up going to a big party in Bungendore last night. They did a car rally all over Canberra.'

'No way, that's awesome.'

'Yeah.'

'And she knows about the accident?'

'Yeah.' He clears his throat. 'She left her phone in Jamie's car last night so just saw my messages ... Anyway, doesn't matter.'

He passes me the unwrapped cheeseburger and turns on the radio, doing an abysmal job of pretending everything is fine.

For once, I don't say a word.

Milo

I told Sal that I missed her, and she said that she missed me too. We said it back and forth a few times through the call, especially after I mentioned the car accident. I shared just enough to paint a picture of a grand gesture that'd gone unbelievably wrong. She gasped and swore in all the right places and seemed happy when I told her I'd been coming to surprise her. I guess I made myself sound like a legendary boyfriend. The sort that steals a car and hits the road for two hundred and fifty kilometres so he can see his girlfriend. A guy of the super variety.

Yeah. And I'm also the new prime minister of Australia. I'm moving into the Lodge on Monday.

Sal knows I'm no hero, but I had to try to cancel out all the weeks we've been apart and make up for lost time. That's why I didn't mention Layla's name again. *Couldn't* mention it. Just like I didn't ask why Sal'd told me she was lying low if she was planning on partying all weekend. And why I had to stop myself asking why Woody's arm is wrapped around her shoulders in every second photo of them together. Our catch-ups need to be full of 'Wish you were here' and 'Wish I was there', don't they? How else are you meant to cram a relationship into a handful of rushed phone calls and texts?

Especially when I've just spent a night in a car with another girl.

A girl who won't stop winking and singing and humming and forgetting to adjust her baggy top, which keeps slipping down over her bare shoulder.

Definitely not a champion boyfriend.

It isn't until I'm chowing into my half of the cheeseburger that I realise Sal didn't bother to dig for details from me either. Not about the family friend I'm travelling with, or what I'd planned for the surprise, or what I did all night in the middle of freakin' nowhere.

She could be as worn out as I am from feeling stretched between two states, or she mightn't have wanted to be the one to ruin the moment. Or maybe she just doesn't care.

At school, all our mates thought Sal and I were meant to be. That we were 'locked in' as her friends used to say. For two years I believed them. It's easy to believe stuff if you're told it often enough. Except, I think as I wind down the window, I haven't been told it for a while.

'D&M skills: five out of five.'

'What?'

'Earth to MD!' Layla tickles my side. 'I said D&M skills: five out of five. Driving skills: two out of five. That one's on me, obviously. Company: four stars. We're excellent sorts, but there's always room for improvement.'

I swivel to face her. '*Please*. Company is at least four and a third. At least.'

'Snacks: three and a half,' she says with a laugh. 'We had some tasty choices, but we stuffed up the sweet-to-savoury ratio. And those jelly snakes have left the weirdest taste in my mouth. Music: half out of five. That one's on both of us, although we didn't count on the whole sleeping-on-the-side-of-the-road thing. Next time we're bringing a speaker and batteries.'

'Next time?'

'I'm focusing on the positives. My survival guide for Durnan is all about the positives.'

'Oh, yeah.' I roll my eyes. 'We've stuffed the car, you lied to get out of training, my girlfriend doesn't give a rat's, and for some reason you won't call your boyfriend for help. Remind me where the positives are?'

I suck in a breath. I hadn't meant to explode like that.

'Wow. Anger management much?'

My palms sweat as I wait for her to say something else, but she only stares ahead, tapping her fingers on the wheel.

'Lay …' She doesn't leap to finish my sentence like she often does. This is bad.

'Nah, it's true. It's a big rotten mess.'

'Stop. *You* were right.'

She arches an eyebrow as if to say *go on*.

'And that other stuff — the lie, your boyfriend — none of that's my business. And yeah, there's been stuff happen that I wish didn't, but … but last night was still somehow fun.'

I glance at her, trying to gauge if she's soaking it in. It's impossible to tell because she won't look in my direction.

'The most fun I've had in ages, despite the big rotten mess.' *There*. I catch a smile. 'And if *I* have to rate it ... well, overall road trip: four and a half out of five. I think we could've done without the whole accident part. But the rest? The rest was perfect.'

Pause.

Pause.

Pause.

And then.

'Overall trip: four and a half stars,' she says. 'I agree. Anyway, what's the time check, good sir?'

She's back.

'Two thirty-three, Miss Montgomery. We'll be home in about fifteen. Mum and Dad will be at the races, and Trent's not back 'til tomorrow arvo, so we've got time to spare.'

'What a finish. Legendary, some might say.'

'And some would be correct. I reckon we swing past mine for like two minutes so I can drop off my stuff — you know, after "staying the night at Murph's" — so Mum and Dad don't freak that I've bailed for Sydney with him or something. Then it's straight to the mechanic.'

'Your parents love you so much it makes me sick. And by the way, I love this plan. It's genius.'

* * *

We slow to a stop in front of my house. Layla spots Trent tearing across the veranda before I do.

'What do we do? MD? Should we get outta here? Shit!'

I'm frozen.

Trent was supposed to be away camping for another night, but there's no time to wonder why he's back so soon. He's seen us, which means he's also seen the giant dent in the bonnet and the crack yawning across the windscreen. If he was going to be annoyed about us taking his work car, he's going to go postal about us banging it up.

I unbuckle my seatbelt, wondering if it's too late to escape and start a new life thousands of kilometres away in Darwin or Byron Bay. As he barrels down the driveway, I can see he's barefoot, shirtless and ruddy — maybe blistering from too much time water-skiing with the boys, or maybe so angry his body is close to self-combusting.

Layla's widened eyes search mine for guidance, but I've still got nothing. After months in overdrive, my brain has chosen this instant to take a sick day.

Trent's arms pump back and forth at his sides as he storms towards us, shouting so many obscenities our neighbours will have enough material to talk about for the next six months.

He opens the door before I can, now so close I can see a vein pumping in his forehead.

Hand gripping the top of my T-shirt, he yanks me out of the car and pins me against the back passenger door.

'I can explain!' I say as the door handle digs into my lower back. 'Let me explain!'

'Go on then.'

I strain away, pushing at his hands, body wilting against the car. 'Let ... go ... first.' I feel pathetic and bet I look it in front of Layla too.

'What happened to my car, mate?'

'Trent, let him go.' Layla circles around the car to stand behind him. 'Let him go then I'll explain.'

'He's a big boy, Montgomery.'

Without warning, Layla throws herself on Trent's back. She wraps her arms around his neck and jerks backwards, putting all of her weight into it. He sways on his feet, but finds his balance, grunting for her to get off him. Her knees and feet dig in around his waist, her hands clutch at his throat, his shoulders, his collarbone, anything she can make contact with. Trent's grip on me loosens, slipping a little every time she pulls.

'Montgomery, relax!' He chokes out a laugh. 'Jesus, I'm only messing around! I'll let go! I'll let go!'

She doesn't though, and with a final tug from her, I manage to twist out of Trent's grasp. I fall to the side and my hip slams into the open car door.

Trent walks over to join Layla, who has flopped onto the grass, panting. The two of them sit side by side, arms wrapped around their knees. He's always like this — exploding, then relaxing within a few minutes. A human firecracker.

I plonk down next to Layla, rubbing at my side. 'You're a real jerk, Trent, you know that?'

'*You* stuffed the car, bro.' He shakes his head. 'Mum and Dad are going to blow up when they see it. What were you doing?'

'Relax, you two, it's my fault,' Layla interrupts. 'Tell him, Milo, tell him we could've died. I didn't see a roo coming, but it was an accident. Just an accident.'

'I love ya, Montgomery, but he flogged my car.' Trent leans back on the grass so his shoulders and biceps pop.

I sit up straighter. 'It's technically mine too.'

Trent laughs. 'You're mucking. Well, the old man's not gonna let you in a fifty-kilometre radius of it now anyway.' He tugs at a blade of grass, swearing to himself. 'So a roo, huh? Poor bugger — did it make it?'

I swallow. 'I don't know.'

'There's some big ones out this way. You alright? How 'bout you, Lay?'

He got there in the end.

'We just need a mechanic,' Layla says, and shoots me a reassuring smile.

'Not sure why,' Trent says. 'It's gotta be a write-off.'

'Why are you even home?' I ask, eager to get the attention off us. 'What happened to camping?'

'Raj's missus showed up and it changed the whole vibe so we called it early.' He shakes his head again as he looks at the car. 'Unbelievable. The front half of that crapbox is a disaster.'

'I'm getting it fixed before anyone else finds out.'

'Better scram then, bro. Mum's inside.'

'What? Why didn't you tell me? I thought she was at the races.'

'Calm ya farm, her hair appointment went over or something.'

Freakin' Trent. As insightful as a tick.

Mum's voice pipes up behind us. 'Thought I heard a commotion out here. Hi, you three!'

Perfect.

She teeters towards us in heels and a fancy dress, adjusting a ridiculous hat in the shape of a flower. Oblivious to what's going on with us, she rattles on about her new hairdresser and Dad's tickets to the VIP marquee.

'It's so gorgeous to see you all lined up like that,' she gushes. 'Just like old times. I swear I have a photo somewhere just like it.'

Layla hurries to her feet. 'Ah, you look great, Jen ... I was, ah, just leaving.'

'So soon?' Mum takes us all in before her gaze rests on the car. 'Jesus Christ on a cracker! What happened?'

She totters over for a closer look, running her manicured hand over the dented bonnet, gasping when she sees the windscreen.

'I can explain everything,' I say. 'We're okay, but we hit a kangaroo and —'

'*You* and Murph did this? You took the car?' Mum's voice is trembling.

'No … not Murph. Just me.'

'And me,' Layla adds. Even her voice is shaking a little. 'I was driving.'

'I'm the only one to blame here,' I add.

Mum clears her throat. 'Inside the house now, Milo.'

'But, Mum, let me explain what —'

'I said now.' Her tone is hard. 'Trent? Are you also involved?'

He keeps his head down. Despite his flaws, he's not into ratting anyone out.

'Milo, I said *inside*.'

I haven't moved 'cos I'm still processing if there's a way to get out of this without dragging Layla through it too.

Mum grabs my arm, nails digging in, and pulls me towards the house. I don't bother to resist this time; I just hurry to keep up with her.

She pauses for a second and turns to face Layla, who's still standing on the lawn, one boot kneading the grass. 'Is someone coming to pick you up, Layla?'

'I don't think so, but I can walk home,' she says. 'I'm so sorry, Jen.'

Her voice is quiet, barely a murmur. She wouldn't ever have seen Mum like this. I don't think I have — not towards me anyway. I float under the radar most of the time. It was always Trent who got grounded or suspended. Never me.

Layla's eyes widen as Mum barks at Trent to drive her home in her car. She insists she's fine, but that doesn't mean squat to Mum, who tells Trent to put on a shirt then do what she says.

I'm not even sure why Mum's taking her frustration out on him right now. Maybe habit. Maybe disbelief that it's me who's stuffed up for once. As Trent heads up the driveway to grab a T-shirt, she turns around to drop her most cutting glare on me.

'I am barely keeping it together right now,' she says, disappointment oozing from every pore. 'Taking the car without permission, worrying me sick at the thought of what could've happened … don't even think about lying to me when we get inside, Milo. Don't even consider it.'

Layla catches my eye. Her look is apologetic, watery. *I'm sorry.*

Layla

'Here's fine,' I say, pointing at the rundown park around the corner from my house.

Trent slows the car to a stop. 'Which joint is yours, Monty Burns?'

I hop out, bag slung over my shoulder, and slam the door shut. 'Thanks for the lift,' I say, smirking at the nickname but ignoring the question. The fewer people who see the shabby old house I'm stuck in, the better. It's bad enough Milo saw it yesterday.

'Hey, wait a sec.' Trent leans out the window. I stand on the footpath, body heavy on my feet. 'So I acted like a massive tosser before.'

'You think?'

'Well, yeah. That's why I said it.' He clears his throat. 'Let me make it up to you.'

'Just make it up to Milo, dude. He's the one you attacked.'

'Says the ninja who put me in a chokehold.' I try not to laugh. 'Look, I was goofing around, just trying to scare him. That little muppet nicked my car, remember? And he wasn't the only one.'

'I know, I'm sorry … but go easy on him at least. He misses his girlfriend. You get that, right?'

He nods. 'But I don't get you two.'

'There's nothing to get. I have a boyfriend, Trenticles.'

'Oh, really? Didn't you used to scribble our initials all over your school books? LM and TD forever? Stuff like that?'

A laugh slips out.

'You did though, right?'

'I'm not admitting anything, no matter how much embarrassing stuff you bring up. And be nice to your brother.'

'Okay, but I *know* you used to like me.' He grins again. 'I know it.'

'Past tense, dude. Doesn't count any more.'

Jay and Mel are spooned on the couch watching Netflix when I walk in. It's their favourite position from the afternoon onwards.

'Hey, guys, what's doing?' I ask, dumping my bag in the hallway. 'Good day?'

'Kurt's not here, doll,' Mel mumbles.

'Oh?' Nice to see you too.

'Yeah,' she continues. 'Him and Ryan went out.'

'Where?'

Jay turns up the volume, captivated by the screen.

'Dunno,' Mel says. 'Out.' She notices my bag heaped on the floor. 'You going somewhere?'

'I literally walked through the door, like just then. I've been gone all night.' Deep breath. 'Has Kurt been home? I texted him heaps yesterday but haven't heard from him.'

Mel shrugs. 'No idea.'

'Okay … well, do you guys wanna grab a late lunch? I'm starving. And you wouldn't believe the past twenty-four hours. I was driving to Canberra and this car behind us kept swerving and —'

'Hang on.' Jay sighs, making a big show out of pressing pause. 'Alright, go.'

I stare at the frozen screen. 'You know what, it's a pretty boring story really.'

'Sorry, doll,' Mel chimes in. 'It's the season finale. Chat after this eppie?'

They don't even notice when I don't bother replying.

* * *

Nothing has changed on the whiteboard. There are no new messages or drawings, no additions to my scribbles. Looking at our unmade bed, I can't even tell if Kurt has been home since I was last here.

The clutter on top of his bedside table catches my eye. There are now two joints, thin and tapered, among the rest of his junk. My throat tightens as I remember the pot sprinkled across Mum's photo yesterday afternoon. It's like it's multiplying around the room.

I suck in a loud breath, trying to calm myself.

Creeeak. The bedroom door is opening.

Startled, I hurl myself onto the bed. Not suss at all, Lay, way to play it cool. I'm still flushed with surprise when Kurt walks in.

'Babe?'

I sit up, trying to be casual. 'Hey.'

'Hey,' he says, in between smacking gum around his mouth. His hair is thick with oil and he's wearing the same rumpled T-shirt from earlier this week. He throws me my bag. 'You left it out there. So, how was your … you had a thing, right?'

So he got my messages.

'I had a thing.'

'How was it?'

He bends down to kiss me on the cheek, but I pull away. I'm not in the mood for another fight, but there's only so long that frustration can bubble below surface level before it explodes anyway.

'Babe?' Alarm registers on his face as he looks at my messages on the whiteboard. 'Are you pissed 'cos I didn't write back to your texts? I just forgot.'

I wriggle across the mattress, lean over to his bedside table and pin one of the joints between my fingers. I gesture for him to join me on the bed, then bring the joint up to my nose, sniff it and cringe.

'I've been thinking and … and I think I want you to stop.'

'Huh?'

I hold the joint up in front of his face. 'This. Stop selling it. Please.'

He scoffs. 'You're crazy.' He snatches the joint from me and tosses it back on the pile on his bedside table. 'Easy money, remember?'

'Stop saying that. Besides, I've got a job now. We'll get by somehow. You don't need to do this.'

'Why? I'm low profile, don't let customers come to the house, my stash is secure … all the stuff I promised ya.'

'Yeah, you're a regular employee of the month. Don't you want more?'

'Customers? Babe, I'm working on it.'

'Oh God, no. More than this.' I gesture with both hands to the room. 'You don't want more?'

'Sounds like *you* do.' There's a fracture in his voice. 'Ya really want me to give it up?'

My jaw hardens. 'It was all over Mum's photo, Kurt, and you didn't even care. *Mum's photo.*'

'You know I've been there for ya every step of the way, from the cemetery to anniversaries to … okay, you know what — I hear ya. I stuffed up. I'll stop. I'll make some more calls about sparkie stuff.'

I mumble, 'Thanks,' but he looks away, so I lie on my back and stare at the ceiling, my eyes following a deep crack running from one side to the other.

'We have an alright life, babe. I don't know why it's stopped being good enough for ya.'

I keep staring at the ceiling until my eyes lose focus. I've got what I wanted — *he's said he'll stop* — but this doesn't feel like how it's supposed to go. Because I can't figure out why it's stopped being good enough for me either.

Layla: *Hi. So are you grounded for life?*

Layla: *I'll take that silence as a yes*

Milo: *Close enough*

Layla: *He's alive! Hooray! Sorry about the grounding tho*

Milo: *All good. Nothing to do in Durnan anyway*

Layla: *Well, I'm sorry. Let me know if I can do anything*

Layla: *OMG. I put my hand up a roast chicken's bum this week*

Layla: *Cluck my life*

Layla: *When did you get so crap at replying to texts?*

Layla: *I know you're grounded so I MIGHT forgive you*

Milo

One hundred and twenty hours and seven family meetings later, Mum and Dad finally have my punishments sorted for, in their words, 'lying, stealing, joyriding and abusing their trust'.

Grounded. *That's a first.*

Taking on extra shifts at the bookshop. *At least I'll get paid.*

Covering the cost of getting the work car fixed. *There goes the extra money.*

Then there's the lucky-last punishment: working through my goals for the year with Dad, who's made the whole me-taking-the-car situation about him. He thinks he's not 'present' enough in my life, so he wants to bond. Not only that, but he wants answers. What am I doing with my life? Where? *When?* Apparently he's done waiting for me to sort it, so he's going to figure out my 'life plan' for me. Bloody self-development books.

This is it. I've found it. The purest form of torture: my life planned out by Dad.

And I thought Trent's BO was bad.

Triple zero? Hi, Milo Dark here, I have an emergency. Please send help immediately.

Quickly losing the will to live through another Durnan day, I lie on the couch in front of one of those generic breakfast shows where everyone looks like a clone of each other. All white teeth and boofy hair. I hate myself for watching it, but I'm too lazy to reach for the remote.

While I stare mindlessly at the telly, Mum's in the armchair across from me, mulling over a sudoku. After a few minutes she gets up in a huff and snatches the remote.

'It's drivel, Milo, rots brains,' she says, turning it off.

'Mum, it's just telly.'

This is what my life has come to: fighting to watch a show I don't even like. Maybe my brain has already rotted to the core.

'Your father and I meant what we said: something's got to change around here.'

Mum likes talking, not listening, so I don't say anything else. If I do, I'll just be getting in the way.

She straightens a picture frame by the window that reads *Follow your dreams*, then stops to peer through the glass. 'Darling, have you seen the Robinsons' place across the road?'

'Course I've seen it.'

'*Tone*, Milo. Well, it's been on the market for seven months now. Can't budge it. Such a shame for them.' She pauses. 'Have you … have you thought about what you might do with the money you're saving?'

She looks out the window again, then back to me. And then I get where she's going with this. Oh.

'Er ... not yet,' I say, sitting up straighter. 'That's kind of the point though. Probably uni once I know what I want to do, or —'

'Uni?' Mum claps her hands together, beyond thrilled to hear that word come out of my mouth. 'Yes, wonderful. I was thinking, you're good with technology and computers, aren't you? You could study that.'

She says it like I'm the next Bill Gates, when I've only ever helped her to update her laptop software and introduced her to YouTube.

'Er, maybe, Mum. But one of Sal's friends went on an exchange to Scotland and —'

'Or there's always property.' She waves me over with a manicured hand.

I heave myself off the couch, hating myself for not sleeping in longer and avoiding this conversation.

'It's one of the benefits of staying here in the country ... and if you ended up studying via distance education then you could move in across the road,' she adds. 'That way I'll always know you're looking after yourself. We could still have dinner together every night. Can you imagine?'

I stare at the house with its double garage and overgrown tree in the front and shabby brick finish. It's one of the few unrestored homes on the block.

Oh, I can imagine.

Mum rushing over unannounced to make sure I have enough clean boxers for the week. Dad berating me for not mowing the lawn often enough. Trent scabbing the keys to throw a piss-up for every dropkick in town.

But mainly I can imagine my whole future mapped out for me in an instant. Durnan forever. No surprises. Just an endless life of same-same: work, sleep, lectures from Mum and Dad, repeat. It's enough to make me want to hurl myself through the window.

Suddenly the only thing that seems worse than having no plan is having a plan I don't want.

'Something to think about anyway,' Mum says, wrapping an arm around me.

I swallow. 'Ah, maybe.'

She roughs up my hair and says, 'Good boy,' like I'm a toddler nailing potty time.

My head aches. It's too much to think about at seven forty-eight in the morning. I collapse back on the couch and pull out my phone to reply to Layla.

'Who are you texting?' Mum asks, sitting next to me.

'No-one really.'

Her lips tighten into a straight line.

'Mum, whatever you're thinking, stop. I begged her to drive me. Anyway, the car's getting fixed and I'm paying for it.' Trust me, I'm paying for it in every way. 'She's telling me about her job, okay? That's all.'

'I thought she was going out with someone.'

'So? Guys and girls can be friends, Mum. We're not all sex maniacs.'

Shouldn't have said 'sex maniacs'. Should *not* have said that.

'Sometimes they can be friends,' she says, side-stepping my last sentence with the skilfulness of an acrobat walking the high-wire. 'I have a good memory though. Even as kids, you followed Layla around like a puppy dog, back when she was all about your brother.'

I snort.

'You did. And she was.'

'Good pep talk, Mum. We done?' I stare at the blank telly screen, scared of what she might see etched across my face.

'I don't want you to get hurt, my darling,' she adds, her voice softening. 'Or Sal. You two have been through a lot together. Two years of dating, that fancy couples award at the formal —'

'It was just a stupid award, Mum. Relax. Trust me, Sal is fine. I mean, we're fine.'

Trent stumbles into the living room scratching at his left armpit. I've never been so relieved to see him. Anything to get Mum off my case.

She cringes as he grabs the remote, turns on the television and collapses into a chair, almost in a single non-stop motion. Releasing a yawn, he plonks his feet on the coffee table with a thud. Mum gestures for him to move them and he releases a deep grunt as he readjusts himself.

Once Mum's headed into the kitchen to make breakfast, Trent rolls around to face me. 'So you *do* have the horn for little Montgomery. Although I guess she's not that little now, huh? Pretty crazy-hot these days.'

'Yeah.' I freeze. The word fell out of my mouth before I could stop it.

Trent hoots with laughter. 'You sly dog, you *have* been paying attention. She's a legend. Can't blame you.'

I throw a cushion at him.

He catches it and laughs. 'Hey, don't be mad at me for your unrequited thirst. It's not my fault she threw herself at me for like forever.'

'You're dreaming.'

He plants his feet back on the coffee table. 'Why do you even care?'

'I don't.'

Mum pokes her head into the living room. 'Poached or scrambled eggs, boys?'

I have no idea. And now I've lost my appetite.

* * *

Layla: *You ignoring me? Or dead?*
Layla: *I'll feel pretty bad if you're dead*
Layla: *But if you're NOT dead, I stand by what I said. Bad. At. This*
Milo: *Just busy. Still grounded. Still working. Fun times*
Layla: *So what's up? How's grounded life?*
Milo: *Spectacular*
Milo: *Heard you were in love with Trent back in the day*
Layla: *With Trenticles? Please*
Layla: *I was like two*
Milo: *Ha. But you liked him?*

Milo: *Trent?*
Milo: *TRENT?*
Layla: *Thought you were busy with work?*
Milo: *I am. Going … going …*
Layla: *Gone*

* * *

Milo: *Hey stranger, how bout a visit at work tomoz?*
Layla: *Hey, sorry, can't make it. I'm working too. Boo but $$$*
Milo: *Alright. Cluck you*

* * *

Milo: *24 hours. Now who's crap at texting?*
Layla: *Sorry! This is prob past your bedtime so you won't get it til later*
Layla: *Grandpa*

* * *

Milo: *It's 7 — I'm up*
Layla: *You're UP? Flirt*
Milo: *Mind out of the gutter, flirt*
Layla: *Back chat! Detention for you! See you after class*
Milo: *Can't wait, Miss Montgomery*
Layla: *Now who's the flirt?*

Milo

I'm cleaning my teeth after breakfast when Trent barges into the bathroom without knocking.

'I'm in here,' I say through a mouthful of white foam. 'Wait a sec.'

'Sorry, bro, can't. Tastes like something's died in my mouth,' he says, rubbing at an eye with one hand, fumbling for his toothbrush with the other.

I spit in the sink, then turn on the tap to wash the gunk down the drain. Yawning, Trent pushes in front of the mirror until we're shoulder to shoulder. I notice his hand is shaking as he runs water over his toothbrush.

'Big night again?' I ask.

He nods.

'I can tell. You look like crap.' I grin.

Watery toothpaste dribbles down his chin. 'You too. What's your excuse?'

I spit again. 'Just trying to be like my big bro.'

A laugh rumbles from him. 'How was work yesterday? The old man still being a punish?'

'What do you think? He was all, "Computer science sounds like a great idea" and "Where's your life headed, Milo?"'

'Worst.'

'I don't know how many other ways I can tell him I have no idea. You're older than me — why don't you cop this?'

'Lost cause, bro. You're the golden boy letting them down.' Trent leans over and spits into the sink, then bolts upright. 'Geez, nearly forgot! How about Sal's tattoo?'

My eyes meet his, which are glassy as hell, in the mirror. 'What tattoo? She hates them.'

'Not any more.'

'She does. She paid me out when I said I'd get a tatt one day.'

'As she should — a tatt would look rubbish on you. I don't know what to tell ya, but she's got one.' He wipes his mouth with the hand towel, leaving a milky smear, then crams it back through the hand rail. When he sees my face, he shakes his head, looking sorry for me for once. 'Wait, you didn't know? That was days ago, after an obstacle course or some lame uni thing. I swear I saw it on Facey — think it was on her wrist.'

* * *

There's no sign of the tattoo anywhere in Sal's photos online. There's plenty of new pics of her from the car rally — laughing, doing star jumps, eating a burger dripping with cheese — while wearing a pink leotard, running shorts, a bib with *Got Wood?* emblazoned across it and a sparkly gold sweatband. I look for any trace of a tattoo on her wrists but it's nowhere to be seen. Not even in the photo of Sal scaling Woody's back and pumping the air with two thumbs-up. My head pounds, annoyed that I let Trent mess with me like this.

I go back to my and Sal's messages in case I've missed something. Layla's name catches my eye as I'm scrolling down. Her most recent texts stare back at me.

I read them.

I read them again.

I catch myself reading them a third time, tiring out my cheeks as I smirk to myself.

And then I read them again.

* * *

Three hours later and I still can't block out the noise, both outside and inside my head. The Robinsons' dog is having its usual ten o'clock barking fit, which has set off every canine within a few streets. Trent's snoring and snuffling roars through the house. Mum's watching an old episode of *Law and Order* at full volume. Dad's on the phone in their bedroom, which is three rooms away but his voice bellows over everything else. I'm still wondering about Sal's tattoo. Trent wouldn't make up something like that — there's nothing in it for him.

When I call Sal, she picks up almost straightaway. Her voice is cracking with weariness. We make small talk for a bit, chatting about work and uni and not being able to fall asleep, and then a lull hits.

I go for it. 'So … your pics look like you're having fun.'

She groans. 'That's one word for it. I'm never partying again.'

'That good, huh?' I'm trying not to jump ahead. 'Yeah … that car rally looked pretty epic.'

'Oh yeah, some of the dares were wild. I thought I told you about that?'

'Yeah, I think you did … what happened again?'

I have no chill.

'At the car rally? My team won the most points — hello, free pizza for two months. Totally worth skinny-dipping in the lake … oh God, and getting a photo with a police officer later that night. She was rad. Nearly forgot that part.'

'You skinny-dipped?'

She laughs. 'Yeah, our whole team did, otherwise we wouldn't get full marks for doing the dare. It was the middle of the night so it wasn't too bad.'

I force a chuckle out.

'You right?' she asks. 'You sound sorta funny.'

'I'm good. Just hanging out and listening and …' Screw it. 'Er, so … random question, but Trent mentioned that … well, I know I probably sound like a weirdo, but … did you get a tattoo?'

No freakin' chill.

She groans. 'Oh, you *did* see the photo? Woody had a brain-fart and tagged me in a photo of it, but I made him take it down. Like, Mum is friends with me on there.'

'Wait, so you actually got one?'

'Oh.' Pause. 'Yeah. I did.'

I swear out loud.

'Pretty crazy, right?'

'Yeah. In a good way.' I mean it. I wish she'd told me, but I mean it.

Sal sighs in relief. 'Well, it was worth fifteen hundred points. I almost chickened out, then I just went for it. And we won!'

'Nice. Can I get in on that free pizza?'

'Oh yeah,' she says. 'I was going to tell you, but celebrations got a bit out of control, and you had the accident and … I was just working out *how* to tell you. I'd made such a thing about *not* getting one. I was worried you'd be mad.'

'Nah. Send me a pic.'

'I will, but … well, the other thing is we had to get tattoos that related to the car rally, so our crew got initials. So Britt got an S for Sal, Woody got a J for Jamie, Jamie got a B for Britt and I got a —'

'W.' For Woody.

'But it sorta looks like an E or 3 from certain angles, but I like to think of it as an upside-down M. For Milo. Kinda cute, don't you think?'

Now I feel like I'm hanging upside-down.

Just say it's cute, just say it's cute, just say it's cute.

I swear again. 'You seriously got a freakin' W?'

'Yeah. What's the matter?'

'His name is on your body? Permanently?'

My chest has tightened so much it feels like someone is scratching through the skin.

'It's not really his name. Just the first letter. It was just this big, crazy night. It doesn't even mean anything.'

I don't see red when she says that. I see scorching, blistering, bloody red. And I let her know.

I've never spoken like that before. I don't even know where this anger is coming from.

'Get over yourself, Milo. He's friends with everyone. *Friends.*'

'And now you've got the tattoo to prove your friendship.' My voice leaks with sarcasm. 'He looks like a really, really good *friend.*'

'What's going on? You don't even sound like you.'

'What do you expect?' I reply, my voice shaking a little. I know I should stop talking, take a walk, sleep it off, but I don't. The redness has spread from the ache in my chest down to my stomach. 'I'm here by myself in Durnan thinking about you like a loser and you're off doing *that.*'

'Yeah, I am. I'm trying something new. Making friends. Give it a go sometime.' She's not even trying to hold back any more. 'And it's not my fault you stayed behind. That one's on you.'

'At least I'm not pretending to be someone I'm not. And I bet the tattoo looks terrible.'

It's Sal's turn to swear at me.

'You're a mess, Milo.' Pause. 'Yeah … you really are, so I'm going to make this easy for you. We're done.'

She's hung up.

I stare at my phone, willing her to ring back.

Nothing.

I try to remember everything I said, every accusation I hurled, every hurtful comment I already regret saying. But I can't.

I dial her number. It only rings once before it cuts out.

Layla

I angle myself under the showerhead so the water strikes my right shoulder and scrub at my skin with a face-washer. Every pore of my body has absorbed the greasy chicken stench from Joe's.

The bathroom is heavy with steam and the smell of coconut, and with everyone else asleep or out, there's an unusual calm in the house. Jay isn't banging at the door for me to hurry up; and Mel isn't ducking in, hand over her eyes, to retrieve her hair-straightener. It's so peaceful that it almost feels like being at home. My old home, where it was just Mum, Dad and me rattling around a house big enough for a family of six. Maybe midnight showers aren't so bad. Maybe they'll be my time. If I can ever get rid of this chicken smell.

The work itself isn't that bad. Nice enough people. Free hot chips and gravy on my break. Six and a half hours of getting paid. But squelching through our front door at eleven forty-three at night with fat in my boots and oil in my hair isn't pretty.

I step out of the shower and grab the two ratty towels I've laid out for myself. They don't match, but none of our stuff does. It's all hand-me-downs from everyone else's parents or hand-me-acrosses from Mel's friends. I wind one around my hair and one around my body.

I'm tiptoeing back to the bedroom when I bump into Kurt in the hall.

'Hey, you're still up?' I whisper.

'Yeah, hey, babe,' he whispers back.

I've barely seen him today. He was so wrecked after a party last night that he slept for most of the afternoon, then it was time for me to go to work.

'Heading to bed?' I ask. Then it clicks. He's in jeans, a T-shirt and sneakers. A backpack is slung over his shoulder. The only place he's heading is out.

'Nah, the Richards twins are having another party. Just got a late call-up — Ryan's gonna give me a lift over there.'

'But it's after midnight.' I tighten my towel. 'And it's dark out.'

'That happens at night.'

'But —'

'Lay, you'll be asleep here anyway, right?'

I shrug.

'You look tired, babe. I'm off.' He pecks me on the cheek, then heads down the hallway towards the front door.

I pad into our bedroom and pace around in my towel, side-stepping his mess to get to the wardrobe. As I pull out a singlet and boxers from the top drawer, I notice the bottom drawer is slightly ajar.

Kurt's drawer.

He's never left it unlocked before. He even refuses to tell me where he keeps the key, but now he is gone and the drawer is open.

I swallow.

He promised me that he'd stop dealing. No harm in making sure. Heart pounding, I drop to my knees and yank open the drawer.

Shit.

My body surges with rage as I stare at the dried greeny-brown leaves and buds, as though staring will somehow make them disappear out of our house. I can already picture Kurt spinning it, telling me everything is okay, that I'm overreacting, that whatever he's doing it's for us. Yet I can't believe any of it any more. He's left me with no choice.

I snatch my phone from the bedside table, my hand tightening around it as I consider calling him and ending it right now.

But then I toss the phone onto the bed.

If I break up with him, I have nowhere to go. I followed him here like a failure, and he knows it. Besides, he's the only one who's even tried to be there for me in the past few years. Everyone always tells me how much I owe him for staying with me through the tough times, and maybe they're right.

Sucking in a breath, I stride into the kitchen and yank open the fridge. Diet Coke. Red Bull. Water. Mel's cheap cask wine. 'Cat's wee' she calls it 'cos she thinks it tastes that bad.

I pour myself a small glass and gulp it down, hating every sip but craving numbness. I refill the cup, drops splashing onto the tiles.

I've been on the couch for ten minutes, staring at the full glass, repulsed by the taste in my mouth and the aching feeling in my chest, when I hear a knock, knock, knock at the front door.

I take another sip of wine, then gag, so I pour the rest down the kitchen sink. I tiptoe through the house and open the front door to see an elderly woman in a paisley-print robe. Her face is engraved with lines and her nose is scrunched up in disapproval.

'I found this boy snooping in my front yard — he's lucky I didn't call the police,' she says, shaking her head. 'I believe you know him.'

She moves to one side and the culprit stumbles onto the top step of the veranda. Milo.

His cheeks are red, his hair is dishevelled and his bottom lip droops like a slug crawling towards his chin. He looks tipsy and the hems of his jeans are covered in mud and leaves.

'Dude!' I say, rushing forward to help him into the house.

The old woman totters off home, but not without shooting us another judgmental glare.

'Hey, Lay,' he says, swaying like one of those inflatable stringy-man balloons outside car dealerships.

'What the ... are you okay, MD?' *Stupid question, Layla.*

Milo babbles something under his breath, then plops down on the veranda, hitting the concrete hard, and rests his head against a post.

With a bit of prodding, I realise he tried to call me, but I've been so distracted by Kurt's lies that I haven't paid attention to the notifications coming through.

'It's over with Sal,' he mutters, 'I've stuffed up my life. I had it all and now ...' He makes an explosion noise.

I take his hand. 'It'll be alright.'

'Nah,' he says, eyes watery. 'I can't be in this town any more. I can't.'

I don't want him crashing through the house in the middle of the night, but I can't leave him outside in this state.

'Come inside for a minute,' I tell him. 'A *minute*. You're going to wait in the laundry while I get you some water, we'll talk it out, and then you're going home before your parents realise you're gone and call the police. Follow me and don't say another word until I say so, okay?'

He nods.

It's a start.

His hand firmly in mine, I lead him through the house and steer him into the laundry. It's a small cramped room away from the bedrooms.

I prop him against the sink and press my finger to his mouth. 'Shhh, two of my housemates are still home,' I remind him, then go to fetch a glass of water.

'Hey, you're in your pyjamas,' he whispers when I get back.

'Well done, Captain Obvious. You know what time it is, right?' My nose crinkles. 'Does something ... does something reek in here? What did ... oh, it's on the bottom of your jeans! Quick, take them off and we'll scrub them. It stinks, man. This is why you don't fall over in people's gardens.'

Milo fumbles with his belt.

'Wait, you've got boxers on too, right?'

He removes his jeans without answering. He does. Thank God. I try not to laugh.

'No more talk until you drink this — you're a mess,' I say, passing him the water.

His expression sours. 'That's what she said.' He slumps down onto the ground, head lolling against the washing machine. 'She used to talk about us getting married one day ... *she* did. Everyone did. Not me. It was her idea.'

'Don't worry about that right now,' I say, dropping to the floor next to him.

'She wanted a dog and a fence and kids and a juicer to make those green drinks and just ... I freakin' hate those drinks.'

I pinch his cheek. 'You're eighteen, MD, forget about all that crazy future stuff for a sec and ...' He stares at me, eyes glassy. 'Just focus on not chucking up in my laundry, yeah? That's the only thing that matters at the moment.'

'My head ...' He slumps lower. 'It got so hard with her. It shouldn't be that hard when it's right ... right?'

'Don't ask me. Everything feels hard.'

'This doesn't.'

'This?' I gesture at the poky laundry, his dirty jeans, the glass of water. 'This feels good to you?'

He laughs. 'Nah. Just this.' He edges closer to me. 'You smell like an island.'

I try not to smile. I hate how he makes me smile, especially when he shouldn't.

'So what happened with you two?' I ask. 'I know the distance blows, but I thought it was going okay?'

Milo shakes his head.

'Come on, you don't know it's over for sure. Anything's possible.'

'Nah.'

I tilt his chin up so we're eye to eye. 'You might forget this by tomorrow, but I'm going to tell you anyway. *You* are making your life suck right now by sitting around freaking out about how your life sucks.'

'No.'

'Yes. Anyway ... that's enough tough love. Drink more water. Please.'

'Stop saying stuff like you know what's going on with me.'

I clench my fists to stop myself from shaking him.

'I do know what's going on, Milo Dark, which is why I know you're horrible with change, but the sooner you realise things change whether you want them to or not, the better.' I pause, fighting the tightness building in my body, running higher up my chest and around my neck, into my throat, down my arms. 'Sometimes you've got to harden up and get on with it. Move on.'

I'm not sure if I'm even still talking about Milo.

Then he does something I'm not expecting. He laughs.

'Damn, you're right. I hate that you're right. So ... so do you think we should be broken up?'

'I didn't say that.'

'You said the thing about getting on with it ... and moving on. You said those words.' He licks his top lip, so I press the water to his mouth. He takes the glass. 'Why do you like him, Lay?'

'Huh?'

'Or love him? I dunno. I forget his name.' Milo's voice is barely a murmur now. 'Your boyfriend. You never talk about him. You never bring him up.'

My jaw tightens. 'Maybe you should go, sleep this off. We'll talk tomorrow.'

'Yeah, okay. You know ... you're the best, Lay, you are. I'd be going crazy in Durnan without you here.'

'Crazier than this?'

He inches closer and folds his hand against mine. My hand with its chipped nail polish and fingernails chewed down to the quick; his, pale and bigger, rougher than I'd imagined, though his touch is still gentle.

The room is so cloaked in night that I question if this is even real. Has my brain short-circuited and I'm playing out what shouldn't happen? What can't happen. What I think I want to happen.

I wonder if Milo is taking in everything I'm taking in — the smoothness of the back of my hand, my quickening breath, the sudden silence deafening the space between us.

I turn to face him. 'MD ...'

His fingers trace my jawline. He's still gentle, cautious ... it's like being brushed over with a feather.

It's my turn to whisper. 'What are you doing? And don't say "I don't know". *You know.*'

'I don't know.'

He wraps an arm around me, pulling me towards him like he did on the side of the highway. I hesitate before giving in and resting my head on his chest. His fingertips run up and down my arm, drawing invisible zigzags and loop-the-loops. I'm suddenly aware of every millimetre of my uncovered skin; every curve and arch and freckle. Yet my body is relaxed into his. He feels warm, like home. I nuzzle closer as he strokes my skin and holds me tight.

Damp hair tumbling onto my shoulders, I dare to look up. He's already looking down at me. My lips are centimetres from his chin. I'm frozen, imagining what might happen if I lean just that little bit further. I picture him outlining my mouth with his thumb, then dragging me in closer, our bodies surging against each other. His hands on my body, my hands on his, skin on skin, warm flesh pressing against the cold tiles.

He's slid closer.

Or I have.

Everything has slowed down.

I can feel his heart pounding through his chest. I wonder if he can feel mine.

I push myself up.

Our lips graze and I taste him.

I'm not sure who pulls away first but the kiss is over in seconds. Maybe we broke apart together. We don't say a word but we're still charged, like there's electricity pulsating between us.

'What was that?' he murmurs.

'I don't know,' I say, stealing his line.

'I've thought about kissing you for so long.'

I stay quiet, too scared of every thought pumping through my head right now. Especially the one that says I'm not ready for it to be over.

If we held back before, things move fast now. Too fast to think. Without speaking, I climb onto his lap so we're face to face. His mouth falls open, startled for a second, but then his hands quickly find my skin. I tighten my legs around his waist as I kiss him, slowly then deeper, then edge my hips up and push myself closer to him.

'Jesus,' he mutters, his voice low and rough, then he cups my face with his palms and kisses me hard.

It feels right, like we've been wasting time not doing this. When we pull apart, my toes still tingle, my skin is still hot.

Milo sits there, legs splayed, jaw slackened. Giddy.

'Lay …'

Hearing him say my name jolts me back to reality. I'm alone on the laundry floor with my childhood friend. And I have a boyfriend. A complicated boyfriend, but one who's been there for me in the past even if he's forgetting how to be there for me now. Yet somehow, tonight in that moment, Milo Dark made me forget I have a boyfriend. I am the worst person in the world.

I slide back onto the tiles and shove a damp strand of hair behind my ear.

Milo hangs his head. 'This is … I don't know what this is.'

I nod.

'Lay, that was …' He shakes his head. 'Shit. I don't want things to be weird.'

'Don't be weird then,' I say, trying to convince myself as I pull him to his feet.

I stumble forward and he catches me. We wobble together. Don't look up. Don't look up. I look up. My eyes linger at the sight of him chewing his bottom lip.

'Fine, it's already weird,' I say. His hands are still wrapped around me, resting on my lower back. I reach behind, unlace them and let go. They hang loosely by his body. 'It doesn't have to be though. You were drinking, I was drinking, you were upset, I was upset, you were —'

'Wait, you were upset? Why?'

Milo has no idea how much harder he's making this.

'MD, we've known each other forever, right?'

'Right.'

'And this was like five minutes of weird. Tops.'

'Tops.'

'And five minutes divided by eighteen years multiplied by one hundred equals ...' I pause. 'I have no idea what it equals, but the point is — tonight is a minuscule amount of time in our otherwise long and boring lives together. I say we stop talking about *this* and we reboot. And we never tell anyone. Deal?'

'Deal.' His hand brushes mine, just hovering there until he pulls it away. 'You have a boyfriend. Jesus. A boyfriend. I'm such an arsehole.'

'No, I am. But me and Kurt are breaking up.'

'What?' Milo's jaw drops. ''Cos of this?'

'No. It doesn't matter why — it's just another thing I need to sort out ... but I am. I'm ending it.' My voice trails off. 'Just focus for a sec, okay? You and me, right now. We're friends above everything else. Friends. You've known me my whole life, and I don't want to lose you, so *promise* me it won't change. We're mates.'

Milo's lips are near mine. He could kiss me again but he just nods.

* * *

Layla: *Get home safe?*

Layla: *You okay?*

Layla: *Seriously nothing?*

* * *

Layla: *Dude!*
Milo: *Sorry, been busy. Yeah, got home. How are you?*
Layla: *Figured, it was days ago. What's on this week?*
Milo: *Not much, work and stuff*
Layla: *Wanna hang sometime soon?*
Milo: *Sorry, can't, still grounded*
Layla: *OK, let me know when you're free*

Milo

I trail behind Trent, who trails behind Dad, who powers ahead, calves hardening, on his mission through the hardware store. I catch a look at our reflections in a mirror for sale: a line of progressively dissatisfied Darks. A terrifying glimpse at my gene pool. My future.

No. Please, no.

I suggested waiting for them out the front, conveniently close to the sausage sizzle, but Dad insisted we stay together, turn off our phones and 'enjoy the moment', so Trent and I endure his search for the perfect pair of secateurs. It's all part of my punishment that'll probably last an eternity.

Dad proves his disappointment in me by expertly weaving snarky comments through his gardening jargon and self-help talk.

A dig at me for not considering Mum's suggestion to study computer science.

A comment about how Bill Burton's twins are getting high distinctions at uni.

An aside about how Jermaine Wright's son — 'who

was in Trent's year, remember, boys?' — is close to making his first million in his start-up business.

Every time Dad says something, Trent shoots me a look, fighting back laughter while silently screaming with his eyes.

For Dad, flooding us with 'kids done good' examples is a group-bonding exercise equivalent to high-fiving each other as we stand on hot coals together at a motivational-speaking conference.

Right now, throwing myself on scorching ashes sounds preferable to listening to Dad asking the sales girl to explain the differences between the anvil, bypass and parrot-beak secateurs for the forty-seventh time.

'The boys'll be starting at Rizza's without me,' Trent mutters. 'You being grounded is nothing compared to this nightmare.'

I pull out my phone to reread the texts from Layla, keeping one eye on Dad as he strides to the checkout. I haven't seen her since the other night, and I'm still filled with enough guilt to flood the river — despite her letting slip about her supposed imminent break-up with Kurt. I'm not the guy who kisses girls with boyfriends. Yet that's exactly who I am. Because when Layla pressed her lips against mine, I gave in to it — to her — within seconds and somehow managed to stifle the roaring of *she's taken* in my brain. Not only that, she's my oldest mate — the only real mate I have left in Durnan now everyone else has bailed. If I blow it any more, I'll complete my gradual downward spiral into Nigel-No-Friends territory. She wants us to be friends, that's it. Which should be easy 'cos it's what we've always been. But friends don't kiss each other the way we did … do they?

'Oi,' Trent whispers, trying to check out my phone. 'Whose Insta photos are you creeping on?'

'Piss off.'

Dad's fake laugh interrupts us — the loud, bellowing chuckle he saves for impressing people — so I slide my phone back into my pocket for later. Ever since he got into the self-help stuff, we've heard that laugh so much I'm considering earplugs.

Secateurs in hand, Dad waves for us to follow him into the car park. He charges ahead, arms propelling him forward. This time, Trent and I trail behind together.

'When did he get like this?' I mutter, watching him wave at every second person like a cheesy salesman. His energy might be impressive if it wasn't so annoying to be on the receiving end. 'And all that stuff about other people's kids — it's like, we get it. We suck. It's not like I don't want to do *anything*. Yeah, it's taking me a while to sort it out, but … damn.'

Trent scoffs. 'He's always been like this. You're just not used to him seeing you like he sees me.'

'Meaning?'

'No big plans, no degree or career goals, no girlfriend to bring round for dinner, too much mucking up — you're a no-hoper in his eyes now. Dad wants kids he can brag about.'

He notices my steely look.

'Sorry to be the bearer of bad news, bro, thought you knew.' He shrugs. 'It ain't too bad once you get used to it. He learns to expect less, then you're free to float along.'

No-hoper. Expect less. Float along. The Trent Dark way. I mull over Trent's words on the walk back to the car. We've always been different, everyone says it: Mum and Dad, teachers, friends, even Sal noticed. Yet somehow, despite going down different paths, we've ended up at the same destination: Loserville.

Trent claims the back seat so I'm forced to sit up front.

Dad buckles his seatbelt and readjusts the rear-view mirror. 'That went well, don't you think?'

Trent clears his throat. I try not to laugh.

'Now, Milo,' Dad goes on, 'turns out the girl at the checkout is related to one of the sponsors I met at the races. She loves her job — *loves* it — and reckons she'd be able to get you in there if you were keen for a second casual job. Whaddya say?'

Trust Dad to turn an innocent trip to the hardware store into a chance to rescue his poor directionless son.

Trent chuckles from the back seat. Luckily Dad is concentrating on reversing out so he can't see the corner of my mouth twitching. It's all so ridiculous.

'Milo, you hear me?' he asks as we head out of the car park.

'Ah, yeah, maybe.'

'Bloody hell, Milo, I'm serving it up for you. You should say thank you.'

'Thanks, Dad.' I stare out the windscreen. 'I'll have a think. I'm already working heaps.'

'These are important foundations I'm trying to lay down for your future. *Me*. Don't forget that.'

Trent snickers. 'Yes, Milo, don't forget those important foundations.'

'Watch it,' Dad says, eyes narrowing in the rear-view mirror.

Trent apologises, fake as anything, but Dad buys it.

When Trent announces he wants to be dropped off to see his mates, I wait for Dad to tell him no, but he simply grunts. Trent flops back in his seat satisfied, like he's proved his point. Maybe Dad has given up on him and I'm still a project with potential, at least while I haven't completely stuffed it. I wonder if it's possible to throw myself out of the car after Trent without Dad noticing.

We drive for a few blocks, listening to the sound of Trent tapping on his thighs.

'Turn left here, Dad, Rizza's place is above the pharmacy,' he says. 'Sweet, there's a park there — yeah, right there!'

In front of Joe's Charcoal Chicken Shop — Layla's work.

As Dad eases into the car spot, I can see two girls behind the counter, neither of them her. Thank you, world.

Trent sniggers. 'Hungry, Milo? You could get yourself some wings and chips. Hang on, you're more of a breast man, right?'

Dick.

'Actually,' he adds, 'you look kinda *thirsty*.' He's straining so hard to repress laughter that his face looks like it might split in half. He jumps out of the car, then looks back in so we're eye to eye. 'Pretty sure the chicken shop's got something that'll quench that thirst, bro. Catch yas.' He throws me a little wave as he walks off.

Dad unbuckles his seatbelt. 'Are you thirsty? I can grab you something.'

Jesus. 'No. Not thirsty. Thanks, Dad.'

'About your mum's suggestion,' he starts, then clears his throat. 'Computer science could *really* be something for you. Emma Hui's daughter does something with computers and now she runs her own business.'

Here we go again.

'Yeah, I've looked at a few unis, Dad.'

His eyebrows shoot up. 'And?'

'It looks okay, I guess. You can start in semester two, but I don't want to rush into —'

'Semester two! There we go!' He slaps the steering wheel as though it's decided. 'Brilliant. Computers! Whaddya say?' Before I can answer, he looks over my shoulder, distracted by a young guy walking past in a suit. 'Hey, look, is that Peter Newbins? I think they've brought him on to try to sell the Robinsons' place. He's a real goer.'

'*Dad, c'mon.* Leave it alone.'

He thrusts a five-dollar note into my hand. 'Go grab yourself a mineral water. Actually, grab me one too. I'm thirsty after all that computer talk.'

Thirsty. I'm going to kill Trent. And Dad. And then myself.

Dad gets out of the car, slicks down his hair and chases after Peter Newbins with the gracefulness of a giraffe. Hope Pete has earplugs stashed in his trouser pocket.

Gnawing on my bottom lip, I look into Joe's from the passenger seat. Still no sign of Layla.

I get out of the car and cross the pavement until I'm close to the entrance. It's simple: get in, get the drinks, get out. But, heart thumping, I panic and make a last-minute detour to the right and find myself staring into the window of the travel agency.

An agent spots me and stands up, gesturing for me to come inside. I mouth 'Just looking', as though this has always been my plan, and scope out the flights with such gusto anyone would think I'm being paid to do it. My brow even furrows in concentration as I pretend to take it all in.

Italy.

Bali.

London.

Fiji.

America.

I size up the prices under the agent's enthusiastic stare. It's strange to think a few thousand dollars is enough to change your life. To get you to the other side of the world. Away from everyone. Away from everything. Start fresh.

As I study the world map on the window, I'm reminded I haven't got one stamp in my passport. It's as crisp and clean as the day it arrived in the mail four years ago. Mum helped us organise them when Dad floated the idea of a holiday to Hawaii, but exchange rates blew out so we went to Queensland for the third time.

The travel agent gestures again, desperate for a sale. I mouth, 'Ah, not today,' and walk back towards Joe's, coiling the five-buck note around my thumb.

That's when I see her.

She's standing on a chair in the back corner of the shop, straightening their specials board. Her curly hair is swept off her face with clips and she's decked out in a Joe's shirt. I smile as I recall her prancing around on the side of the highway in Veronica's Little Bookshop T-shirt. She was hilarious, despite everything, and made the unbearable somehow perfect. *She's taken*, the voice hisses again, and she just wants to be friends.

Suddenly I want to bolt before she spots me lurking outside, but my feet feel bonded to the ground. Not that it matters: Layla's already seen me through the window. She looks happy about it too — all dancing eyebrows and a beam so brilliant it might just light up Durnan.

I can't be here. I can't talk to her like this.

Not when she looks and acts like that.

Not when I'm acting like this.

I don't even know how to freakin' text her any more.

I gesture to the car, pretending I'm in a rush.

Realising I'm not coming in, she cocks her head to the side, confused, her grin hardening into tight, pressed lips.

I hurry to the car and keep my head down until Dad's back. I'm relieved he's too busy waffling about Peter Newbins and life plans and home loans to remember anything about the mineral waters.

* * *

Layla: *Hey!*
Milo: *Was with Dad, had to rush off*
Milo: *Sorry*
Layla: *That's OK, when are you grounded til?*

* * *

Layla: *You there?*
Milo: *Yeah, what's up?*
Layla: *Nothing really, you alright?*
Milo: *Yeah, just at work, bit busy*
Milo: *How are you?*
Layla: *I'm OK. Are you?*

Layla

I push my scrambled eggs around my plate and watch Kurt gnawing at his bacon before gulping it down. I've been pep-talking myself for days, trying to find the right words to break up with him. I thought I had them too. I thought we'd be over by now and I'd be free from the guilt and sadness and frustration. And we probably would've been if Ryan hadn't invited himself along this morning for brunch at Quiche. It's not like I can say, 'Er, Ryan, please pass the tomato sauce … oh, and by the way, Kurt, I don't want to go out any more.' The whole thing is postponed and I'm losing my nerve again.

Back at school, people's friends assisted with break-ups. The unsuspecting boy or girl was pulled aside after class or bailed up in line for the bus home, then the news was dumped on them — usually with a crowd watching it all go down. The *really* chicken people sent a text message, sometimes short and to the point, sometimes long and waffly. Not kind but definitely effective. Over in the speed of pressing 'send'. Not like me, days later, still wondering how to start this conversation.

But school's over and I owe Kurt more than that.

Oblivious, he and Ryan talk loud and fast, making plans for tonight. Another weekend, another party. Kurt doesn't bother to check whether I want to go. Not that I want to. He flashes me a wink: *Thanks for understanding, babe*.

Ryan slurps his juice and waves over a waitress for a water refill. She tops up our glasses with a yawn, unaffected by the swarm of customers winding out the door.

Milo going quiet on me isn't helping any of this drama rattling around my head. I'm trying not to overthink his blunt texts, but it's hard not to when life has been so full of him lately.

The night we spent talking on our road trip to nowhere.

Lips and hot breath and hands in the laundry.

All capped off with his panicked look when he spotted me at Joe's. In one second, I felt like I'd lost my only friend. Maybe I need him more than he needs me.

I push away my plate and slump in my seat.

'Done with that, babe?' Kurt asks, his fingers already touching the rim.

'Yeah. Go for it.'

He and Ryan return to planning their night. I'm back to people-watching and planning how to get Kurt alone.

I notice a group of girls huddled around a phone in the corner, laughing, giggling, elbowing each other. It's been so long since I had that — a tribe. After a while, I guess the ache for it went away.

One of the girls tosses her hair, still cracking up as her friends jostle over the phone, and as she turns her head, her eyes lock with mine across the café.

I think I know her.

Oh my God.

Jill.

I can't look away now. It's Jill and my old group from Year 7 — I forget the other girls' names. We came from different primary schools from surrounding towns so barely knew each other, but we clung together during first term thanks to a few shared classes.

My heart pounds.

Sydney may have been fast and angry, but it's big enough that I rarely bumped into anyone from my life — past or present — in public. Mum always joked she'd see half of Durnan whenever she was at the supermarket, especially if she was in her trackies and hadn't washed her hair. She'd tell me and Dad she was popping out for five minutes to pick up milk and toilet paper, and return an hour later full of stories about the neighbours' anxious cat or her chiro's stepson losing his first tooth. 'It's Durnan's way of knitting us all together, whether we like it or not,' she'd say. As a kid I thought she was annoyed by it, but now I think she might've liked how everyone was forced into each other's lives on their best and worst days. She didn't have a big family of her own, so maybe Durnan made up for it.

Can't say I see the appeal. Especially on a day when my plans to break up with my boyfriend have already imploded.

My natural instinct is to look away from Jill, pretend we haven't seen each other, like so many people do to escape excruciating situations, but my body isn't cooperating. Her mouth crinkles into a smile, then before I have time to look for a hidden trapdoor in the café to throw myself through, she flounces over. I'm stuck — there's no magic carpet or broomstick to fly away on — so I drag myself to my feet and edge towards her. The quicker this happens, the quicker it's over.

My palms are already wet.

'Layla!' she squeals, wrapping me up and squeezing me in. 'Wow, it *is* you! Are you back visiting your dad? How *nice*.'

'Er, well, sorta …' I stammer for the next words, but I needn't have worried. Jill's charging ahead without me.

'Wow, you still look like you — well, sort of,' she says with a laugh, sizing me up. 'Wow, I guess I haven't seen you since, well …' Her voice trails off, but then she forces a big beaming smile. No grim looks here. Just fake smiling. I don't know what's more unsettling. 'How have you been anyway?' she asks, without leaving me time to reply. 'You look so … so city. Very chic.'

I tug at my T-shirt, feeling the complete opposite. 'Er, thanks. You too.'

'Oh, no!' She blushes. 'Wow, you have *been* in the city, right?' She's operating on a superhuman level of happy — big toothy grin, squealing, wild hand gestures. I'm exhausted just being in her presence, especially as we're basically two people who used to know each other pretending we still have something in common. 'Or were you at the coast? I kind of lost track …'

'Five years'll do that. Bit of everything.' I shrug. 'Um, sorry, yeah, I've been sorta hopeless. After everything, I shut down my accounts and …'

'It's fine, I get it.' Jill nods, biting her lip. 'I'm just glad you're doing *so* well now.'

I don't correct her. I hate being fake, but not everyone in this town needs a behind-the-scenes pass to my life. Not if I can help it.

'Thanks. You too. Um …' I search for an appropriate question. I'm so out of practice at acting like a normal human. 'How was the rest of school?' A nervous grin is plastered on her face. 'Sorry, that's a weird thing to ask. Don't answer that. Er, so you're living here too, huh? In Durnan?'

Slightly better question, but not great.

'Here?' Jill waves the idea away. 'Oh, no. Melbourne now, just visiting parents, you know how it is.' She pauses, registering what she's said. 'Sorry … um … yeah, so I'm just here for the weekend, but, ah, let's catch up next time I'm back, okay?'

'Sure,' I manage to say. 'Sounds perfect.'

Surely dishonesty doesn't matter when you're both in on the lie?

'So, ah … bye then.'

Jill lingers on the spot, before hurrying back to the girls. I don't dare watch her go, but I bet they're all taking me in with eyelash-batting interest. Layla, the human sob story.

It's not until I'm seated again that I realise I didn't give Jill my phone number. I can't hear her and the girls laughing any more, so I steal a glance back at the corner. They've huddled in even tighter.

They're not whispering about me. They're not whispering about me.

Jill peeks over in my direction. Busted. Fake smiling again, she gives a small wave when she notices I'm looking, then returns to the huddle.

Yeah, they're whispering about me.

'Who was that princess?' Ryan asks through a mouthful of egg. 'Her friends are cute. Introduce me.'

I screw up my nose.

'What? I'm a catch.'

He and Kurt swap laughter, then start trading stories about last weekend, seeing how much they can one-up each other.

Nibbling on my nails, I stare through the window. Between the boys and Jill, I'm running out of safe places to daydream in this café.

Then I see him through the glass. *What?* Milo's here too? *Here?*

Well, it is Saturday morning and the options are limited in Durnan, I remind myself. Brunch, play sport, hit the shops, stay in bed.

I shouldn't have come out from under the covers.

Milo doesn't see me. He's staring down, gaze slicing through the footpath with laser-like precision. His hands are pushed deep into his shorts and he walks like he's dragging himself through mud, like someone with nowhere to go.

'Y'alright, babe?' Kurt asks, nicking some of Ryan's food.

I glance at him. 'Sorry, what?'

'Doesn't matter,' he says, stuffing his spoon into his mouth as he looks out the window, wondering out loud what's caught my attention.

I follow his gaze, worried, but Milo is already gone from sight.

I last another minute while the boys order milkshakes with extra whipped cream, then excuse myself to pop outside to make a quick call to Joe's.

My heart pounds as I jog to catch up with Milo. He walks on, kicking at the cement, unaware I'm coming for him, fuelled by a stressful morning. The full weight of every messy thought is crashing down on me. I should go back to the café, back to Kurt, end it right now.

Should.

Instead I hurry on, feet pounding the concrete, until I'm in front of him. I swivel around, hair whipping out around me. 'You,' I say, poking him in the chest.

He steps back, startled. 'Jesus, Lay.'

'You were supposed to be one of the good ones.' I poke him again.

'Ow,' he says, rubbing his chest. He glances around to see if anyone can hear us. 'Whaddya mean?'

I refuse to break eye contact.

He shakes his head. 'What? What's going on?'

My jaw juts out. 'You tell me. What happened to you and me being friends above everything else? That was the deal.'

'Nothing's happened. We're mates, like you said.'

I scoff. 'You've been blowing me off.'

'Jesus,' he mutters, throwing his hands in the air, fed up. 'Lay, are you still with Kurt?'

'Yeah, but I'm —'

'Then you've still got a boyfriend. I'm trying to do the right thing.'

'I just want my friend back.'

'I'm outta here before I screw this up even more.' He strides off, but only makes it a few metres before he reels around and comes back. 'Fine, yeah, we were meant to be okay, but I don't how to pretend nothing happened when *something* happened.'

He's close enough for me to see glints of gold in his hair that I've never noticed until now.

'I came to your place when I shouldn't have ... and I could've stopped it and I didn't ... I didn't want to stop it.'

'Same,' I admit, stepping in closer, crossing my arms. '*Same.*' I pause, poised to tell him every crazy thought that's been spinning through my head. But now's not the time to say things that can't be taken back. Not when everything is still so muddled with Kurt.

'I ...' he starts, and it sounds like his voice is caught in his throat. 'Look, between this and Sal and my parents ... I just don't want to ruin anything. The timing is —'

'I know. It is.'

He sighs. 'I want things to go back to the way they were. This used to be easy. But it's not when you look at me like that.'

'This is my face.'

He shrugs.

'*Milo*.'

'Stop looking at me like that.'

I force a weak smile. 'Then you stop it too. We're just two friends looking at each other in an ordinary, average way.'

'Yeah ...' He pauses. 'I need to shut up now, and I need you to let me shut up.'

I nibble my fingernail. 'Okay. How about this: we both need to be careful about the looks we give each other — that's rule one.'

Milo nods.

'Rule two ... no eye contact for longer than a second. And no skin contact. Too risky. Definite rule three.'

'Definite.'

'No lip contact for rule four.'

'*Lay*.'

'Just flagging it. You're standing too close to me now. I wouldn't want you to trip over and land on me mouth first.'

'No flirty banter — that's rule five.' He points at me, shaking his head. 'None.' Then he raises his hands in the air and takes a step back. Then another. 'This better?'

'Much safer. Hey, maybe to suffocate all this weirdness we need to list the stuff about each other that's really annoying? Like, to repel each other.'

'You made me jump from that stupid tree into the river.'

'*Hey*! You thought of that *way* too quickly. And you conquered a fear that day — you should be grateful. And how about you? You nearly napped in my neighbour's pansies.'

He snorts with laughter.

'You didn't hire me for a job at the bookstore either.'

'I knew you were cut about that.'

My mouth splits into a grin. 'I think we're gonna be alright.' Already close to breaking rule three, I link my fingers together instead. 'It'll be weird, but we'll have our rules and we'll be alright.'

Something over my shoulder catches Milo's attention. 'Lay, I, um, there's something I need to explain.'

Before I can ask what's going on, a girl strides up next to me. She has a shock of long strawberry-blonde hair and a big toothy smile, although it seems plastered on her face, like it's hiding something beneath.

'Oh my God, Sal,' I blurt out. 'I mean, hi.'

'Hi ...?' She's still smiling but her tone has a shaky, unsure note to it. That's when I realise: she has no idea who I am.

'Sal, this is Lay ... ah, Layla,' Milo says, finding his voice. 'She's my, ah ... well, she went to our school ages ago — I don't think you had classes together. And she's, um, a family friend.'

Sal clears her throat. 'Oh? Like, *the* family friend?'

I wonder from her squeaky pitch if I'm a secret he wanted to keep, or at least a secret he didn't know how to tell.

He nods. 'Lay, Trent and I grew up together. She lived next door for a bit.'

A bit. Try thirteen years. He's playing this down, and I have no idea why he didn't tell me Sal was back in Durnan.

Sal releases a laugh. She sounds a little nervous or maybe I'm projecting.

'Cool, hi,' she says for the second time. Not awkward. Not at all. 'Well, I'm Sal, but I guess you know that. Um ... I just got in from Canberra this morning, so thought I'd surprise Milo. But I guess you knew that too.'

'Er, no, I didn't.' I really didn't. 'That's nice.'

'Yeah, I, ah, I had some things to pick up from my parents'. You should've seen the look on his face,' she says. 'Complete shock.'

'I bet,' I manage. I know the feeling. 'Um, what's on today then?'

'Hanging out, maybe more shopping.' She holds up a few bags. 'We haven't worked it out, but I was thinking a movie ... or maybe a trip to the river.'

Milo's eyes widen.

'We've never gone there together,' she says. 'The pool was our year's thing — but Milo told me how he went with a family friend. Which, now I'm connecting the dots ... is probably you?'

I suck in a breath. 'Yeah, that's me. It's awesome. Awesome. Very beautiful. The river, I mean. Very beautiful. I said that already, didn't I?'

I grit my teeth, hoping the concrete cracks open and sucks me down into the abyss.

'You know, it's probably too cold for the river,' Milo says.

'A movie sounds nice too,' Sal says. 'Layla, do you want to come with us or ...?'

'Oh! No, I won't,' I say in a rush. 'I'll leave you to catch up. My boyfriend's waiting for me back at the café so ...' I can't read Sal's expression after I've mentioned Kurt. Milo looks green. 'Anyway, have fun at the river. I mean, at the movies. Bye.'

I turn on my heel and head for the café, waiting until I hit the car park before checking over my shoulder. Even from a distance, I can see Sal clutching Milo's arm, dragging him towards the shopping centre across the street. I watch for a little longer, foot kicking at the kerb, waiting to see if he turns around to look at me like people do in the movies.

He doesn't. Of course he doesn't.

Because I have a boyfriend. Just.

And it looks like he has a girlfriend. Again.

No wonder he's been acting so cagey about us.

Not that there is an us.

I look one final time. He's already disappeared into the Saturday morning shopping crowd. So that's that.

Bzzzzz.

A message.

Bzzzzz.

And another one.

Oh God.

* * *

Milo: *Hey*

Milo: *So that was pretty weird with Sal just then, I'm sorry*

Layla: *All good*

Layla: *Have fun*

Milo: *She really did surprise me, I didn't know she was coming*

Milo: *I don't even know what to think*

Layla: *So stop thinking*

Layla: *And take note of Rule 6. It's new*

Layla: *Reminder of how L & M can stay friends:*

Layla: *1. Mind your looks. YES, THAT ONE*

Layla: *2. Eye contact kept to a second or under. LOOK AWAY*

Layla: *3. Skin contact. NONE*

Layla: *4. Lip contact. NEVER*

Layla: *5. Flirty banter. STOP IT*

Layla: 6. *No talking about bfs/gfs.* TOO WEIRD

Layla: *Safe topics: puppies, the weather, pizza versus burgers, Joe's health-and-safety code, pimple-popping, Netflix*

Milo: *Got it. Thanks, Chicken Girl. So ... puppies are pretty cute, hey?*

Layla: *Puppies > everything*

Milo: *Btw she's not my gf. We broke up, remember? She's visiting her parents*

Layla: *OK ...*

Layla: *PS: Please refer to rule 6*

Milo: *Netflix and chill a safe topic?*

Layla: *RULE 5*

Milo: *Sorry*

Milo: *Good weather we're having*

Layla

'There y'are!' Kurt cries. 'Quick, we've gotta run, babe. Now!'

'What?' I say, still sitting on a wooden bench outside the café. 'Why?'

Kurt grabs my hand and drags me through the car park. When we reach my car, Ryan is already in the driver's seat with the motor running. Kurt hurls open the front passenger door and nudges me in, before throwing himself onto the back seat. Ryan checks the rear-view mirror, then tears away, narrowly missing hitting a van.

I struggle with my seatbelt as Kurt and Ryan cheer. 'What's going on?'

Ryan howls with laughter as he slaps the steering wheel. 'That was close, man. Few minutes more and you'da been busted for sure.'

I scowl at Kurt. 'For what? What did you do?'

'It's more what we *didn't* do.' He holds up the bill.

My mind races. 'Turn the car around right now. We have to go back and pay.'

'It's fine,' Ryan says, winding down his window. 'They won't even care.'

'I want to be able to show my face in this town. Go back.'

Kurt shrugs — *whatever* — and looks out the window.

I slump in my seat, feeling suffocated, wishing I was anywhere but here, with anyone but him.

I hunt around the car for my sunnies, partly to block out the glare, partly to block out everyone and everything. They aren't in the glovebox with my lip glosses, or in the side compartment with old junk mail. Sighing, I check the armrest between the driver and passenger seat. There's no sign of them on top, so I rummage through to see if they've fallen down the side.

Kurt blurts something from the back seat, but it's too late to distract me. I've already seen it.

A zip-locked bag filled with rainbow pills.

I hurl the bag at him.

'Shit, it's a mate's, babe!' he says, waving it in the air. 'I dunno how it got in ya car. I swear.'

'You told me you'd never touch that stuff.'

'Believe me. I'm done.'

'Which is it?' My voice is sharp. '"A mate's" or "you're done"?'

'Ya getting me all confused. Just trust me, babe.'

'God, I *can't* … how can I? And you shouldn't trust me either.'

'What?'

I take a breath. 'I can't do this any more.'

Kurt rolls his eyes. 'Babe, come on, you're overreacting. It's just a little —'

'No! It's not. This is too much. I ... no. I'll move out, okay? Just ... just give me a week to sort something.'

'You're seriously doing this? Now?' There's not a trace of softness left in his voice.

My fists tighten in my lap. 'Yeah. One of us can sleep on the couch while we —'

'I'm not sleeping on the couch again.' His jaw clenches. 'You're making a huge mistake.'

Ryan keeps driving, and turns up the radio while Kurt and I argue about lies and broken promises and every stupid thing we've ever done to each other. We scream until my throat burns.

* * *

Milo: *Hey, friend. How was the rest of your day?*
Layla: *Just friggin' peachy, friend*
Milo: *Nice*
Milo: *Sweet dreams, friend*
Layla: *Slippery slope, friend*
Milo: *Dear Miss Montgomery, I hope you have adequate sleep tonight and feel well-rested on Sunday morning. Regards, your friend, Mr Dark*
Layla: *Better*
Milo: *That's what friends are for*
Layla: *Cluck you*

Milo

Sal steps onto her tippy-toes as she strains to look through my bedroom window and the pitch-black into the Perkinses' backyard.

'That's where she lived?' She turns to face me. I'm leaning in the doorway. I've been there for a while. 'Just there?'

'Yeah. She, um, left when her mum passed away.'

'That's awful. It sounds kind of familiar but you've never mentioned any of this to me.'

'Really? I guess, we had neighbours ... and then we didn't.'

Sal nods.

'Like, I don't know anything about your neighbours,' I say, feeling the need to explain myself. 'Well, except that guy who always steals your mum's newspaper.'

'Mr Ridge isn't a pretty eighteen-year-old girl,' Sal says, plonking back down on my bed. 'Are you planning on coming anywhere near me today?'

'Sure.' I sit down next to her. My head feels heavy, swollen, like someone has stuffed wet sand into every crevice of my brain. I edge myself back against the wall. 'Sal, I need to tell you something.'

'You like her. I know.' She says it in a calm tone, as if she's listing grocery items she needs to pick up from the shops.

'What? *No.*'

'I saw the texts. You and Layla.'

I feel my breath quickening. 'You what?'

'When you were packing the dishwasher. Sorry, your phone kept buzzing.'

'No, but … they're nothing. We're just joking around.'

Sal smirks. 'Look, lie to me about *whatever* is going on there — that's fine. But don't lie to yourself.'

I swallow hard, searching for the right words.

'Milo, you don't have to tell me … things happen. That's kinda the point of being broken up, right?'

'So did you and that guy …?'

'Who? Woody?' She rolls her eyes. 'Guys and girls *can* just be friends.' She glances back at the treehouse. 'Although now it's clear why you stopped trusting me — you had a little friend on the side. Classy.'

'*Sal*,' I say, my finger tracing the tattoo on her wrist. 'Nothing happened while we were together, I swear. Jesus, nothing's happening anyway. It's not.'

'*Milo*,' she says. 'It's fine.' She sighs, leaning in so we're forehead to forehead. 'I don't know how to say this next part, but I'm okay with this. All of this. Aren't you?'

I want to say yes, but it sounds so final. So awful.

'You're going to explode one day if you keep holding everything in.' She edges closer so our knees scrape together. 'I *know* you know what I mean.'

209

'Why'd you come here if you're so okay with it?'

'I had to make sure. You told me you loved me and I told you I loved you, and ... well, everyone was screaming in my head to make this work, you know?'

Far out. *I know.* 'Yeah.'

'We had this life mapped out, this plan ... but it just stopped feeling right.'

I manage to nod.

'Then I saw the way you looked at her ... I should've been sick with jealousy. But all I felt was nothing. Like, nothing.'

I clear my throat.

'Sorry, that came out wrong. I felt something, I did ... but ... but not enough.'

Ah, man. Same. *Shit.* Same.

'So we're doing this?' I ask.

'I think we've already done it.' She bites her lip. 'You'll always be my first.'

'Lucky you,' I say, forcing a laugh to try to break the tension. 'And I guess I can say the same about you.'

She cracks a smile. 'You can.'

We drift into silence again, Sal staring at the stain on the carpet where she spilled orange juice during an argument a year ago, me staring at the alarm clock. After a while, she announces she's leaving so I walk her down the driveway to her car, knowing Mum is standing in the kitchen, elbow-deep in soapy water, squinting through the window as it all plays out.

Sal and I don't bother with any more talking. We hug, we mumble, 'I'll miss you', but neither of us promises to stay in touch.

* * *

Dad pokes his head into my room. 'Knock, knock,' he says, not bothering to actually knock.

I take out an earphone in anticipation for the lecture ahead.

'Free for a chinwag? It's been a few days since we've had a yarn about your plans. Kettle's on.'

'Er, thanks, Dad.' There's no easy way out of this. 'Can we raincheck? My head kinda hurts.'

'Right. Sal. Your mother told me.'

'Yeah ... Sal.' And every other aspect of my life, but Dad already has enough reasons to think I'm hopeless.

'It's just,' he starts, clicking his tongue as he leans against my wardrobe, 'I looked it up and you need to get cracking with your uni applications.'

'I know. I'm getting to it.'

He nods. 'And, ah, by the way, Peter rang earlier —'

'Who?'

'*Peter*. Peter Newbins. Pay attention, Milo. He reckons he can swing us a good deal on the Robinsons' place, exclusive for us — *for you*, as a starter home. Trent, too. The four of us, together. Your mother and I would help you boys out financially at the start to get things moving. It'd be perfect.'

Jesus. 'Dad, I don't think —'

'Why not? I'm working with what I've got here.'

I swallow. 'That house is your dream, not mine. And definitely not Trent's.'

'Then get your act together, Milo, and get those applications done. I've had it with the waiting.'

'I'm trying. I'm working my arse off. But I don't want that house. I don't want something that just seems convenient.'

'Watch your tone.'

My heart rate quickens. 'I am taking this seriously — I promised you I would. I'll study once I work out what I want to do. Maybe computer science, maybe not. Or travel the world, or learn how to be a photographer, or volunteer somewhere, or, I dunno, take Japanese lessons or *move* to Japan ... who knows?'

'Who knows? Yeah, who bloody knows.'

'Whatever it is, I want to care about it and I want to get there on my own. It's the reason I'm here, saving money, with no friends, no life ... I'm trying to pull it together. Like you said.'

'Oh, give me a break,' Dad says, his voice low and angry. 'Photography? *Japan*? I expect this sort of navel-gazing and slacking off from your brother, but not from you. Are you applying for uni or not? No more of this wishy-washy crap, Milo. I want a straight answer.'

I look at my feet, but can still feel Dad's eyes boring into the top of my head. I give a small nod.

'Good. Because if you go any slower working out what your next step is, you're gonna start falling backwards. And your mum and I won't be there to catch you.'

* * *

Milo: *Any chance I'm adopted?*

Layla: *Huh?*

Milo: *Dad's doing my head in*

Layla: *OMG don't even TRY to challenge me to a dad-off (But hope you're OK?)*

Layla: *PS: You're up late, grandpa*

Milo: *I'm fine. Just can't sleep. What's up with you?*

Layla: *Watching a doco on Netflix*

Layla: *Did you know oysters change their gender at least once in their lifetime?*

Milo: *Nup*

Milo: *But I know seahorses mate for life*

Layla: *Like, ONE seahorse forever? That's it?*

Layla: *Seriously, no other seahorses?!*

Milo: *Apparently*

Layla: *Better than black widows. They eat their booty calls*

Milo: *Ha! You're basically David Attenborough right now*

Layla: *Who?*

Layla: *Hey, MD, you still up?*

Milo: *Now I am*

Layla: *DUUUUUDE*

Milo: *Rule 5*

Layla: *My bad, sorry*

Layla: *Not sure if this is against the rules to tell you, but Kurt and I broke up*

Milo: *What? When? You alright?*

Layla: *Before. I will be. Gotta move out soon tho (obvs)*

Milo: *There's a room here*

Layla: *Perve! (But thanks)*

Milo: *A spare one, I mean! It's here if you're stuck. Mum'd love it*

Layla: *'Mum', hey?*

Layla: *Wanna catch up soon? (AS FRIENDS)*

Milo: *Sure (AS FRIENDS)*

Layla: *I was thinking at the treehouse*

Milo: *Why there?*

Layla: *It's on my list. Pants are compulsory*

Milo: *Is that now a rule? 7?*

Layla: *Yep. How's Thursday?*

Milo: *Cool. 5.30's good at mine. Night*

Layla: *It's technically morning now*

Milo: *Then morning, Layla Montgomery*

Layla: *Morning, Milo Dark*

Layla

Knock, knock.

I tap my foot as I wait at the Darks' front door, cringing at the sign hanging there: *Families are like fudge — mostly sweet with a few nuts.*

No-one answers.

I check my phone. It's now 5.45 pm and I don't have any missed texts or calls from Milo. I plop down on the steps and rest the tub of gelato on my knees. It's starting to sweat, sending droplets of water down my legs and onto the concrete.

'Lovely day, isn't it?' calls an elderly man hobbling along the footpath with a tiny dog. He's the fifth person to spark a conversation with me since I arrived.

'Perfect,' I call back.

Friendliness from strangers is one of the biggest differences between Durnan and the city — well, Durnan and most places I've lived. Everyone's up for a chat here. I've already spoken with four other people in the fifteen minutes I've been waiting: a cheerful mum pushing her baby in a pram, two kids on bikes handing out supermarket catalogues, and the woman who showed up to mow my old backyard.

So much for hanging out in the treehouse today.

Alone with my thoughts on the step, I have enough mental space to contemplate the idea of being squashed in a treehouse with Milo. Maybe him *not* turning up is the best outcome.

Because me and *Milo*.

Both single.

Alone in a tiny space.

Oh God.

If we survive without breaking any of the rules, we'll deserve a gold medal.

* * *

Layla: *You're late and I have gelato*

Layla: *Hey, jerkface! Coming? PS: A lady's mowing my old backyard. Roar!*

Milo: *Sorry, Dad's bailed me up at work. That sucks*

Layla: *I'm here — should I go?*

Milo: *Didn't realise how late it was! No, don't. Give me 10?*

Milo: *Actually, 20*

Layla: *C'MON*

Milo: *ASAP, promise*

Milo: *Key's behind the pot plant*

Layla: *I'm eating ALL the gelato without you*

I lick my fingers, sucking the last of the gelato out from under my thumbnail. Dragging myself from the couch in the living room, I wander over to a cabinet. It's covered with photos in matching white frames: the Darks smiling at Christmas, the Darks smiling in a garden, the Darks smiling at Sea World, the Darks being the perfect smiling Durnan family.

'Monty Burns! Didn't know you were visiting me today.'

I turn to see Trent standing behind me. He's flushed, and wearing a singlet and shorts with a towel draped around his neck.

'Trenticles. Didn't hear you come in.'

'Back door,' he says, gesturing down the hall. 'You breaking in or what? All the expensive stuff's in the folks' bedroom.'

I smile. 'Oh, totally. Milo's running late but he told me to wait inside ... that alright?'

'Yeah, course. Always. How's Kurt by the way? Saw him at a party the other night.'

'We broke up so he's ...' I shrug. 'I have no idea.'

'Ah, sorry. Didn't know.'

Clearing my throat, I return to looking at the photos. Trent edges over. I can smell his muskiness.

'Talbingo?' He laughs and snatches up a shot of the Darks smiling by a lake. 'Isn't that where you confessed your love to me once? At the cabins?'

'No.' I snatch it back.

Trent grins. 'I reckon I still have the letter you wrote me. Filthy it was too.'

I laugh. 'Dream on.'

'Deny it all you want. I think you're still angry I turned you down for Valerie Rhodes. Biggest mistake of my life.'

'Shut up.'

'As you wish.' He pauses. 'But, ah, has Milo confessed his relentless thirst for you yet?'

'I said shut up. We're friends.'

'You two are as in denial as each other.' He smirks. 'Anyway, I'm jumping in the shower. Big workout today. *Huge.* Make yourself comfy, Montgomery.'

He goes out, leaving behind the stench of sweaty armpits.

* * *

Layla: *Save me! Trent's talking about his HUGE workout*

Milo: *Ha! Run! I'm about 5 away*

Milo: *This bus is taking forever*

Milo: *Save me any gelato, Chicken Girl?*

Milo: *You ate it all, didn't you?*

* * *

I kick off my thongs and help myself to chopped-up mango in the fridge, before lying on the Darks' couch again. It's like it's ten years ago and Mum's in the next room playing cards with Jen.

My head presses into a cushion as I buzz through the TV channels. Boring. Funny but seen it. Hundred years old. Dumb and seen it.

'Hey.'

I sit up, startled, and see Milo standing behind the couch, backpack slung over one shoulder.

'Hi,' I stammer, suddenly nervous. Being nervous around Milo is so out of the ordinary it's like we're in another dimension. 'What *is* it with you Dark boys and sneaking up on people?'

'Huh?'

'Back door, right?'

'*Huh*?' He walks around the couch and eases himself down next to me.

'Trent came in the same ... doesn't matter. How are you?'

He's careful to keep about a metre between our bodies while we talk, but not *seem* like he's keeping a metre between our bodies while we talk. We chat a lot about a little for a few minutes. Well, he does, while I nod along, pretending to listen while wondering what happens next.

'So, no treehouse today, huh? Damn.' He scratches his head. 'Um, you want a juice?'

'Sure. I'll help you get it.'

'Er, thanks.'

I spring to my feet, grateful for something — even something as trivial as juice — to focus on rather than the silence that creeps in every time one of us runs out of ways to stuff the air with small talk.

We head into the kitchen, and he fills my glass to the top with orange juice until nothing but a dribble comes out. He holds up the bottle: *empty.*

I point at it. 'That's dangerously familiar.'

'What, the juice?'

'The empty bottle.'

It's what we used to play spin the bottle before we discovered empty wine bottles in the recycling.

He flushes a little. 'Oh. Yeah. True.'

'Yeah.' Warning: rules down. 'How's Sal?'

I repeat: rules down.

'Well, I'm totally, one hundred per cent, definitely single.' He clears his throat. 'And, ah, you?'

He already knows I am. My lip curls into a smile. It's too late to fight it.

'Yep. Definitely, totally. One hundred per cent.'

'Interesting …' He hasn't let go of the bottle. 'About you and me the other week …' His cheeks are still flushed. 'I was thinking and … well, it wasn't *that* big a deal, was it? We can stay friends *despite* that … right? No weirdness. I can't deal with the weirdness.'

Every time he says 'weirdness' it only amplifies the weirdness.

I hoist myself onto the kitchen counter. 'Here's what I think. We kissed once, and now we're here and we're friends and I've got juice and everything's normal, so yeah … no big deal. No weirdness.'

'Well, technically it was two kisses in one day.'

'True. Well, maybe that makes it even less of a big deal. Twice and all is still okay.'

'Better than okay. In fact …'

'Yeah?'

I'm bursting for him to finish the sentence. His body is close to mine now. He's leaning in towards me so slowly — *painfully slowly* — that it's barely obvious it's happening. But it's happening.

'I might be wrong,' he begins. 'But maybe three times wouldn't be *that* different.'

I raise an eyebrow. 'You know, you're right. If anything, it would just *prove* how much we can handle it. The kissing. As friends, I mean.'

'Right. One hundred per cent.'

I can see his chest rising and falling now.

'Maybe we're friends who kiss sometimes. What a revelation. Who cares?'

'I don't get why everyone's not doing this.'

'It's genius,' I say and readjust my position on the counter, leaving my legs slightly splayed … just another space for him to stand in. 'So, ah, what do we … oh! I've got it.'

I take the bottle from his hand and lay it on the counter next to me. Then I give it a spin. It whirls around, sliding across the bench, before slowing to a stop, the lid pointed towards the fridge, the base pointed at Milo's stomach. The lid's not pointing at him. *It's supposed to be the lid.*

He leans in for a better look. 'Now what?'

I look at the bottle. 'Well ...'

He steps in closer until I can feel his body against mine.

'Well ...' He leans in and brushes my lips with his, just for a second. He breaks into a small smile. 'Oops, I fell.'

'Rules four and five,' I mumble, feeling a flutter flow through my body. I link my bare feet around his waist to pull him closer. 'See, we're friends.'

'Totally,' he says, before moving his lips against mine again, faster this time, like he's been holding it in.

My fingers slip up the back of his T-shirt, while his hands move over my jeans then slide up towards my shoulder blades. I press one palm onto the counter and wrap my other arm around his neck, when I hear a clatter. We look down to see the empty bottle on the tiles.

Then we hear slow clapping behind us.

Milo

Trent tells us not to worry. To chill. That he's seen it all before. That it looks like I'm using too much tongue.

'Relax, bro, we're all friends here, right?'

He's brought out his laptop to show us a video of the three of us playing together as kids. Layla flashes me a lopsided grin as we take seats at the opposite ends of the couch and Trent is all over it.

'Well,' he says, giving her a wink, 'some of you are more than friends, hey, Montgomery?'

'Shut it, Trenticles.'

I notice she's blushing. I don't know why but it kinda makes me happy. That maybe I'm not the only one into this. Whatever this is.

I roll my eyes. 'Are we gonna watch this stupid thing or not?'

'Damn straight we are, Casanova. Still can't believe I found this gem on Dad's old hard-drive. Haven't watched it all the way through yet, but what I've seen is gold. Trust me.'

He presses play.

Suddenly we're toddlers again.

There's our backyard with its patchy green lawn and overgrown garden before my folks got it landscaped, and we're giggling as we take turns running through a sprinkler. The camera work is shaky and Dad's voice booms off screen, telling us to calm down, take turns, be careful of bindies. The video goes in and out of focus — there's even a bit of muttered swearing as Dad fumbles to find his grip — then Trent and Layla come back into the shot. Trent's undies are so drenched they're hanging low on his lily-white body, while Layla's hair is thick and curly and dark, the way I remember it. She's waddling around in a striped one-piece, and then I trundle into the shot behind her, starkers, wearing my soaked undies like a floppy hat. Trent squats down on the sprinkler, laughing as the water bubbles up in his undies, and we all shriek like we've been hooked up to an IV of red cordial.

'Look at ya little thingy!' Trent points at the close-up of me sprinting across the screen, bare body on show for all to see. Layla tries to hide a cackle behind her fist. 'Bit cold that day, mate?'

'Where's my Layla?' a woman's voice calls off screen.

I suck in a sharp breath. Shit. I know that voice in the video. It's her.

Trent's still hooting at the footage, swearing as little Layla dacks him on screen, oblivious to the fact we're not laughing any more.

'Where's my Lay-Lay?' the sugary voice says. 'It's time to go, sweetie.'

My heartbeat quickens as I dare to look over, hoping

I'm overreacting, but Layla's lips are tight as she watches her mum walk into the frame holding a beach towel.

I clear my throat. 'Lay, we can turn it off —'

'No, leave it,' she says, not taking her eyes off the laptop. 'I'm fine.' Trent's no longer laughing

'Lay-Lay,' her mum sings on screen. 'Lay-Lay, come to Mummy. Ready to go?'

The three of us are silent as little Layla sticks out her tongue at her mum, who crouches down to eye level, sweeps her thick dark plait over her shoulder, and tries again.

'Sweetheart,' she says, extending her arms. 'We've gotta go. Mummy's gotta finish marking her school reports and I need you to come with me.'

Little Layla roars and stamps her foot on the grass, then runs in the opposite direction.

'I mean it, Layla. I'm counting to three, okay? One ... two ... Layla!'

More screaming. Then crying. Then a shot of her mum wrestling a wriggling, kicking, shrieking Layla over her shoulder. Her tiny little arms hit and punch at her mum, but she only grimaces, chewing on her bottom lip.

Layla's eyes fill with tears as she watches the video. 'Turn it off, Trent,' I hiss.

He's startled and slow, and we hear little Layla's repeated shrieks of 'Hate you, Mummy!' through the speaker.

Swearing, Layla snatches the laptop from Trent's hands and slams the lid shut.

Layla

I mumble that I have to go, that I have other plans, that I'll see them later. Thongs in my hands, I run through their living room and swing open the front door, ignoring their voices begging me to stay and talk about it.

I sprint across their lawn onto the hot cement. Gravel pierces the soles of my feet but I barely notice. I don't stop running.

* * *

Milo: *Hey, I'm so sorry. Wanna talk? I'll come to you?*

* * *

I make it to the alley behind the supermarket a few blocks from my house before I stop to draw breath. Well, to draw breath, kick at the cracked slabs of concrete and think about consequences. I've clearly underestimated the damage of allowing the Dark brothers back into my life.

Before Mum died, I didn't think about consequences. I never tried to trace a problem back to its cause. Back then, life felt almost forgettable; a series of moments of varying degrees of mundane: sleeping, flossing, reaching for the remote, kissing a boy behind the bike shed, buying potato gems on the walk home from school, lying on the trampoline with Milo, sleeping again. If only I'd known how much I'd miss that close-to-bored feeling.

Now all I do is think about consequences. It's how my brain's wired.

I know a look mightn't just be a look.

A little white lie mightn't just be a little white lie.

A woman driving to the bakery to buy a poppy seed loaf mightn't just be a woman driving to the bakery to buy a poppy seed loaf.

At the time, the moment might seem like nothing, but it could end up being everything.

The butterfly effect.

Because a woman driving to the bakery to buy a poppy seed loaf *also* mightn't be watching the road because her little girl is screaming in the back because her doll has fallen out of her hands. Maybe the woman left the house forty-five minutes later than she planned to because the washing machine flooded. Maybe she didn't sleep well the night before. Maybe her cousin has been diagnosed with cancer and it's stressing her out. Maybe she lingers in the rear-view mirror two seconds too long to cringe at the dark circles beneath her eyes. Maybe she's driving eight kilometres above the speed limit — even though she can't afford to lose any more points off her licence — because she wants to make it back home in time to greet her son when he gets back from camping with his dad. Maybe all of that has added up to this exact moment in her life — driving to the bakery to buy a poppy seed loaf.

That woman made it to the bakery. I know 'cos she told the police, the police told Dad, and Dad told me. When her little girl wouldn't stop screaming, she pulled over to let a ute speed past, picked up her daughter's doll, took a minute to collect herself, then drove to the bakery, bought her poppy seed loaf and made it back in time to greet her son. She didn't know until six hours later, while watching the news, that the ute sped on for three more blocks, clipped the median strip and hit a mother of one crossing Butcher Street to watch her thirteen-year-old daughter play softball.

Turned out the driver of the ute was still off his head after a party the night before. He lived though. He saw his family again. Stayed in the world.

The mother of one wasn't so lucky. She passed away in the hospital an hour later.

To this day I wonder if the woman driving to the bakery ever thinks about consequences. How, if she hadn't pulled over to let the ute past, maybe everything would've played out differently.

Or maybe it would've been exactly the same.

There's no way to tell.

All I know is I was still wearing my softball uniform when Mum took her last breath in the hospital that day. And I never wore it again.

The news of her death swirled around me faster and faster, until I fainted from shock. Apparently the nurses sat me in a chair and swathed my forehead in a wet towel, then they told me again 'cos no-one was sure if I remembered the first time.

Dad sobbed uncontrollably in the corner, already withdrawing into himself.

It didn't hit me then — that she was truly gone.

It didn't feel real until later.

We never got to make cupcakes together at midnight 'cos I had a sugar craving. We never stayed up late gossiping about boys, swapping stories about crushes and first kisses. I could never ask her for advice, or lean on her again, or ask her who to call to say, 'Help, my mum is dead, what do I do now?'

The only person I ever wanted in those moments was her. And she was the only person I could never see again.

In all the chaos at the hospital, my tattered old softball mitt got left behind and I only realised a few days later. Not that I ever bothered going to collect it. I couldn't even look at the bouquets of flowers piling up on Butcher Street.

* * *

Not all moments in my life are that sharp.

Not all moments rip away everything in an instant.

Sometimes they add up, multiplying quietly over the years, building, growing, until one day they rise up at you like a thundering wave, drag you out, pull you under and smack your head on the sand.

Like what happened at the cemetery with Kurt.

Like what happened today at the Darks'.

Like what happened with Milo in the laundry. *What keeps happening with Milo.*

Once those moments arrive, you wonder how you didn't notice them coming sooner. Why you couldn't see what now seems so clear.

I gag once, twice, then heave up foamy bile onto the concrete.

* * *

Milo: *Lay, where are you? Want company?*
Layla: *I'll be OK*

Layla

I lap the block three times before I've calmed down enough to go inside the house. The lounge-room curtains are drawn and the lights are dimmed. Mel's head rests on Jay's shoulder as they're curled up together in the armchair, Ryan's lying on his back on the floor by the coffee table, and Kurt's stretched out on the couch. My bed for the night.

'Hey, Lay,' Mel says.

Everyone else mumbles hello. None of them have spoken much to me since the break-up, not that I've gone out of my way to make small talk over Weet-Bix either.

'Hey,' I say, coughing from the smoke clogging the air.

I look at Kurt, waiting for him to catch my eye, but he doesn't. He's already like a stranger. Or maybe I'm the alien.

With the couch taken, I march to the bedroom and stand in the doorway, looking in. There's not long before I have to move out, but I feel even further away from a plan. Where do you go when the most familiar places are too painful but nowhere else feels like home?

I rub at my eyes. *Hold it together. Don't crack now.*

'Lay … ya really don't have to leave.'

I turn to see Kurt standing there. His eyes are red and his clothes smell smoky — the way they always have, I guess.

'I mean it, babe. Stay. It was a stupid fight, that's all.'

'No, it wasn't.'

'Where ya even gonna move to? You belong here.'

My stomach lurches because I know I don't. Surely I belong somewhere, but not at this house with these people living this life.

I look at the floor. 'I'll work it out.'

'We both said stuff we didn't mean. Can't ya forgive me?'

'I meant everything,' I manage, voice trembling.

'Babe.' Kurt wraps his arms around me. 'C'mon.'

I flinch. 'Ow, you're squashing me.'

He lets go, swearing under his breath. 'I've been there for ya … for years. Through all that stuff with ya mum. That should mean something. That should be enough.'

I swallow. My silence says it all. It's not.

Kurt sighs and crosses his arms over his chest. 'Fine, do it. But stop putting it off. Can ya just leave?'

'What?'

'Ya heard me, babe. Leave. Like, now.'

He hurls open the wardrobe, pulls down my suitcase and throws it on the bed.

'I can't,' I say, voice shaking. 'You promised me a week. I've got nowhere to go. Not yet.'

'Ya had me, but ya don't want that, do ya?' He shrugs, jaw hardening. 'Call ya dad if ya have to and tell him ya've blown it again. Just leave 'cos I can't even look at ya. *Now.*'

* * *

I feel like the last girl in the world.

The car park at the river is deserted. The trees make striking silhouettes as the sky darkens behind them.

I breathe in a gulp of fresh air, soaking in the scent of the river — *our stupid river* — before winding up the windows. My bulkiest, softest jumpers and tracksuits are piled on the back seat. A makeshift bed. I crawl onto them and lie down, burrowing my cheek into my pillow. Cool air sends goosebumps across my thighs and calves so I pull one of the hoodies around my legs.

In my rush to leave, I forgot to throw in a sleeping bag or a sheet. I didn't even stop to say goodbye to my housemates. They'd all disappeared into their bedrooms when Kurt started yelling and I wasn't about to knock on their doors on the way out. Not with Kurt breathing fire. And it wasn't like they came to my rescue.

How weird to think I may never see and of them again. Not if they want it that way.

Not if I want it that way.

Durnan is small, but it's easy to disappear if you know where to hide.

One final check that the car doors are locked, then I pull my eye mask down and hug the downiness of the pillow again as my phone buzzes.

* * *

Milo: *Hey again, Chicken Girl, what's doing tonight? Any more oyster facts for me? PS: Trent and I feel like arseholes after today. Let us make it up to you! You OK?*

Layla: *Oysters produce pearls. PS: Thanks, I've been better, but I'll be OK*

Milo: *Knew that one! PS: Wanna talk about it?*

Layla: *Crazy that something so awful can produce something so beautiful. PS: Maybe*

Milo: *Awful? They're delicious. PS: OK*

Layla: *And an aphrodisiac*

Milo: *Not at all related **

Milo: ** Busted*

Layla: *Hey Milo?*

Milo: *Hey Lay?*

Layla: *Thanks*

Milo: *No worries. (What for?)*

Layla: *Just thanks*

Milo: *It was the kissing, wasn't it?*

Layla: *Ha!*

Layla: *That part didn't hurt, friend*

Milo: *Catch up soon, friend?*

Layla: *When were you thinking? I'm kinda busy right now*

Milo: *River. Saturday. 1 pm. You free?*

* * *

Bleep. My phone battery's nearly done.

Bleep, bleep.

A quick look through my backpack and suitcase for my charger reveals I left it behind at the house. Friggin' hell.

I want to see Milo too. I want to feel his fingers trace over the creases of my palm. I want him to pull me close, in that way only he does so my face buries itself in the warmth of his chest. I want my friend, but I don't know how to be with him as long as my mum's memory plagues every corner of his world. It only hurts me. And that'll only hurt him.

Besides, I haven't showered and brushed my teeth since this morning. If my hair was a bird's nest earlier, it's a haystack by now. I also forgot most of my toiletries in my rush to bail out of the house. Anything that wasn't on my chest of drawers or in the wardrobe didn't make the cut.

Bleep, bleep, bleep.

My phone's screen goes black.

Dead.

Milo

There are no customers in the shop, so I put down the cleaning rag and spray I've been using and sneak a look at my phone. Nothing but a text crammed with typos from Murph that proves his night was way messier than mine. Not a single message from Layla. Just when I thought things were untangling themselves.

I shake my head, as though that'll somehow shake her out of my system.

I know she was upset. Even Trent, who has the emotional IQ of a tractor, knows that. But why is she freezing me out?

Giggling explodes through the store and I look over to the counter. A group of girls who graduated from Durnan's private school last year have swarmed through the door, and Trent, who's meant to be balancing the till, is flirting hard, like it's a competitive sport.

He invites them to hang with him and the boys tonight. One of the blondes leans across the counter, chest spilling out of her top, and tells him to put his number in her phone. She winks, he grins, then there's a lot of hair tossing and pouting and teasing from her friends.

I return to wiping the bookshelves, trying to trick myself into thinking about anything but Layla and wondering if the cleaning spray has seeped into my brain.

* * *

At five thirty I switch the shop sign to *Closed* and lock the door.

Trent smacks gum next to me. 'Coming with, bro? Those girls are keen, I reckon.'

'Nah, might sit this one out.'

'Why not? Is this about Montgomery?'

'Nah, course not.'

'Well, the old man's been riding you hard. Let off some steam, bro, it's Friday.'

'You want to go out? Where people will see us? Together?'

'Let's roll,' he says. 'It's about time the Dark brothers tore up this town.'

* * *

I've barely sat down in the beer garden when I spot the blonde with the phone squeezing past crowded tables to make her way towards Trent and me.

She waves at me, I elbow him.

'Don't shit yourself, bro, I'll handle it.'

Moments later we're surrounded. The girls fight for Trent's attention as he leans back against the pool table, his shirt straining at his chest. I may as well be draped in an invisibility cloak. I check my phone. Nothing. Layla can probably smell the desperation seeping through her phone.

A collective 'Oh wow' erupts within our circle. All the girls' goopy-mascara eyes are pasted on me. One of them — maybe Denny? — places her hand on my knee. I sit up, startled.

'Milo, I can't believe you nearly died,' she says, clutching her chest. The others all nod, sucking hard on their straws. 'I mean ... it's so ... *scary*.'

I try not to stare at the piece of mint caught between her teeth. 'Sorry ... what?'

'Trent told us what happened to you at the river,' she continues. 'When you almost ... *drowned*.' She whispers the last part, like she's filling me in on a top-secret mission. 'Lucky he was there to save you. I mean, can you imagine?'

I look at Trent who gives me a quick wink. 'That's what he said?'

Denny nods. 'But he was more humble than I'm making out.'

'I bet.'

'Tell them about the car accident, Milo,' Trent says, slurping his beer. 'This guy has nine lives, I swear.'

I try to catch his eye to tell him to shut it, but he's too busy smiling at the girls.

Another girl gasps. 'An accident too?'

'Nearly wrote off a car but pulled it together,' Trent

says. 'I was pretty freaked out.' Freaked out? Yeah, right. 'I'm just glad he's okay, you know?'

I take a sip of my cider, mainly so I don't combust right there.

Trent calls the girls into a huddle. 'Bet you ten bucks he says I'm lying, playing it down to impress you all. Doesn't want to seem like a big-shot.'

'Ah, can you give me a sec?' I say, holding up my phone and pretending I have a call.

I leg it to the bar. Trent trails behind me, waiting 'til the girls are out of sight before clipping me over the ear.

'Oi, I'm pulling hard for the two of us back there. Which one do you like?'

I head into the pokies room. 'Geez, you're a tool.'

He follows me in. 'What?'

'You "saved me"? That's your new pick-up line?'

'It's just a story, no harm fudging the details,' he says, pulling up a stool. 'They're loving it.'

'Can you hear yourself? It's pathetic. From what I've been told, you didn't "save" anyone. You just stood on the side of the river watching me bob around face down.'

'Back up, mate, I was a kid too. What, you buy into the whole "Trent nearly ruined our lives" theory? I know Dad's been pumping it for years, but you?' He puffs out his chest a little. 'Low.'

'No, I didn't mean …' I sigh. 'I don't know what I freakin' mean. But why are you even bringing up that stuff? Durnan's small enough without complicating things.'

239

'Just trying to help you out. Throw you a bone. Maybe literally.'

I sigh. 'Jesus, man. I'm sure they're nice but … nup. No way. Not going there.'

'Let's have a boys' night then. For real.' Trent clinks his glass against mine, then inhales half of it.

We sit for a bit and let the pokies' jingling and whirling fill in the quiet.

'No-one blames you for what happened to me,' I say. 'Not even Dad.'

'Bro, I was the lump who almost let you die.' He gulps more of his drink. 'Ask anyone, especially the old man. But you know I'd never deliberately hurt you, right? Right?'

My cheeks feel warm. 'Yeah. Course.'

'Good.' Trent slaps the counter. 'Now … enough mushy crap.' He raises his beer. 'Cheers to the Dark brothers and turning your crappy little life around. If anyone can do it, it's you, golden boy.'

I roll my eyes and look at my phone again. Big fat nothing.

Trent glances at me. 'Montgomery?'

'Nah, she's ghosted.' I raise an eyebrow, ready for him to give me crap for caring.

He shrugs. 'Relax, bro. Sal's left you all paranoid. She's probably just working.' Pause. 'Or maybe she's phased you after she realised you've got a micro-penis.'

'Is that why she ruled you out in high school?'

Trent roars with laughter, then pulls me towards him into a loose headlock, ruffling my hair 'til it's spiking out in every direction.

* * *

Milo: *Life update: I'm eating Joe's chips in bed on a Friday night #foreveralone*
Milo: *Are we on for the river tomorrow at 1 or ...?*

Layla

Stars hanging from the sky are my only company tonight.

My phone is still dead so I'm lying on the back seat, drawing circles with my left big toe on the roof. They start off small and tight, then grow wider and loopier. The seatbelt-holder digs into my right hip but I don't care.

I stare into the dark, adjusting to the blackness. I wriggle around on my back to adjust my underwear, then press my right foot against the roof to leverage my body weight. My period's come, and it's the kind where you feel like there's someone pummelling your lower stomach with sharp tiny punches. Raiding the bathroom for pads and tampons didn't come to mind when Kurt was yelling at me to leave, so I've wound toilet paper from the loos by the river around my knickers. I'm basically thirteen and hiding in a cubicle at Mum's funeral again. Only this time Jen isn't here to whisper instructions to me about what to do next.

Reaching out to Dad for help isn't an option; he's probably still away for work anyway, so Shirin would be forced to shoulder the burden. She'd hug and squeeze and fuss, then she'd want reasons for everything: why Kurt and I broke up, why I can't go back there, why it ended. Why, why, why. I can't tell her I've blown it again.

I can only imagine what Mum thinks, watching me from wherever she is. I like to imagine it — her place — as a comfortable couch in the sky with a milk bar that serves strawberry milkshakes that never run out and perfect wi-fi so she can stream all her favourite shows without the TV freezing every five minutes. Maybe she has some new friends to squash up on the couch with, or her own parents, Grandma and Grandpa. And maybe she never sleeps 'cos where she is no-one needs sleep 'cos there's so many other better ways to fill the hours instead. Whenever I picture her, slurping her third milkshake for the day and laughing with Grandma over something only the three of us would find hilarious, my mind worries about her witnessing all my stuff-ups. But it's an even worse thought to imagine her not being there at all.

I definitely can't talk to Milo. Being in the car like this reminds me of him more than ever: of our road trip; of squeezing into small spaces; of staying up all night and wondering if everything is going to be okay when all signs point to no.

My mind is flooded with can'ts.

I've considered driving to his place so many times, but the more hours that pass, the harder it is to do.

'Truth or dare?' I mumble to myself. My head is foggy now.

'Truth, please.'

'Layla?'

'Yes?'

'Do you have any idea what to do next?'

'Truthfully?'

'That's the game.'

'Not a clue.'

'You're so screwed. Oh, and you're talking to yourself, you fool.'

'Whatever. You got me into this mess.'

Knock, knock, knock.

Someone's rapping on the car window.

I sit up in shock, sucking in a breath as a silhouette fills the space. Instinct kicking in, I grab the car handle and pull at it. I can't remember if I locked the doors.

'Hello?' a male voice says. 'You alright in there?'

'Fine! Thanks, okay, bye,' I say in a rush.

'It's the police,' a husky female voice adds. She sounds stern, tougher than the guy. 'Can you wind down your window, miss?'

'Um, how do I know you're really the police and not an axe murderer?'

I hear stifled laughter from the guy, so I wipe at the condensation on the window, creating a sphere of clear glass.

A big round face appears in the circle. 'Evening. No axe murderers here.'

I gasp in fright at the sudden sight of eyes, a nose and knitted eyebrows pressed up against the window. His breath fills the glass.

I wipe again and he holds up his badge. 'Here you go. The name's Constable Bill Dutton.'

Shit. When I was in Year 7, he was in Year 10. 'Tiny' we called him, because he was anything but. I'm not positive, but I think he went out with Jill for three weeks before she broke up with him for buying her scented soap from the two-dollar shop for Valentine's Day. Mum died not much longer after, so I haven't seen him since then.

'Hang on,' I mumble.

Plunging my hand into my bag, I find my perfume and drench myself in it, then I ease out of the car. The moon is lighting up the night.

The cops stand a metre back, Bill's arms are crossed over his chest, the woman's are on her hips.

'You by yourself, miss?' she asks.

I nod, keeping my head down. Maybe she won't notice my bloodshot eyes from crying.

'It's awfully late. Can we grab a name, please?'

'Layla. It's Layla.'

'*Layla*? Montgomery?' Bill asks, taking a step closer.

'Hi.'

'Well, goddamn ... I haven't seen you since ... well, school, I suppose. I didn't even know you were back in town.'

I throw him a pinched smile. 'Forgot to send out flyers, I guess.'

'You know this girl, Dutton?' the female officer asks, throwing him a questioning look that suggests there'll be a conversation at the station later.

'Used to.' Bill clears his throat. 'So what are you doing here, Layla? It's not safe at night.'

'It's fine, no axe murderers, remember.' I gesture around the empty car park. 'Pretty peaceful really.'

The woman sniffs the air. 'Your eyes are pretty glassy, miss. Aren't they, Dutton?'

He gives a curt nod.

'Alright, Layla,' she says. 'I'm Senior Constable Minch from Durnan Police and it seems you already know Probationary Constable Dutton. Let's start with some ID.'

That wakes me up. 'What? Why?' I ask, passing her my licence. 'Am I under arrest?'

Minch steps closer. 'Calm down, please, miss. Now, you don't have anything on you that's going to hurt me or my partner here?'

'Hurt you?' I swallow. 'As if. I don't want to hurt anyone. I'd never —'

'Layla, just answer the question,' Bill says.

I narrow my red-rimmed eyes at him — a habit when I'm cornered — but he stares back. Then I get it. He's pleading with me to shut up. Do what Minch says. Get this done for the both of us.

I give in. 'No, I don't have anything on me.'

'Great. Now put your hands up please,' Minch says.

'*What*? No! I said I don't have anything!'

'I'm going to search you quickly, Miss Montgomery,' Minch says. 'Please stay still and it'll be over before you know it.'

I fight the urge to run that's prickling my heels and stretch my arms out wide. Her hands run over me, patting me down from top to toe. Her palms bounce over my ribcage, stomach and thighs, and I bite down hard on my lip to distract myself, so hard I taste blood.

They let me off with a caution.

Minch snorts with displeasure but concedes there's nothing on me and no reason to take things any further. She tells me I'm lucky this time, that it could've been worse.

I barely hear the words spitting from her pale, thin lips 'cos I'm trying to stop my hands from trembling behind my back. Every cell in my body was convinced Ryan and Kurt had stuffed more of their awful junk through the car and Minch was going to pin their stash on me.

Bill tells me they're going to drive me home. I shrug it off, making a flimsy excuse about loving the quiet, but he insists, says it's not safe to stay there alone.

My jaw stays stiff as I refuse for a fourth time.

When Minch saunters off to take a call, Bill steps up again. 'Level with me, Layla. I can tell you've been crying. You can't call your dad?'

'I think he's at the mines.'

'What about a friend?'

I shake my head.

'Why not? You've got plenty of mates.'

Silence.

'Okay … a neighbour? Another relative?' He waits for an answer. Nothing. 'There's got to be someone.'

'I'm alright here.'

'Look,' he says, voice low so Minch can't hear, 'I'm pretty new to this job but I've already seen some bad stuff. It's rough around here at night. It's not like when we were kids. Just believe me, okay?'

He opens up the car, wincing at the musky smell. 'Throw your stuff into your bags. We'll work something out.'

* * *

Minch stays in the car while Bill walks me up the driveway with my suitcase and backpack. When Shirin opens the door, tightening the belt on her leopard-print dressing gown, she gasps at the sight of the police car.

After thanking Bill for dropping me off, Shirin takes my suitcase from him and leads me down the hallway to the last room on the left — the guest room. My story tumbles out in nonsensical snippets as she turns on a small lamp in the corner, which casts a warm glow across everything. There's still not much in there: a single bed, a bedside table, a small desk, a chair and a wardrobe. No photos. No clutter. It's like stepping into a furniture catalogue.

'Come on, hon,' she says, waving me into the room.

I mumble thanks and tell her I'm sorry again for waking her in the middle of the night.

She tut-tuts at my rambling, then disappears out of the room and returns moments later with a towel, face-washer and bottle of body wash. Pressing it all into my hands, she tells me to have a hot shower and get some sleep.

'We'll talk tomorrow when you're rested.'

I'm overcome with a strange feeling of remembering what it's like to be looked after. Cared for. I don't think I realised how much I needed it until this moment.

My head is bowed. All I can think is how terrible I must smell, and how I hope Shirin has some spare pads in a bathroom drawer, and how I feel like a stranger in my dad's home.

But Shirin doesn't comment on the redness of my eyes, or the late hour, or the cops showing up at the house, or the fact I haven't returned her calls since our last catch-up. She just tells me it's good to have me home.

I hold back the tears until I'm in the shower.

* * *

I pick at my grilled cheese on toast, popping holes in the stretched-out melted cheese oozing over the edges onto the plate. Shirin watches me from across the kitchen as she sips her second coffee for the morning. We still haven't spoken about last night; a miracle considering Shirin loves to flood silences with her every thought.

In the daylight, I take a second to look around. It's not like the Darks' place, which Jen has styled to look like a spread in a high-end glossy magazine. Here it's like life has vomited over every square metre of the house except the guest room. There are photos everywhere, crammed onto every shelf, the walls and even along the hallway. When I look closer, I realise how many there are of me. Dad pushing me on a swing as a toddler. Me sitting on Dad's shoulders after a swimming carnival. Me and Dad raking leaves on the front lawn at the old house.

Mum isn't in any of the photos but she's still tied to them. She took them, bullying Dad to hop into the shot 'cos he hated posing, and refusing to be in them herself 'cos there were 'enough photos of her'. It's the biggest lie she ever told us.

I stop looking.

Shirin takes a seat opposite me and I can almost see the mechanics whirring inside her head. I'm swamped with guilt that she has to muddle her way through this.

'So,' she begins, taking another sip of her coffee. 'Let me get this straight, hon … you've been kicked out?'

I nod.

'And you and Kurt have broken up?'

I swallow. 'Yep. Done.'

'Okay …'

Her lip twitches. I bet she wants to ask why, but she respects my privacy and doesn't push me for details. In an unexpected way, it actually makes me want to tell her everything. I silently work through my 'Layla screws up her life' checklist: homeless, broken up, busted by the police, Milo … oh, yeah. The other thing.

'I also … I missed work, I think. Definitely one shift. Maybe even another one today, I can't remember.'

A light flickers in Shirin's eyes. 'You have a job?'

'At the chicken place. But everything got so crazy with Kurt, and I think I left my uniform at the house and ...' I clear my throat. 'Anyway, I tried calling Joe from your phone this morning — I hope that's okay — but it's ringing out. I'm fired for sure.'

She points at my plate. 'Don't forget the crusts. We could drive there today? Work it out in person.'

'It's not like I have a good excuse.'

'I dunno, it sounds to me like you have a lot going on, hon.'

'Yeah.' Not that I want to explain any of it to my boss.

'Look, I have to be honest with you. Your dad is worried about all this.'

'He knows?'

'Of course. Some of it anyway — I was *creatively selective* when I spoke to him,' she admits. 'The thing is, I want you to stay here with us. We both do.'

I swallow. The last time Dad and I lived under the same roof it was a disaster.

'You're eighteen — I get it,' she continues, steamrolling over the silence. 'You're old enough to make your own decisions. But the *police*? And sleeping in your car? Let us look after you, for God's sake. You've tried doing it alone. It hasn't worked. *Enough.*' Her voice is shaking. 'If you want to leave, then there's nothing I can do to stop you. But that room down the end is yours.'

'But Dad —'

'Wants this too.' Her hand rests on mine. 'He does. He's not the man he was back then.'

251

'He doesn't even text me.'

She sighs. 'Oh, honey. He works too much and has made plenty of questionable decisions involving you, you're right, but I think he gave up on you ever wanting to be near him again. But you're here now, and … well, maybe you two can start again. He needs this second chance … and I think you do too.' She pushes my plate closer to me. 'And he loves you silly. Please treat this place like it's home because it *is* your home.'

I mumble thank you and agree to stay for a bit. Not for long. Just until I'm sorted.

Shirin lifts her cup to her lips and I notice a satisfied smile stretch from the corners of her mouth, like she's just solved the most complex mystery in the world.

Milo

Music pounding in my earphones, I head out the front door. Block after block, I run through how Layla and I might greet each other, what we might say, whether we'll hug, or kiss on the cheek, or launch ourselves at each other with so much PDA that it horrifies all the families hanging by the river.

Then I remember. There's still no word from her. She might not even show.

At the entrance to the car park, I hoist myself over a waist-high fence to take a shortcut. Long grass scratches at my calves as I wind my way down to the water. My heart starts to race as I conjure her in my mind. Messy hair. Skinny jeans. That voice that slices through a room.

I spot her car wedged between two SUVs.

Holy crap. She came.

* * *

I circle the car, tongue pressed against the top of my mouth, and peek through the windows. Nothing looks out of place. There's a little extra rubbish littering the back seat, but that's about it. It's locked. I've checked twice.

Palms cupping the back of my head, I look around, half-expecting to see her bounding over, calling me 'jerkface'. But she's not down at the river bend, or splashing by the willows. She's not up high near the rope swing. She's not on the grass under the trees. She's not chatting with the duo who've run the tourist centre for the past ten years.

I even wait outside the ladies' for fifteen minutes, but the only person who comes out is a weathered woman in a sarong, jumper and thongs who tells me to scram before she pads back to her caravan.

I wander up to the main street to suss out if Layla's at Joe's, or stocking up for us at the gelato shop, checking my phone to see if I've skipped over something.

Nope. No messages or missed calls.

An hour has passed since I first arrived but this is all I know: she's not here.

* * *

Milo: *Hey, where are you, Chicken Girl?*
Milo: *I'm back at your car*
Milo: *Are we playing hide'n'seek?*
Milo: *Have we done that thing where you're at your car while I'm by the water, or you're in the bathroom while I'm up at the main street?*
Milo: *Well, that's an hour and a half*
Milo: *Seriously, you OK?*

Layla

The bedroom door creaks open. Shirin edges her way in, harem pants first.

'Wanna watch a soppy movie? I've got tissues and snacks.' She waves a heaving bowl of buttery popcorn in my direction.

'Sure.' I sit up on the bed, tugging my hoodie further down over my forehead.

'You can invite a friend over if you want?'

I shrug. 'That's okay. Er … that popcorn smells good,' I say, keen to change the topic.

'The movie's just an excuse to eat it. Dinner didn't touch the sides.' Shirin crunches on a fluffy kernel. 'So, quick update: I've picked up the car for you and a girlfriend dropped off her extra charger, 'til we get you another one.'

Using her spare hand, she eases it from her pocket and places it in my hand.

'You're the best. Thanks.' I sit it on the bed next to me.

She raises an eyebrow. 'A few months back you would've killed me for a charger. Should I call a doctor, hon?'

'It's cool, I'll check my phone later.'

I feel bad for disappearing on Milo, but maybe the space will make him realise how chilled things can be for him without me dropping atomic bombs all over his life.

Shirin zeroes in on my suitcase, which is wide open on the floor in front of the wardrobe. A waterfall of jumpers, hoodies, shorts, T-shirts, dresses, skirts and knickers cascades over the edges.

'You haven't unpacked.'

She plonks the bowl of popcorn next to me on the bed, and heaves and huffs at my suitcase until it's out of the way and she can open the wardrobe. Even from the bed I can see it's already crammed with boxes. Boxes scrawled with *Layla* in black marker. I'd recognise Dad's terrible loopy handwriting anywhere.

'Your father was supposed to move these into the garage months ago. Luckily for us, he's hopeless and forgot.'

'What's in them?'

She runs her hand over my name. 'Your things, honey. You don't remember?'

I stare at them, wondering what could be inside.

'They were all boxed up years ago, right after it happened. Your father wasn't himself though, so I can't imagine they're very organised. You've never looked in them?'

'I never knew about them.' I wonder if Shirin hears the crack in my voice. 'What happened to Mum's stuff?'

'Oh … I don't know, hon. Why don't we unpack these and make space for your clothes in the robe?' She reaches for a box.

'That movie was sounding pretty good,' I say. 'I can get to them tomorrow.'

'Alright, your call.' She glances at the bare walls. 'We should get some colour in here too. Ever painted?'

'Once maybe … not really.' I'm pretty sure watching Kurt graffiti a public toilet wall doesn't count.

* * *

My phone's screen glows in the dark. Now that it's charged, messages are flooding through. A missed call from Joe's. Mel telling me she's sorry about how it all went down. Another missed call from Joe's. A long-winded novel of a text from a clearly out-of-it Kurt saying he never loved me anyway, followed by another four messages saying he's sorry, missing me like crazy, didn't mean any of it and wants me to move back in. A voicemail from Joe telling me I'm fired and not to bother coming in again. *Shit, shitty shit.* A short message without any flowery bits from Dad saying he's glad I'm home and he's sorry he's still away for work. He does sign off with 'love you' though.

I save Milo's messages until the end.

I have to reread them because I'm too frazzled to take them in the first time.

The second time, I savour every word.

It hurts to think of him wandering around the car park, confused and wondering why I wasn't there, but I don't know how to reply now. Not after everything that's gone down since I last saw him.

I imagine how it might play out: *Um, hi, sorry to stand you up. After I lost my mind at your place, my jerky boyfriend kicked me out so I had nowhere to sleep. I totally stuffed up my one source of money, then the cops had to drive me home, but I'm not a total head case, promise, so let's be friends-who-kiss-sometimes and swap funny oyster facts soon, yeah? Lx*

Yeah, no.

But putting off texting him forever won't work either. If I ignore his messages for too long, he'll eventually stop trying. Just like Jill did. Because with me gone, his life might loosen itself out of the knot we've created until it's back to normal and he'll realise he was better off without me after all. And that's just about the bluest thing I can imagine happening right now.

I can do this. My fingers hover over the keys.

Hi Milo.

Delete. Too formal.

Hey, you.

Delete. Too breezy considering what I need to tell him next.

Chicken Girl here. Do I win hide-and-seek?

Delete. Too flippant. Too lame. Too fake-happy.

I fall asleep without replying to anyone, not even Milo.

I take a knife from a drawer and head into the bedroom. Earlier this morning Shirin pulled all the boxes out of the wardrobe so there's space for me to store the clothes I rescued from Kurt's.

I crouch down to the first box, which is puckered around the edges after years of storage, and slice through the masking tape. Nothing but baby clothes that I'd thought Mum and Dad had given away years ago. I rifle through it and hold up a pair of knitted booties, barely as big as a credit card. I close up the box, keeping the booties next to me.

My hands shake a little as I reach for another; it's like stepping into a time machine. I tug at the tape, trying to ease it off without ripping anything. It doesn't work so I knife through it. This box is crammed with primary school stuff — old assignments, notebooks and report cards. *While Layla excels in her studies and shows potential well beyond her grade, she could do better at being quieter in class so she doesn't distract the other students.* I flush with pride when I see my Year 6 teacher begrudgingly gave me an A.

I tear through the next few boxes. Old toys. More assignments. Birthday cards. Even more clothes. A jewellery box filled with necklaces, a charm bracelet, stud earrings and my signet ring. It's so small it doesn't even fit on my pinkie finger. On a whim I check every compartment to make sure Mum's bracelet isn't tucked inside a deep crack. Nothing.

The second-last box is full of books. How I'd adored them. I remember staying up with a torch under the sheets until Mum came in and begged me to get some sleep before school the next day. I take out book after book and place them to the side until my fingers wrap around the one I'm looking for: *The Very Hungry Caterpillar*. I stroke the cover and open it to the first page. There it is: her handwritten words to me. *To our little butterfly. Love Mum and Dad xox*

I slip the book under the booties.

Fighting back tears, I rip open the final box to see my old swimming gear stuffed inside. Flippers. Goggles. Cap. A Teenage Mutant Ninja Turtles backpack that Mum used to fill with my favourite toys to lure me to class week after week. *Property of LM* is scribbled on a raggedy foam kickboard wedged down the side of the box. It's Dad's writing this time and the water has washed most of it away.

I stack the boxes in a corner. As I pick up the box of swimming gear and try to heave it onto the top of the pile, the backpack topples out and hits the carpet. Scooping it up, I unzip it, wondering if Dad held onto my Daffy Duck floaties.

I almost drop the bag when I see what's inside.

My tatty old softball mitt.

* * *

The sun belts down on my skin as I squeeze my fingers into the mitt as far as they'll go, rub its leathery exterior, read the personalised ID tag a hundred times. *Layla.* This time it's in Mum's scrawl.

My cheeks ache from smiling so much.

I don't know how the mitt made it into the box. Back then, after the accident, Dad was in no position to get it back for me. I send a big thank you to the sympathetic neighbour or kind-hearted nurse who returned it 'cos I now have another piece of Mum. Another memory.

Maybe I do want them all.

Maybe she is with me again, *just.*

I look up, heart swelling at the bright buttery orb glowing in the sky.

No, I tell myself, she *is* with me.

That's how Shirin finds me: flopped on the grass, fingers tracing over the stitching on the mitt, staring up at the blue.

'Sorry to interrupt the daydreaming, but what would you like for dinner, hon?' she asks, playing with the beaded necklace hanging around her neck. 'Green curry or fish tacos sound good? Or do you have a favourite dish? Keep in mind you're on dishwasher duty.'

Mum used to cook a rotating schedule of meat and three vegies and spag bol, while Dad was lucky to manage boiled eggs when it was just the two of us. I've never been asked what I want to eat before. I've never had green curry or fish tacos.

'Um … you choose. Whatever you make will be great.'

'Tacos at Casa del Layla and Shirin it is. I think you'll love them.'

'Cool … where's that?'

Shirin grins at my confusion. 'It means House of Layla and Shirin. So basically … here. Our home. Your home.'

'Oh.'

'It's so lovely having company in this big old house while your dad's away,' she says in a soft voice. 'I don't know if I've told you, but it makes it feel like a real home for me too.'

I feel a lump in my throat.

'Speaking of which,' she continues, maybe sensing from my watery eyes that I'm not going to reply, 'what colour should we paint your room? We'll pick up some paint from town tomorrow if you like.'

I swallow down hard, then manage to tell her that I'd love that.

And I want to paint my bedroom yellow.

Like the sun.

Milo

Should I text Layla again?

I've asked myself that question too many times as Trent screams at the zombies lurching towards him on the screen in my room.

Since my latest lecture from Mum and Dad, I'm meant to be smashing through uni applications, but instead I'm doodling on paper and telling myself to sort my head out — all to the sound of gunshots.

When Layla never showed on Saturday, I decided to suck up the blisters and walk home past her place — okay, fine, I caught a taxi to her place — but no-one answered the front door and her phone went straight to voicemail. I only made it halfway up her neighbour's lawn before the old woman came hobbling out onto the veranda, flapping a rake and crowing at me to stay away from her garden bed.

Can't say I've ever been a fan of mysteries.

'Suck it!' Trent's knuckles are white as his fingers grip the controller. More gunshots. Then a bloodcurdling scream. He flops back onto my bed, swearing so much you'd think he'd actually just faced an onslaught of bullets.

'Owned again, huh?'

'Can't get past this freakin' level.' He glares at the screen. 'Not all of us can be gamer geeks like you, bro.'

I snort. 'It's a blessing and a curse bestowed on a special few.'

I draw a line down the middle of the page with two clear headings at the top of each column: *Text her again* and *Don't do it, dickhead*.

My mind runs over what I could write in the first column.

Because the last time I saw her, she was upset — and with Lay there'll be a reason why she's blowing me off.

She's my mate and that's what mates do.

The car was where I asked her to meet me — but she wasn't there.

I'm worried something's happened to her.

A solid list.

I look at the next column. All I can think about is one big fat reason why I shouldn't.

Because she clearly doesn't want to see me again. If she did, she would've texted back days ago, loser.

I stare at the empty columns, then scrunch up the paper and toss it at the bin by my desk.

I miss. Of course.

'Wanna game?' Trent asks.

'Nah, man.'

'Whatcha doing over there?'

'Nothing.'

I walk over to pick up the crumpled paper and aim for the bin again, but it flies past and bounces off the bed. Trent leans down and snatches it up. He goes to throw it, then catches the look of urgency on my face. I'm primed, on the balls of my feet, ready to pounce. I've given away that I care what's on the page and he knows it.

'What is this?' he asks, uncurling it.

'Give it here.'

He's taller and wider and manages to hold it above my head. 'Montgomery again? Nah, enough! Can't let you do it.' He scrunches up the page and lobs it at the bin. It strikes the inside before hitting the bottom.

'She's disappeared,' I tell him. 'I reckon it's our fault — that video tipped her over.'

'Righto, Sherlock.' He snatches my phone from the bedside table. 'It's just Monty Burns. Text her.'

I stand up. 'I have. I'm leaving it for a bit.'

'Fine, I'll do it then. Hey, let's just call. She's probably had her phone on silent or something.' Trent punches a few numbers into the phone to try to crack the password.

'Give it back.'

But he keeps fiddling with it, swearing to himself as he stabs for the magic number. Still wrong. Then he snorts with laughter. He's in.

'Mum's birth year? Bro, cut the cord.'

I lurch at him, trying to snatch the phone out of his fingers, but he's too fast. He leaps onto the bed, bouncing up and down as he scrolls.

'I'm dialling, mate, I'm dialling!' He laughs. 'Whatcha gonna do?'

'Shit, Trent!' I swat at him. 'Man, I'm not messing around. Give it here.'

He throws himself into a sloppy star jump, then lands on his back. He passes me the phone, triumphant. 'It's ringing.'

I snatch it from him and slam the 'end' button. 'What the hell?'

'Chill,' he says, sitting up so he's perched on the edge of the mattress. 'There's no need to cry about it. It's just Lay — sheesh. You can go back to sitting home alone with the little general ... or we can try again!' he adds with a laugh, snatching the phone back.

I grab for it and my hands shove his chest, knocking him back onto the bed.

'What the ... can't ya take a joke, bro?'

He leaps up, nostrils flaring, and pushes my chest, sending me arse-first onto the carpet.

I struggle to my feet. 'You're pathetic.'

'You pushed me first.'

'It's like you're proud of being a prick. I'm done. It's pathetic, all this.'

Trent puffs his chest out a little more. 'Say it again.'

'What?' I say, adrenaline surging through my body. 'You didn't understand me the first two times? I said *path-et-ic.*'

'Me?' Trent fakes a laugh. 'Ever think maybe Montgomery's bailed 'cos *she doesn't like you*. Get a life, 'cos you're the pathetic one.'

I swing my right fist, not sure what I'm even aiming for,

but he swerves out of the way and I strike his collarbone. My knuckles sting. Not surprising considering I've never thrown a punch in my life.

I haven't thought this through.

Trent hurls himself at me, slamming us both onto the carpet. We're a flurry of fists as we pant and grunt and wrestle on the floor. My wrists are flimsy as I try to push him off me. His body feels as hard as concrete.

'Just … relax,' he huffs out while struggling to pin my arms down next to my sides. 'What … are you … doing? Stop … shit, bro … stop being … a cockhead.'

'Get … off … me, man.'

Eyes half-shut, I shove upwards but hit nothing. I try again with everything I have. *Crack.*

Trent yells out in pain, grabbing at his nose. Even through the blurriness I can see red.

Red smeared down his chin.

Red on my palms.

* * *

Layla: *Hey, MD, so I've been MIA. I'm so, so sorry. Things have been weird … too hard to explain on texts. If I'm not already phased, wanna catch up tomoz? The river? 1 pm? (Yeah, I'm copying.) Lemme know, Chicken Girl*

Layla

Painting the bedroom walls isn't distracting me from the fact Milo hasn't texted me back. It's been hours. I shouldn't be surprised — I was the one who stood him up.

Taking a deep breath, I dip my brush in the paint can and wipe off the edges, sending yellow droplets spilling onto a crumpled old sheet of Shirin's. I move the paintbrush down the wall and back to the top again, trying not to wobble on my toes too much. But I reach too high and the brush slips from my hand and sprays my feet with sunshine.

My phone buzzes.

Milo is calling me.

Wait. *Milo is calling me?*

I wipe my hands down my shirt and lunge for the phone, sucking in a sharp breath before I answer. But I should've sucked in two 'cos it's not even Milo on the other end.

'Hi, Layla. Jen Dark here.'

Perfect. He's roped in his mum.

'Er, hey, Jen … um, what's going on? Everything okay?'

My attempt to stay light and breezy is a flop.

'I'm sorry to bother you, but I'm minding Milo's phone and your text came through and I couldn't bear to leave you hanging so …' Her voice cracks. 'The boys have, ah, got themselves in trouble. We're at emergency.'

'Where?' I say, before realising she means the hospital. Oh God. *That emergency*. The place where they took Mum after the accident. The place just behind Butcher Street.

I haven't been there since she died.

I'm immediately hit with an image of Milo lying on the side of the road. A millisecond later I'm carrying a coffin, preparing a eulogy, escorting Jen to her spot in the front row of the church, and pouring tea at the wake for all the elderly relatives that the Dark family haven't seen in years. Somehow even an imaginary world without Milo becomes full of him.

My voice sounds strangled as I ask for more details, pulling and twisting at my hair, fingers smearing yellow through the strands. I'm straining to listen to Jen's reply, but everything is buzzing, like there's a swarm of bees between my ears. I catch a few words — 'fight', 'Trent', 'still waiting for the doctor' — but can't piece together what's happened or how badly hurt they are.

I hang up, mind racing, and rush into the living room to tell Shirin I need to go to the hospital.

She holds my hand as I rush her through the muddled story, at least the parts I know, before announcing she's getting her car keys and driving me there.

'No.' I shake my head. 'I can handle it.'

'I'll wait in the car park if you want, but you're not doing this alone.'

She says it with such insistence that I only manage to whisper, 'Thank you'.

'Now, who is this boy again?' she asks, pulling on her coat. 'Have I met him?'

'No. He's just a boy I know.'

Defining what we are right now is an impossible request, but what I've said isn't enough — not even close — so I correct myself.

'He's just a boy I know, but he's a boy I've known forever and I need to see him right now.'

* * *

Shirin and I stride towards the hospital entrance, my breath catching as we pass the oversized red and white emergency sign. I'm on alert; I can feel it in my guts and in the amount of saliva building up in my mouth. The familiar pungent smell inside the hospital stings my nostrils.

We reach the waiting room and I search for Milo in the sea of people — some grimacing in pain, others slouched in their chairs, red-eyed, blotchy-skinned, their discomfort dulled by their tiny screens. I can't see the Darks.

'Maybe they're in with the nurses,' Shirin says, giving my hand a squeeze.

Doctors stroll past, clipboards in hand, not hurrying and barking orders like you see on medical dramas. It's nothing like TV, where problems are resolved in forty-five minutes. In real life, time stands still in hospitals; there's more waiting than anything else. And all the waiting gives your mind way too many hours to wander and worry. And ask why. Why him? Why her? Why me?

Once again I battle an image of Milo twisted at a strange angle, his blood drenching the road. I remind myself this has nothing to do with a car — nothing to do with Mum — but my brain doesn't want to cooperate.

'I'm just gonna grab a water,' I mumble to Shirin.

I hurry down the hallway, avoiding eye contact with anyone who walks past. The emergency department seems like the one place in Durnan where I'll be let off the hook if I don't say hello as I pass someone. I keep my head down to avoid staring into patients' rooms. The people with no visitors by their bedside are the hardest to walk past. Eventually I find a quiet corner by the bathrooms and hang there, wondering how long I can stay before Shirin comes looking.

I hear rattling, whimpering. It's getting louder.

Two nurses are wheeling a patient wrapped in head bandages on a trolley towards me. I press myself against a cork noticeboard littered with flyers to get out of the way. They hurry past, consoling the crying man, and disappear around the corner. I can't help wondering if he has a family on their way, or if his story will have a happy ending.

A woman with weathered rosy skin and silver hair peeking out from beneath a broad-brim hat — a farmer, has to be — sips from a foam coffee cup as she strides past, her Blundstones muddying the tiles. I turn away, pretending to read something on the noticeboard behind me. A purple brochure in the centre of the board catches my eye. I lean in for a better look: it's for the Durnan Counselling Centre — DCC. I glance around to make sure no-one's watching me. The farmer has rounded the corner and I can hear her chortling to someone, but I'm alone again.

I inhale and steal another look.

The logo has a rainbow butterfly design woven into it, so of course I think of Mum. Well, think of Mum *again*. Since stepping into the hospital, I've struggled to *stop* thinking of her. Standard really, only multiplied.

According to the brochure, the DCC is just off the main street. I figure it mustn't be far from Joe's. Guess it's the kind of place you don't notice if you're not looking for it.

I look to make sure Shirin isn't approaching. I don't have a good reason to explain why I'm hovering in this hallway. With no-one in sight, I pry open the glossy purple paper with my thumb. I see more butterflies flitting in the corner of the page. More rainbows sweeping across the top of the brochure.

I skim the paragraphs, lingering over certain words.

Committed to quality counselling and care.

Experienced professionals.

Consultations in strictest confidence.

Assistance with issues including anxiety, body image and grief.

* * *

I crouch on the tiles back in the waiting room, flipping through a box of magazines creased and ripped over the years by patients and their families. The same ones I remember from five years ago are stuffed way down at the bottom. Typical Durnan.

'Lay? Holy crap.'

Milo's T-shirt is smeared with red, like someone has swiped a bloody hand across his chest. He's alone, no sign of his family.

'Hi.' I spring to my feet and throw my arms around him. 'You okay?'

'I'm okay.' His arms slide around my waist and he lifts me up, just a little. I feel tiny, light, in his arms as the tips of my boots kiss the floor. 'What are *you* doing here? Where have you been?'

'Your mum called … and we'll get to the other thing later.'

I bury my nose into his neck, soaking in the smell of his cologne, until I remember Shirin can probably see us from the other side of the waiting room. I pull away from him and glance over in her direction. She hurries to pretend to check her phone and knocks over her coffee cup.

'But *you're* okay?' he tries again.

I smile. 'I'm fine. Now shut up and tell me why we're at the hospital.'

Milo laughs, then winces and his hand races to his bottom lip. When I raise an eyebrow, he shakes his head. 'Maybe don't ask.'

I inspect his chin closer and see the beginnings of a bruise. 'Oh, I'm asking. Don't make me interrogate you. Did Trent hit you?'

He groans. 'Come in a bit closer. I don't want all of Durnan hearing about the dysfunctional Darks.'

His face flushes as he talks me through it, especially the bit about hearing Trent's nose crack.

I swear out loud. *Milo fighting?* This has to be a parallel universe. '*You* hulked out? You?'

'Sorta, but it was an accident. Trent wouldn't shut up about ... well, some stuff and then he kept pushing it and pushing it and ...' He swears, gesturing to the blood on his T-shirt. 'One minute we were sorta joking, the next there were fists and knees and freakin' elbows and ... I was just trying to get him off me. I didn't know what I was doing!'

'I believe that, Rocky.' I bump my hip against his. 'So where's Trenticles? Is he mad?'

'Surprisingly, no. He's in with Mum and Dad and a nurse down the hall. I mean, his nose is busted a bit — but he gets that we both stuffed up. Everything went wrong *fast*, it was stupid. It's more Mum and Dad ...'

I lean in closer.

'If I was *on* the crap heap before, now I'm an insect suffocating *in* the crap heap. Running away to Timbuktu's sounding damn good right now.' He sighs. 'Wanna come with?'

'Oh yeah. Smuggle me into your suitcase.'

'Why do I get the feeling we'd be on Interpol's watch list within twenty-four hours?'

'Because.' I fold my hand around his. He winces a little. 'Sorry.' I let go. 'Timbuktu, huh? Better get packing.'

'I've heard the weather in Timbuktu is brilliant this time of year.'

'Then I'll race you to the airport tomorrow.'

'Holding you to that. Hey, there's yellow on your cheek.' His finger traces over the paint.

My heart pounds a little faster. 'Oh.'

His eyes lock with mine. 'Where have you been? One minute we were texting, the next ... shit, it took Mum calling you from hospital behind my back to see you again. You can tell me anything, you know that, right?'

'I know.'

'So tell me *one* thing then. I'll take just one. I've been going kinda crazy.'

A laugh slips out. 'I can see that.'

Silence.

I tell him one thing.

Then his hand tightens around mine as I tell him everything.

* * *

275

Milo: *Morning, didn't see you at the airport …*

Layla: *Haha! Guess I missed the flight. Next time? PS: Rest that body of yours pls and tell Trenticles to do the same*

Milo: *SO bored*

Milo: *I could go some Joe's wings …*

Layla: *I've lost all Chicken Girl rights. (Fired, remember?) But yes to future lunches and second-lunches*

Milo: *Cluck them for firing you*

Layla: *I clucking stuffed it up. Not meant to be, I guess. Catch up tomoz?*

Milo: *Sorry, busy*

Milo: *WAIT. No, I'm NOT. I'm chained to bed and grounded again. Maybe YOU should smuggle ME into a suitcase and take me to the airport?*

Layla: *Let's start at your place and see where Sunday takes us*

Milo: *I'll be here*

Layla: *Then I'll be there*

Milo

Play Again? flashes on the screen. Trent looks over at me. 'Want in this time?'

'Yeah.' I take the spare controller. 'How's the nose?'

'If my honker's crooked under here, you're buying me a new one, bro.' He says it with a grin. 'Anyway, I can smell your arse from here so I guess it's on the mend.'

The two of us have been bunkered down in my room playing video games, surfing the net and talking crap since we got home from the hospital. Any tension has evaporated.

If only I could say the same about Dad. He can barely get through a sentence without looking like fire's about to spark from every orifice. It's going to take a diligent regimen of hard work, profuse apologies and sorcery to get him back on side. Although after the past few months, I'm not convinced I'll ever win him over. I'm no match for Jermaine Wright's son.

'You know I'm sorry,' I tell Trent. 'Damn, I still can't believe it even happened.'

'*You* can't?' He hoots. 'Bro, the boys reckon I'm lying — they're convinced I got a nose job, for real.'

I snort with laughter.

'What's going on in here?'

We turn to see Mum in the doorway. Again. She's been hovering since we left the emergency department, probably worried she's going to find Trent and me brawling on the ground.

'Not much,' I say.

'Not much what?'

I shrug. 'Just hanging.'

'Well, dinner's ready. I've made Nan's famous potato bake.'

'Hell, yeah,' Trent says.

I walk to the door. 'I'll set the table.'

'You rest,' Mum says. 'I mean it. You too, Trent.'

'I'm not in pain,' I say. 'I can do it.'

'*I mean it*. And if you need me to type up your uni applications later, just ask.'

She hangs close behind as Trent and I head down the hallway towards the dining room.

'Where are you going?' she asks when I veer off to the bathroom.

'The toilet?'

'Oh, of course, that's fine,' she says. 'I'll be out here if you need anything.'

Jesus. I trudge off before she offers to wipe my bum.

* * *

'Chops are getting cold,' Dad says, pointing at my plate.

'More beans, darling?' Mum asks in a forced breezy voice.

'Nah, I'm fine … thanks.'

I feel a nudge against my shin and look up to see Trent shaking his head and mouthing, 'Nightmare', before shovelling potato bake into his mouth.

I look at Mum and Dad. 'Um, can we talk normally for like one second?'

Mum raises an eyebrow. 'What do you mean?'

'Okay,' I begin, 'we all know what happened was stupid, but —'

Dad grunts. 'It was stupid alright. Willie Diaz was at the hospital for his daughter's bunged-up appendix. How do you think I felt trying to explain why we were there?'

I sigh. 'I get that, Dad. That's why I'm trying to say —'

'No. You said you wanted us to talk, so I'm bloody talking. Do you have any idea what the town will be saying about the two of you? About me and your mother? I'll tell you: *They've raised idiots. Those Dark boys are idiots.* That's what they'll be saying.' Trent and I swap looks. 'That's why you're both pulling your heads in, or the door's that way. You hear me, Milo?'

I nod, jaw tightening.

'I asked you if you heard me, Trent?'

'Yes, sir.'

I know things are serious 'cos Trent hasn't pissed himself laughing.

'There are more chops if anyone wants them,' Mum says in an anxious sing-song tone, a fruitless attempt to lighten the mood. 'You know what, I'll bring them out now *just in case* you want them. That way they're here. You know. In case you want them.'

Dad shakes his head. 'See, your mother, she gives and she gives and ... Jesus Christ, boys, it's like you don't care about anyone but yourselves.' He powers on. 'Coward punches, they're called. *Coward* punches. These sorts of fights can leave people with brain damage. Or dead.'

Trent clears his throat. 'Nah, Dad, a coward's punch is different. It's when —'

'I don't want to bloody hear it.' Dad slams his cutlery down. 'I know what happened. And it's a disgrace on this family.'

I sink back in my seat. I wasn't expecting sympathy or even forgiveness, but I was hoping Mum and Dad would at least give us a chance to explain and set things right.

This is how I'm going to go.

Not caught in a current in the Durnan River.

Not hitting a kangaroo on the highway and narrowly missing a tree.

Like this. Whittled down bit by bit, little by little.

Vale Milo Dark: suffocated in a cocoon of his own creation.

Layla

'Hi, is the manager here?' I ask the girl behind the counter at Quiche.

'Ah, she's somewhere,' she replies with a laugh. She's about my age, wearing twice as much make-up, and doing that thing where someone looks you up and down, focusing on a detail — old shoes, a short skirt, a fresh pimple. It's a habit that usually makes me feel smaller than small, but her mouth breaks into a big pearly beam at the sight of the colourful streaks through my hair and I can't help but like her.

She presses a hand against the door into the back room, then pauses and says over her shoulder, 'Hope you don't mind me saying, but we were totally preschool buddies, right?'

I stand up straighter, draw my shoulders down and raise my chin. A glance at her nametag. *Amvi*. 'Um, maybe.' It's slowly coming back. 'Did your mum help out during storytime?'

'Sure did. With your mum. They Meryl-Streeped the hell out of all the animal voices in every book, remember?'

I swallow. 'Yeah.'

She grins. 'Those were the days, huh?'

'Pardon?'

'Afternoon naps, no responsibility, someone to cut up our fruit.'

'Oh, yeah. Totally.' I smile, feeling silly for thinking she was alluding to anything else. 'It's Layla, by the way.'

'I know. Hey.' She points at her nametag. 'Amvi, duh. I'll try to find my boss for you.' She turns with a flick of her hair and disappears through the door.

I pull up a seat at an empty table, my stomach churning twice as hard now. Knowing someone here wasn't part of the plan. I rifle through my bag for my wallet, double-checking the money is still in there.

The manager barrels through the door and heads in my direction. I hurry to my feet, the chair scraping beneath me.

'Yes?' she says. The nametag hanging from her shirt says *Gayle*.

'Er, hi,' I mumble, trying to forget that Amvi is smiling at us from the counter as I empty the notes and loose coins onto the table. 'This is for you.'

'Great. Love money. But what's it for, darl?'

I swallow. 'Well, the other day I was here with my boyfriend and housemate — well, ex-boyfriend and ex-housemate — and they ... ah, we, I guess, I was in the car — and we ... we ... forgot to pay.'

Her arms are crossed now. 'And that's the money?'

I scoop it off the table and into her hands. 'Some of it. It's all I have.'

'Fair enough. Well, thanks for coming back. Accidents happen every day.'

'They do. Except ... well, what I said's not true,' I blurt out.

Gayle raises an eyebrow.

'The boys bailed, but I let them, and they don't care but I do and —'

'Stop right there,' she says, holding up her hand. 'You're telling me you did a runner? From my café?'

I hate that I'm lumped in with Kurt and Ryan, but I force myself to nod.

'You from around here?'

I nod again, not daring to make eye contact with Amvi.

'Parents too?'

'Just Dad. Reg ... Reg Montgomery.'

Gayle's eyes widen. I can tell she's heard of him, heard our family's story. It's probably Durnan folklore by now. 'You're ... Layla? I mean, you don't know me from a bar of soap ... I didn't know you were back in town.'

'Guess I tried to keep a low profile.' I clear my throat. 'Well, tried and failed.'

Her mouth melts into a warm smile. 'Yes, it seems that way, darl. I think my mum went to high school with your dad a long, long time ago, although I guess everyone crosses paths in Durnan one way or another. I wouldn't have recognised you, not from the photos in the paper. I mean, with the spunky 'do and all.'

'Isn't it cool?' Amvi chimes in, before rushing to wipe down the counter to hide her obvious eavesdropping.

I run my hand through my hair self-consciously, twirling the strands between my fingers. 'Um, thanks ... anyway, I better let you get back to work. Sorry again about the money.'

I push my chair under the table and head for the front door, which is when I notice the sign: *Waitress wanted. Experience necessary.*

I glance back at Gayle, who's now behind the counter showing Amvi how to use the coffee machine. She likes my hair, knows Dad and hasn't kicked me out of the shop for telling the truth. Maybe she won't have a laughing attack in my face.

Just ask.

Do this one hard thing.

Just ask.

I take a breath and walk over to Gayle, who's now rearranging the salt and pepper shakers on the tables. 'Um, hi.'

'Hi again.'

'I know my timing is terrible, but I saw the sign for a waitress and ... and I was wondering if I could maybe hand in my CV?'

'Ah, Layla, we filled it a few days ago,' Gayle says, gesturing to Amvi, who mouths 'Sorry' to me. 'We were supposed to take the sign down.' Now it's her turn to eye me up and down. 'You got any experience?'

'As what? Oh, as a waitress?'

'No. As a train conductor.' She tries not to chuckle. 'Yes, as a waitress.'

'No. None.' It sounds bad, so I try to remember everything on my CV. 'But I've worked in a bakery, and at a supermarket, and at a chicken shop and with a pet shelter — but that one was too sad, I couldn't bear it when they weren't re-homed.'

She nods. 'Tough job.'

'It was! Did you know hundreds of thousands of animals are put down every year? It's the worst.' I pause. 'I don't know why I said that.'

'You like animals, huh?'

'Sometimes more than humans.' I hear Amvi snort with laughter from behind the counter. 'I don't know why I said that either. I'm bad at this.'

'It's fine,' Gayle says. 'Humans test my patience too, especially when my girlfriend burps after dinner. You know, a customer once told me their toasted cheese sandwich was *too cheesy*.'

'There's no such thing.'

'Exactly,' she says with a smile. 'Layla, we don't have anything going here, not yet anyway, but … if you're free for a couple of hours tomorrow and want to make a few dollars, I can introduce you to my friend Max. He's a bit lonely.'

'Max?'

'Oh yes. Amvi knows all about Max, don't you, darl?'

'We go way back,' she says, then points at my scuffed boots. 'My tip? Wear runners.'

Milo

My hopes of fleeing the cocoon are foiled again: Layla and I only make it as far as the overgrown grass in front of Dad's vegie patch. Sticking her tongue out at me, Layla drags two beanbags from our rumpus room, tussles them into shape, then waves me over. It's quiet in this corner of the yard. Just us two.

Just us two and Max, a half-blind chocolate-brown Labrador digging a hole next to the clothesline.

'I thought you took him for a run?' I say.

Layla's flopped on her beanbag like a rag doll. 'He's a machine. He just goes and goes. If I don't stuff this job up, he'll have me running marathons by the end of the year.'

She fidgets around until she finds the perfect position, then pulls her hat down low. I look over at Max, who's nose-deep into Dad's carrots, then follow Layla's lead, letting my body sink down into my beanbag.

'This is a real job? You're getting paid to babysit it?'

'Yes, Mr Judgmental, and it's called puppy-sitting — and I can now add dog-walker and dog-sitter to my CV. Who knew this job even existed? There have to be hundreds of pooches in Durnan needing extra cuddles and love. It's perfect!'

She flings her arms wide in excitement and our palms brush for a second. We snap our hands back as a jolt of static electricity crackles between us.

'That was you,' I laugh, shaking my hand.

'Yeah, it was.'

Even she knows she has electricity running through her veins.

I stare up at the sky, kicking at the dirt with my sneaker. 'You know what I told you at the hospital? About leaving for Timbuktu?'

'Yeah?'

'I've been thinking about it a bit. Leaving, I mean.'

Tilting her hat back, Layla swivels to face me, her beanbag crunching and shifting beneath her. 'You've had a bad few days. Okay, a bad year. But it doesn't mean you have to leave town and ... everything. Right?'

'I guess.'

'So it's decided: the Durnan dream lives on.' Layla pushes her hat down again so her face is covered. 'Phew, Max, that was a close call, wasn't it? We nearly lost him,' she says in a muffled voice. 'Timbuktu ... you crazy monkey. No more scaring me like that, Milo D — I hate you.'

'Hate you the most, Layla M.'

Layla

'Let's go somewhere, do something,' he says, repositioning himself in his beanbag.

I squash another spoonful of gelato into my mouth. 'Nah, you're grounded. Besides going places and doing stuff is overrated.'

'Since when?' he asks, wrestling the tub back from me.

Max barks, nudging Milo in the side.

'Since ... I dunno. Since I said so.' I shoo Max away with a laugh and he bounds off in the direction of another dog barking. 'Hear me out on why you can't leave. When you run away, everyone misses you ... at first. And it feels good in the new place, like you've discovered this portal to a secret universe — but you haven't ... and suddenly you're in the loneliest place in the world. After a while, you sorta can't even remember why you thought it was a good idea to leave in the first place.' I glance back at the house, where Milo's parents are sniping over how best to prune the vines on the pergola, and laugh again. 'But I can see how it might hold some appeal for you.'

'Dad's gone from pushing me to do something I don't want to do to thinking I'm an oaf who's incapable of anything. Trent's the only person in that house who even comes close to getting it. Bizzare.'

'*No.*'

'Yes. And Mum's always around, nagging, waiting to swoop in. It's like the umbilical cord has grown back.'

I screw up my nose.

'Seriously. If she could chew my food for me, she would.'

'Oh God.'

'So ... let's run away.' He gulps down another spoonful of gelato. 'England, France, the Caribbean — you pick. Anywhere you want.'

'New joke, please,' I say, taking the tub back for more. 'You're making me wanna go on a holiday.'

'I ... I don't think I'm joking.'

I roll my eyes. 'Come on.'

'I mean it,' he says, his voice strong. 'This can't be "it" ... *Durnan*. I can't be Trent, just staying here doing nothing 'cos I'm too lazy to work out what I want. Or Dad, who's this big annoying fish in a small pond, and Mum who puts up with it. I don't know what I wanna do, but I know I haven't found it here. I wish I had.'

I'm sitting up straight now, trying to process it all. 'You're serious.'

'Yeah.' He clears his throat. 'And ... and maybe you could come with me.'

'What? *Dude*. We can't. I have a job now. You have a job. A family.'

'No, listen. We can. Think about it. If we go to London, we can travel for six months without a visa — *six freakin' months*. Do you get how much of the world we'd see in that time? Or ... we can apply for visas and ... well ...' His voice trails off.

'And what?'

'Stay for two years.'

'Two ... no way. I mean ... live in London? Stop it.'

'Lay, we'd be together so we'd never be lonely or bored or have to share a hostel room with some creeper who brushes his teeth without his boxers on.'

'Ew!' I shove him.

Milo grins. 'Hear me out — we'd see the world. Jesus, I haven't even left the state in years. But if we're there ... in London ... we can go anywhere. Like, Paris — for a weekend. *For a day trip*. It's amazing. It's the kinda stuff you can look back on and be proud of when you're a hundred.'

'Yeah, it is ... but I can't imagine doing it. Not really doing it.' I pause. 'You, um, seem to know a lot about this.'

He nods, flicking his plastic spoon against his hand. 'Just try to imagine it, Lay. We could get lost for a while.'

He's been looking into this for longer than he's letting on. I can tell.

Max barks and bounds towards us. He jumps onto my beanbag, squashing us down together. I pull him onto my lap, sucking in a breath at the weight of him.

'What do you think?' Milo asks, reaching out to pat Max, who's panting in my face, all hot stinky puppy breath.

'Aw, look at him,' I coo. 'He's smiling. I think he loves me. I think he loves me more than he loves Gayle and Amvi.'

'Amvi?'

'This girl I met. Well, met again. She's rad. Kinda long story.' I cock my head to one side. 'Sorry, what did you ask me?'

'London. Thoughts? Comments?'

'I don't know. I don't ... I mean, it's huge. Bigger than huge. And you're asking me like you're asking me to go eat sushi. I don't even have a passport ... or money!'

'I'll wait. We can keep saving. It can work.'

I've never heard him fight for something like this before.

'Look, I know what you mean about this town. I'm staying with Shirin and it's kinda routine and quiet ... but I like it.' I heave Max off me and drag out my phone. 'Here: I painted my room yellow. See? Shirin had to fix it up 'cos I stuffed the edges, but I did that. Me.' I pause. 'I just heard myself. Don't tell anyone. Especially not Max. He still thinks I'm sorta cool, and I'm already pushing my luck now that we're running pals.'

'That's a no to London, then?'

'I think so, yeah. I'm sorry.'

'What if I buy you a croissant in Paris?' He flashes a cheeky smile. 'What if I buy you fifty croissants? Two hundred? Three hundred?'

I pause. 'I'm so sorry, MD.'

He nods, plucking a blade of grass from the lawn. 'Nah, it's alright.' He sighs and flops deeper into his beanbag. 'Okay, so London's out. What can I do in this stupid town then? Computer science or buying that damn house across the road aren't happening, I'll tell you that.'

I swallow. I almost don't want to point it out. 'You just said it. And I think you've been saying it a million different ways for a while — I just never heard it until now.'

He locks eyes with me. 'What do you mean?'

'MD, you don't want to work at your parents' shop or follow their path. You don't want to study what they want you to study, or do what they would've done when they were your age.'

He's nodding in agreement as I'm talking. But he doesn't know the next bit's the toughest bit.

'And you don't want to get stuck here with a girl who just happened to float back into your life … even though she's a friggin' legend.'

I want him to smile at my lame attempt at a joke, but he doesn't and his expression is impossible to read.

'I don't want that for you either,' I add. 'I need — want — you here, but I can't bear the thought of you missing out on something and it being my fault. Not when you can have anything. You said it: London. You *want* to get lost.'

'And you don't,' he says, so quietly it's almost to himself.

He leans forward in the beanbag, fingers kneading his temples. I can almost see him weighing it all up in his head. The money. The time. The possibilities. If it's what he wants, he can do this, he can do this right now, and that's the most terrifying part for me.

'I wish I wanted it, I do,' I add, breaking the silence. 'Oh God, I feel like a monster. Gelato? Does more gelato help?'

With a small smile, he accepts the tub. 'Doesn't hurt.'

'Um, I better get Max back before he digs his way to London. Just promise me one thing?'

'I'd say "anything", but I don't think I can trust you with that responsibility, Chicken Girl.'

'Wise choice. Just promise me you won't run away.'

'But you said —'

'Don't *run away*,' I repeat. 'Say goodbye to everyone before you leave. If you do end up leaving, I mean.'

Milo chews on his bottom lip. That bottom lip. 'I'm just talking shit. Besides, you'd always get a goodbye.'

I nod. 'Good, 'cos I heard about this girl who ran off from this guy she was best mates with and they didn't speak for like five years. Bad, right?'

'Shocking.'

'I heard they bumped into each other again though.'

'No way, what are the chances?' Milo says, settling into his beanbag. 'Sounds perfect.'

'Nah. It was a disaster.' I smile, then squat down so we're knee to knee. 'But as far as disasters go, it was pretty friggin' spectacular.'

I unclip the leash and Max bounds into Gayle's arms, nearly taking out the floor lamp in the corner of the lounge room, before he leaps through the open sliding door and chases after a bird. Keeping an eye on him through the window, Gayle pours me a water and tells me her physio is wondering if I could wash her sausage dog every now and then, and her best friend needs someone to walk her staffy every night 'cos she's worn out from juggling three casual jobs.

'You've got yourself quite the booming business, if you want it,' she says, scribbling down her friends' numbers on a piece of paper for me. 'We should start calling you the animal whisperer. Don't tell Amvi, but Max is beyond smitten with you.'

I grin. 'Really?'

'Oh yeah.'

'Awesome. He liked Milo too.'

'Who?'

I hadn't meant for that to slip out. 'Oh ... just my friend.'

Gayle's eyes sparkle. 'Well, your *friend* must be a good egg because Max is a tough judge of character.' She laughs. 'Ever think you could be a vet or work in a zoo, something like that?'

'I dropped out of school last year, so ...'

I didn't mean to say that either — especially so

bluntly — because it usually makes people feel even more uncomfortable than it makes me.

But Gayle poo-poos me with a flick of her wrist. 'So nothing. You're a bright girl and there's plenty of time and ways to make whatever you want happen. Believe me.' She groans when she spots Max digging a hole in the middle of the backyard to bury a T-shirt with the washing pegs still attached. 'That dog ... I just hung up that load.'

I try not to laugh at the sight of him tangled up in the material.

'Anyway,' she says with a smile, 'I think Max is thrilled to have your undivided attention and he'll see you at the same time tomorrow. And maybe your friend too?'

'It'll just be me.'

'Okay, and a quick heads-up before you call my physio — her sausage dog is a cutie but he widdles when he's nervous. Perks of the gig, darl.'

* * *

Milo: *Have you phased me for Max?*
Layla: *Of course*
Layla: *Why? Missing me or something?*
Milo: *Never* *
Milo: * *Incorrect*
Layla: *Ha! Are we still meant to be following the rules or ...?*

Milo: *Maybe, but I forget them so …*
Layla: *Maybe I forgot them too …*
Milo: *Well, if we BOTH forget them, maybe there's no point in trying to follow them. PS: Especially when you love breaking rules 1 and 4 so much*
Layla: *Thought you forgot them? PS: You're the master of breaking 3 and 5*

Milo

I chew my thumbnail as I stare at the prices in the travel agency's window. Mum's at the post office; she thinks I'm getting an afternoon snack from Joe's. Reminder to self: buy something on the way back so I don't blow my cover.

Italy.

Bali.

London.

Fiji.

America.

It's the same list as before, only this time the flights to London are cheaper. It feels like that might be a sign, but I've never been good at picking up signs. My palms are damp and I don't know why. It's not like I'm trekking to Machu Picchu, or standing on the edge of the Grand Canyon, or butchering the French language to a Parisian waiter who doesn't understand a word I'm saying. I'm just a guy trying to work out what to do next. (Hint: not computer science or becoming a teenage real-estate mogul.)

I wipe my palms down the front of my T-shirt, head spinning as I try to absorb all the info in the ads.

Cheap London flights!
Exclusive fares for under 26 year olds!
Never a dull moment!

A young agent with slicked hair and a crisp white shirt catches my eye through the window. He grins a toothy grin. Salesman mode is activated.

I look around; there's no sign of Mum yet.

I walk into the travel agency.

Layla

I lie on my bed, knees up, scrolling through the photos on my phone. I pause on a selfie of me and Milo pulling stupid faces at the river, then crack up when I find the series of Max slobbering and rolling his way around the vegie patch.

And then I see a pop of purple. The DCC flyer from the hospital. I'd almost forgotten I snapped a photo of it.

I flick past it, to photos of Milo goofing around in my cat ears, and Shirin in her overalls splattered in yellow paint, then pause and head back to double-check something.

There *was* a butterfly in the logo. Thought I might've imagined that part.

After a few false starts with the sluggish internet — enough to make me almost want to scrap the whole thing — the DCC's website loads. Information overwhelms the screen. Opening hours. Bulk-billing. Confidential sessions. Phone counselling.

Phone counselling.

My heart races as I imagine talking about my feelings with a counsellor again, especially as my memory has warped as the years have passed. Sorting through the tiniest of details would be like trying to do a puzzle with half the pieces missing.

Shirin's words ring in my ears: *You've tried doing it alone. It hasn't worked. Enough.*

I look at the brochure again. My eyes linger on the word *grief.* I hate that word.

I close my eyes and try to pinpoint what Mum would want me to do. If I can't be with her, then I have to think like her.

Inhale. Focus, Lay.

My only wish is for you to try your best and be kind to the people in your life.

She told me this as she tucked a loose curl behind my ear on the day I missed out on a prize at assembly. She told me this after encouraging me to be nice to the new girl at kindy who'd been sitting alone at recess every day. She told me this the week before she died, when my head was hanging over the toilet bowl 'cos I was so nervous about my softball team's practice.

She wanted me to help others be happy and she wanted me to be happy.

Maybe I am tired of fighting this on my own, like Shirin said. Or maybe, for the first time, I understand there's nothing to be afraid of any more, because the worst has happened and now it's over and I'm still here. Like I told Milo: if he can survive that crappy, crappy thing at the river, he can survive anything. I've already got through the unimaginable, and I'm still going. One scuffed boot in front of the other.

I crack my neck, then, hands trembling, punch the DCC's number into my phone.

A counsellor called Hayley answers on the second ring. I'm shaking so much I nearly hang up. But I cling to the phone, stumble through an introduction, and tell her my name is Sarah. Too many people in this town know Dad, and knew Mum, which means they'll know of me. Plus, I've always liked that name.

I'm talking fast — so fast that I wonder if she can even understand my gibberish.

Hayley's voice is warm when she tells me she's here to listen for as long as I want, for as long as I need.

I suck in a breath. My mouth feels a few too many steps ahead of my brain, but the more I try to stop it, the faster the words seem to pour out. Before I know it, there's another person in the world who knows my story and things haven't fallen apart.

Yet the weight of it is still heavy. Because when I wake up, it's Mum's face I see, I tell Hayley. And when I go to sleep, it's her voice I hear.

The rest of my words get caught in my throat, behind my teeth, under my tongue, and I can't tell her the rest. That Mum was part of the tapestry of Durnan and so loved. She didn't even realise it 'cos that was just how it had always been. Other parents' faces would light up when she told a dirty joke at the school gate when she thought us kids were out of earshot; and she'd have the supermarket in stitches every time she waltzed down an aisle or played puppeteer with the unsuspecting roast barbecue chickens.

I won the lottery: I had her nearly all to myself. Most people aren't lucky enough to say they've been loved with the fierce force of my mum for thirteen years.

Except me. I'm lucky enough to be able to say that.

'I'm ...' My voice cracks. I try again. 'I'm never going to get over this ... am I?'

'Sarah,' Hayley says, her voice gentle, 'no-one's expecting you to get over this. To be alright with what happened. Yes, the days might get a little easier, with time. Your heart may hurt a little less, with time. But what you feel — that pain, that ache — it hurts this much inside you because it's tied to how much you loved each other. And my word, it sounds like you loved each other.'

I can't hold the tears back any longer, and when I try to hide the sniffing it comes out as a gurgle.

'Sarah? Are you there?'

I wipe at my eyes, but there's a million more tears waiting. 'Yeah.' My voice is wispy. 'Yeah, I'm here.'

By now I'm crying so much a snot bubble forms out of my nose and I can't help but laugh. I can almost hear Mum's teasing.

'Ah, God,' I choke out between watery laughs. 'This is crazy — I can't stop.'

I drag my sleeve across my face, mopping my cheeks and lips and chin. Even my neck and chest are wet with tears.

'Sarah, it sounds like your mum loved you just about as much as anyone can be loved. If you keep remembering that, you'll always be connected. And no-one can take that away from you. No-one. She made you *you*.'

My chest tightens as I look over at the framed photo of me and Mum at the zoo.

'Um ...' I begin, voice wavering. 'Hayley?'

'Yes?'

'It's Layla ... My real name's Layla.'

All the truth that's been locked up inside me is out. I mightn't have been able to stand by Mum's grave, but I've dragged myself through the halls of the hospital, and thought of her every day for over half a decade. I might've spiralled after watching the video with Milo and Trent, but I've given myself permission to remember her again, despite the heaviness in my heart that still takes me by surprise every time. And I might've silenced myself for five years, but I've immersed myself in her memory to find my voice again.

'That's a gorgeous name,' Hayley says, not skipping a beat. 'Thank you for telling me. *Layla*. Yes, I think that suits you perfectly.'

I'm all out of words, so she pencils me in for another chat later in the week.

After I hang up, I exhale the breath I seem to have held onto for the entire call. Then I break down crying, buckling in on myself as my mascara stains my pillowcase. For once, I don't try to hold it in.

* * *

Milo: *Afternoon. You free to hang out today/tonight?*

Milo: *Hello ...?*

Milo: *Night, Lay*

* * *

Layla: *Sorry I missed this — everything OK?*

Milo: *Yep, can we meet up soon?*

Layla: *Yeah, course*

Layla: *HANG ON ... why? What's happening? Something's wrong, isn't it?*

Layla: *Oh god. Timbuktu. You're doing it*

Layla: *You're doing it, aren't you?*

Layla: *Please ... if what I think is happening is happening, tell me now so I can prepare myself*

Layla: *Please ...*

Milo: *Lay ...*

Milo: *I REALLY didn't want to do this over text, but ... yeah, I'm going to London, leaving in a month, I think*

Layla: *AS IN NEXT MONTH? But I'll miss your b'day*

Milo: *That's OK. I missed yours!*

Layla: *I wasn't in Durnan then*

Milo: *I won't be in Durnan either*

Layla: *This is too big for texts. Treehouse tomoz at 9 pm?*

Milo: *Sounds good*

Layla: *Night, MD. Is this real life?*

Milo: *Night, Lay. Think so. Pinch me tomorrow*

Milo

The treehouse is bursting with red balloons. As I get closer, crunching on the dried leaves on the Perkinses' lawn, I notice streamers hanging from each corner, loosely plaited together. And then I see her. She has a paper crown on her head — the Christmas bonbon kind.

Layla wriggles to the edge of the treehouse and hangs her legs over the side. 'Surprise,' she whispers through the dark. 'Happy birthday, MD.'

'What is this?'

'Welcome to your early birthday party, silly.' She gestures to the ladder. 'Quick, get up here.'

'This is break-and-entering, right?'

'We're not breaking anything, only entering, so no.'

I climb up to join her. 'Hi.'

'Hi,' she says, squeezing a crown onto my head, jamming a party whistle in my mouth and tossing confetti in the air over us.

I blow on the whistle and the paper tube unravels, nearly hitting Lay in the face. She giggles as she swats it away.

'I can't believe this,' I say, still struggling to take it all in.

She edges closer to straighten my hat, which keeps slipping off. 'You really do have a huge head. Lovely,' she adds with a grin, 'but huge. I never noticed that before.'

I laugh. 'It's my party and you're paying me out?'

'Come here,' she says, swiping balloons out of the way so I can wriggle in further. Closer to her. 'Got you a present.'

'Yeah?'

'Well, you're leaving me and you suck, and I like to give people who suck presents.' She hands me a long slim tube. 'Go on. Open it.'

I pull off the lid and take a look. As suspected there's a large sheet of paper rolled up inside.

'If this is a blown-up photo of us as naked babies in the bath . . .'

I stride out the paper and uncurl it, then flatten it out across my lap. It's a world map, each continent and ocean decorated with pinks, oranges, greens and blues.

Layla leans in, tracing her fingers around Europe and Asia. 'It'll help you get lost ... and found, if you ever want that too,' she says.

Clearing my throat, I lean in and hug her. It's over too quickly.

'This is great. All of this. Thank you.' It doesn't sound like enough, but I don't know if anything will right now. 'You're the best.'

'It is and I am. I do have a confession though.'

'Here we go.'

'I was kinda freaked when you told me you were leaving.'

'You mean when you bullied me into telling you, even though I had a plan for how I was going to do it?' I grin. 'Sounds familiar.'

'There I go, getting in the way again,' she says with a smile. 'Don't worry, nothing you could've done would've made it any easier 'cos ... well ... it just wouldn't have.'

I'm trying to stop myself from filling in the blanks, but it's hard to think straight.

'I feel like an idiot 'cos there's part of me that never thought you'd go through with it,' she admits. 'That you'd stop yourself. But I know what it means to you to walk away from this town, so now you're doing it, despite everything, and it means ...' Her voice catches.

Maybe this isn't about everything. Maybe this is about leaving despite one thing. One person. Or maybe I'm listening for what I want to hear.

'It means ...'

'Yeah?' I say.

'It means you have to go. I know that sounds crazy 'cos you *are* going — it's happening, you've told me — but I want you to know I get it. All my reasons for wanting you to stay can never make you forget all the reasons you need to leave.'

A rustling in the tree above us, probably a possum, interrupts the growing silence.

'That was a good speech,' I say. An embarrassed snort slips out.

'I try,' she says with a small smile. 'Besides, there's thousands of girls who'll be lucky to meet you overseas. But if you stay any longer in Durnan, you know we'll end up with each other.'

I nearly choke. 'Excuse me?'

'You know I'm right. There's no-one else in this town — sorry, Trenticles, love him, but no — so if you stay, then we'll probably get hitched one day 'cos we're bored, stack on the weight from eating all that gelato, then I'll take up chain-smoking 'cos I'm stressed out, and you'll yell at our ratbag kids for not putting away their toys, and then I'll yell at you for not pruning the pergola properly.' She grins and throws a balloon at me. I tap it back towards her. 'I'm thinking of me and my bum. It's a nice bum, but it can't handle a lifetime of our eating habits. We're too good at it.'

'We are high achievers in the field of gelato consumption. Married though? With a pergola? And *kids*?'

'Yep, ratbag ones.' One strap is sliding off her shoulder, but she doesn't seem to notice. I try to stop noticing. 'The kind you see losing it in the lolly aisle. And you'll probably be bald — or at least have a thinning hairline.'

I shoot her a wry look. 'Jesus, who knew it was all downhill from here.'

'It's why you have to go. I'd make you lose your hair. I don't want you to lose your hair. You have nice hair.'

I turn the map around so it's facing Layla and place it back on my lap. 'Shut your eyes and give me your finger.'

'Perve.' But she shuts her eyes and stretches out her left hand.

Gently holding her wrist, I move her closer so her fingers hover over the map. 'Put out your finger — no, not your middle one — and touch the paper. Eyes closed, please, Chicken Girl.'

'If this is a way to make me touch —'

'Piss off!'

'Fine!' She slams her finger down in the middle of Australia. Peeling one eyelid open, she looks down. 'Oops.'

She covers her face with her left hand and swirls her right hand above the map. This time she plonks her finger down in Europe.

We both strain forward.

'Corfu.' Her nose scrunches in confusion.

'Greece. It's an island in Greece.'

'Island, huh? You're going to be one of those people who shares photos of amazing beaches all the time, aren't you? I hate you already.' She smirks in such a cute way it makes me want to sprint home and rip my passport to shreds. Either that or move into this treehouse with her and never leave. 'More than usual, I mean.'

Layla has no idea how gorgeous she looks surrounded by the balloons. Her hair is wavy and wild, and her eyes sparkle in the night. She's radiating a lightness that I've only seen glimpses of recently. I bite my tongue to stop myself from asking her to come overseas with me one last time.

* * *

My arse aches from sitting on the floor, the air's getting cold and our fingers are stained Twisties orange.

There's nothing left to say. Well, nothing left I *should* say.

Faking a cough to get Layla's attention, I pull out the small velvet box that's been pressing against my thigh for the last hour.

'So you've done this amazing thing for me,' I say, gesturing to the balloons and streamers, 'but, ah, I kinda have something for you too.'

Her gaze darts between me and the tiny box. 'Holy … MD, I was kidding about marriage. We're embryos! And what about my bum and your hair?'

'What? No! *Not that.*' I open the box and hold up a fine gold bracelet, then thrust it into her hand. 'Just take it.'

She stares at me, stunned.

'It's fine if you hate it. I kept the receipt. I wanted to get you something for when I told you the news, and now I'm looking at your face and I should've gone with something that doesn't scream "desperate loser" and —'

'Shut up. I love it.'

'Yeah?'

'It's similar to another one that was … well, it was special,' she says, trying to do up the bracelet. It slips from her hands, wedging itself into the wooden planks of the treehouse. '*Crap!*'

This is so 'us'.

Layla swears as she struggles to tug the bracelet out from between the boards. After careful manoeuvring, she frees it, then wraps it around her wrist again.

'You know, it's been alright hanging out with you, Mr Dark.' She grins. 'Maybe for a second anyway.'

'Just a second, huh?'

'Yeah, a split one. After all, you did come into my life — again, I mean — at the worst possible time, and we somehow made it here despite that.'

'Rules *annihilated* … but we're here.' Her lips curl upwards into a smile. 'You're becoming as soft as a marshmallow, Miss Montgomery, you know that?'

'Hey, take that back! Although it was bound to happen, I suppose, spending time with a dorkatron like you,' she teases, before leaning over and pressing her lips against mine.

I'm caught off guard but I sink into the kiss, my hands running through her hair. Tonight there's nothing blurring the edges so everything is sharp: from the urgent feel of her hands tracing over my back to her warm breath as she nuzzles into my neck. When she pulls away, she's slightly out of breath.

I wonder if I'm as flushed as her.

Layla rests her head on my legs like she did at the river, knees pointing to the sky, but this time I relax at her touch. I even let my fingers trace her forehead and wipe away a twist of hair threatening to tangle with her eyelashes.

'This whole friends-who-kiss thing is kinda nice, hey?' She holds up her arm to admire the bracelet again and releases a sigh. 'I've gotta say ... you're not even leaving yet, so why does this feel like we're saying goodbye forever?' She exhales again.

'It's not forever. Just a bit.'

'You'll be shacked up with an English supermodel in no time. And if I ever leave Durnan, I'll be a movie star on her way to winning an Oscar.'

'That's ... specific.'

'How do you *know* we'll see each other again?' she asks, twisting around to face me. 'All this was a fluke. It aligned perfectly. If one little thing had gone differently that day, or every day since — if I'd thought, stuff trying to get a job at the bookshop, or I'm going back to Sydney on my own, or a million other little choices — then we wouldn't have to say goodbye 'cos we'd never have said hello.'

She's quiet. Sad, I think.

Jesus, I want to kiss her again.

Forget the islands. Forget adventures. Layla makes me want to stay in Durnan despite all the reasons why I shouldn't. Despite all the reasons why I can't.

Because I can't. *I can't.*

'Lay … here's what *I* think's going to happen.'

'This'll be good,' she mumbles. 'This'll be great.'

'I'll be back in six months. Done. That's it.'

She rolls her eyes. 'You don't know that. You don't even know where you're going to be in six weeks. Months will pass, then instead of coming back you'll get a visa and live overseas and get sponsored to stay then … *poof!* Gone.'

'Okay, say that happens — just hypothetically — and years pass. I reckon you'll be walking along one day — I don't know where, somewhere good, doesn't matter — and you'll see a familiar face. And you'll think, *Damn, I know him. He looks like this hot guy from Durnan who I always wanted to —*'

'Your point?'

'Just saying you might remember he was a bit of alright. Good friend, great kisser.'

'Loved nuding up at inappropriate times.'

I laugh. 'Anyway, you'll come up to this guy and —'

'No, he'll come up to me, he'll definitely come up to me.'

'*You'll* go up to him, this familiar guy, and you'll say, "Milo Dark, is that you?", and then he'll say, "Do I know you?" Then you'll kiss him to try to make him remember and —'

'No way, *you'll definitely kiss me* and —'

'Then we'll …'

'What? We'll what?'

'That's all I have so far.' I grin. 'But you'll see me. And you'll kiss me.'

313

Milo

I wait until Dad's in a good mood before bringing up London. Don't know why I'm surprised it takes a few days. If anything, I'm glad a slot's opened up at all. It could've been decades.

Loud laughter from the patio is the first sign it's go-time. He's with Mum and Trent and work's done for the day, which means there'll be cheese and bickies. If Dad's on the patio, there's always cheese and bickies. Throw in that I've been on my best behaviour, Trent's still lying low, and Mum's happy 'cos Dad's happy, and conditions are as sweet as they'll ever be.

As I creak open the flyscreen and step outside, it feels like I've entered the lions' enclosure at the zoo without safety gear. Dad's bellowing laugh is echoing around the yard, and I consider whether it would've been easier to pay a doppelgänger to cover for me while I'm in London rather than telling my parents I'm leaving Durnan.

Maybe.

Or maybe I'm just the biggest coward in Australia.

I choose the seat next to Trent, who's sneaking glances at his phone between his knees, and opposite

Mum, whose eyes are glistening as she strains to keep them open while Dad drivels on. They don't know it, but they'll come in handy if Dad blows up like Vesuvius.

White froth spits from Dad's mouth as he tells us, hands thrashing around, that his brain was *literally* exploding with excitement over the shop's numbers this week. I remind myself to break it to him what 'literally' means the next time he's in a good mood. Which could be never.

But first, London.

I wait for Trent to finish punishing Mum with questions about what's for dinner, and for Dad to slice off a hunk of blue vein and smear it on the last cracker, and then I blurt it out.

My hunger to see the world. The feeling of treading water in Durnan. The need to push myself. To try something on my own.

The toothpaste is out of the tube. But I'm hit with nothing but silence from my family.

Even Trent looks like he's about to choke. 'Wait, are you serious, bro?'

'Yeah. Hundred per cent.'

'Holy ... England! That's freakin' awesome. Can we visit? Mum, we'll have to visit.'

'Um ...' Mum falters, lost for words. 'I ...'

Dad clears his throat. 'Jen, shall I clear these plates and get dinner started?'

Trent scoffs. '*Dad*. Get ya head out of your bum and say something.'

'Trent …' Mum warns.

'Nah, Milo's talking about leaving and visiting the Queen, and Dad's worried about his next meal.'

'Let's all calm down,' Mum says as Dad just glowers into his stubby. It'd be easier if he yelled at me. 'Milo, darling, you can't think this is a smart idea? You're just a boy.'

'I know I've been useless around here, but it's like you can't see I'm trying to do something about it.'

Dad finally speaks. 'You're only eighteen. You don't know what's good for you, and you've proven that time and time again.'

'Yeah? Well, eighteen's old enough to buy fireworks. To sue someone. Freakin' hell, *I* can be sued. To get married. To buy a place — and you were gagging for us to do that. I'm not a kid. It's not even like I need anything from you — I'm paying for it myself.'

Mum sighs. 'I know you think you're independent, but —'

'People can join the army at sixteen, Mum, *sixteen*,' Trent says, before elbowing me. 'You gonna spot me a ticket, bro? Imagine us Dark boys tearing up Edinburgh.'

Jesus. Not helping. 'That's in Scotland, man.'

'Same diff, isn't it?' he says with a shrug.

'You stay out of this, Trent.' Mum's eyes set on mine. They're still glistening. Dad's avoiding eye contact again. 'You don't want to go to uni?'

'I do, just not yet. One day.'

'And you don't want to stay here?'

'Not when I don't know what else is out there.'

Dad gets to his feet, collects the plates, then leaves the table without saying anything.

'I'll talk to him,' Mum whispers. She reaches across the table and takes both my hands in hers. 'We'll just need some time to adjust.'

Should've hired a doppelgänger.

* * *

Milo: *Hey, so more news ... tix are booked! I leave on the 3rd at 4 pm outta Sydney (if Dad doesn't kill me first)*

Layla: *Oh my god! That's huge*

Layla: *btw 3 is my fave number*

Layla: *WAIT! THAT'S YOUR ACTUAL B'DAY?!*

Milo: *I know but cheaper tix. (Pov, who me?)*

Layla: *This feels real*

Milo: *Too real?*

Layla: *The right amount maybe*

Layla: *I looked at my list — we still haven't yelled at idiots lapping the main street*

Milo: *You mean ... EVERYONE IN DURNAN? We should do that today*

Milo: *Actually I can't. Forgot that Trent's helping me buy a new backpack. Soon tho?*

Layla: *Sure, have fun #bromance*

Milo: *You too*

* * *

Milo: *Evening, Chicken Girl, how's your day?*
Layla: *Max crapped in my shoe! Still love him tho*
Milo: *I'd never do that*
Layla: *Ha! Good to know. And you?*

* * *

Milo: *Sorry for delay! Hopeless. Life update: my map fits in my new backpack. Tell me more things bout you*

* * *

Layla: *Sorry, now I'm battling with replying. Puppy-sitting is booming. Making it RAIN*
Milo: *Dollar dollar bills! CEO of the year*
Layla: *Layla Enterprises, baby. Will write back properly ASAP*

Layla

Milo and I haven't texted for eleven days.

After the treehouse, things got stuck in the in-between again.

We've never been more in the grey.

I got swamped with dog-walking, catch-ups with Amvi and hanging with Shirin and forgot to write back at some point, then he didn't nudge me for a reply, and now he seems to have forgotten too. He's busy planning for his new life overseas; I guess I'm busy living mine here. Or maybe we're getting used to missing each other. After all, the more time we spend together in the grey, the more time I want to spend together in the grey. Every talk and kiss and in-joke only pushes us in deeper, making me sick at the thought of ever saying goodbye.

I still think of him on and off all day. There's no cure for that. When I admire my bracelet or feel its cool metal press against my forearm. Or when I run along the river with Max on the leash, heart pounding in my chest. Every time I stroll past the gelato shop, or when Shirin tells me she's about to do laundry. If I walk past a eucalyptus, I remember how we clung to the branches of the tree at the river, laughing and shrieking as we swung from the tyre swing.

It all feels like a different lifetime. Like someone's pressed reboot and our time together is already fading into chalky pastels and fuzzy memories.

I don't know if he's thinking of me.

I go to message him whenever I think of him, but when I pick up my phone, I stop myself. What is there to say to a guy who is leaving to start again? To a guy who wants to get lost? What is there to say to a guy who was only nearly right?

All my words will only make it harder for him to leave.

Twelve days until he goes.

Milo

I don't know how to text her. Everything I type seems too full-on or romantic or boring or wanky — *Meet me outside Buckingham Palace?* Such a tosser! — so I delete them all.

Soon, not seeing each other will be the new normal, so maybe we're bracing ourselves.

I glance at the map of the world again, swearing to myself as I take in the big blue of the ocean stretching across the paper, a staggering reminder of how far away London will be from this life.

Reminders like this, of her, make me want to cancel the trip, but I know that won't make me happy either.

I've learnt the lesson and it blows: no-one can get everything they want. At least not at the same time. That's the fantasy. The fairy tale.

But c'mon, I don't want everything — just *two* things. Travel and her. Surely that's not too much to ask.

I turn on my phone. No messages. I turn it off.

Maybe it's better this way.

I wonder if she thinks it's better this way.

* * *

Milo: *Hey, stranger. When can I see you before I go?*

* * *

Layla: *Hey, whenever you want. Sorry I've been MIA!*

* * *

Milo: *That's OK. Same! Things are pretty hectic. How's the day before I fly out?*
Layla: *Perfect. Come to mine if you want. Shirin will be at work*
Milo: *Yours it is*

Milo

We've already said all the things.

Well, *nearly* all the things.

I look around the room, taking in the lemon walls and photos pinned to the corkboard next to her bed. Me. Max. Shirin and her dad. Her mum.

'This room suits you,' I tell her, finally letting myself look in her direction again. I notice the bracelet dangling from her wrist. 'It's like living on the sun. Well, without the third-degree burns.'

Layla releases a soft laugh. 'Hey, by the way, I've gone through my old stuff and you've definitely stolen my Teenage Mutant Ninja Turtles blimp. You owe me a blimp, jerkface.'

'You flogged it from me to start with.'

There's an old softball mitt on her chest of drawers. I pick it up for a better look.

'Hey, careful with that,' she tells me in a rush, taking the mitt out of my hands and putting it back in its place.

Before I can ask why she pushes me towards her bed, but instead of tipping me backwards onto the mattress, she pins me against the wall.

'What? What's wrong?' I tilt her chin upwards. 'You mad at me for leaving?'

'No ... yes.'

'Fine. That's cool. I'm mad at *you* for telling me to leave.'

'*Fine.*'

'So we're both mad.'

She steps in, hair brushing over her collarbone. 'Furious.'

I'm fighting kissing her tonight. That laugh, that fieriness, that ability to turn the most mundane thing into an adventure. And she has no freakin' idea how pretty she is, which somehow makes her even prettier. That and the potty mouth. The dimple in her chin. The banter. The spongy curves of her body.

Jesus.

The thought of getting on the plane is hard enough without being close enough to smell the raspberry smeared on her lips.

'Um ...' I begin, already feeling weak as piss for what I'm about to say. 'I ... I better go. I've still gotta finish packing and the drive up to Sydney tomorrow's gonna be a bitch. Dad reckons we're heading off at like 6 am, so ...'

'So. This is it then. Go.'

Another step closer.

'Yeah.' My hand finds her waist. 'My official goodbye, as requested.'

'Nup. Changed my mind. Don't want one.'

'We'll still talk.'

'Yeah … until we don't.'

'You planning on deleting me from your phone? Hey, maybe we really will bump into each other again. Someplace exotic. Or back here, like the first time. Or in the middle somewhere.'

'The middle, huh?' She nods. 'I was thinking and … well, I think you need something to remind you that things weren't so bad here.'

'Oh yeah?'

She laces her fingers through mine and we melt into a kiss so soft it's like she's trying to savour every detail of my mouth.

'Hmm, I see your point, Chicken Girl, I do, but I think my memory *already* needs jogging.'

'You're very forgetful, Mr Dark. Ever thought of getting your head checked?'

'Only every day. Why do I like Durnan again?'

My heart flip-flops as she twirls over to the bed, edges onto one side of the mattress, and gestures for me to lie down beside her. My body's curled up next to hers, and our T-shirts and jeans and Cons twist around each other like pretzels.

I don't know how long we lie like that; wound into one. Eventually our lips part, breath punctured, but Layla doesn't uncurl herself from the nook she's made her own.

Then, later, a whisper. 'Don't freak out,' she tells me, 'but I think you've got part of my heart now.'

Too late.

Freak-out commenced.

'Just a part?' I want to make this easier, I want to hear her laugh — *and she does* — because I have no idea what I'm supposed to say next.

'Yes, just a part. *Greedy.*'

Pause. 'So … like your right ventricle? Or your aorta?'

Layla snorts. Success again. 'You dag, I take back everything.' But she wriggles in closer and her fingers don't unlock from mine.

'Same though,' I tell her.

'Same what?'

'Just … same. All of it.'

'I don't want to do this.'

Another pause. 'Same. Same.'

We say goodbye in her bedroom, in the hallway, on the veranda, then side by side on the gutter outside her house. Her neighbours are washing their ute two doors down and the foamy water streams along the kerb and around our sneakers.

I listen to Layla tell me she'll miss me *just a little* as she presses her heels down on the white bubbles.

It's happened. We're out of goodbyes. I pull her in and she wraps around me like a vine. Neither of us seems to know how to end it so the hug goes for way too long yet it's somehow still not even close to being long enough.

Eventually we unlace our bodies. Her fingertips find mine again, brushing my palms and the backs of my hands for the shortest of moments. This time when we pull away, it sticks. I leave her alone in the soapy suds as I trudge off down the street.

When I look back, she's halfway up the lawn and headed for her front door. I wait a second. She turns around and our eyes meet. Her lips crease into a smirk and I can almost hear her voice in my head. *Piss off then, Mr Dark*.

Layla

Milo: *Got to the airport without the family killing each other*
Layla: *Hey, b'day boy. Missing me already, huh? PS: Fine, you got me, I miss you too. PPS: Good day so far?*

* * *

I've been sitting on the grass in front of Mum's grave for a few minutes when the sky opens. Rain falls, sparse and sharp at first, before filling the air with fat droplets. *Don't complain, it's good for the farmers*, I can almost hear Mum saying as I hurry to my feet and fumble with my umbrella.

I swipe at my hair; it's already saturated. The few people straggling at nearby graves run for the car park, their feet skidding across the manicured lawns.

In a few minutes I will be alone in a cemetery.

You'd think after five years of avoiding coming here I'd have given it some thought, but I'm unsure about what I'm supposed to do. I stare at the plaque on the grave again. Mum's name is etched in the bronze: *Cate*

Montgomery. She always thought Catherine sounded too posh for her; I thought it was perfect.

My eyes trace over the words on her stone: *Loving Wife, Mother and Friend.*

I try not to take in the hundreds, maybe thousands, of other graves lined up in every direction around me.

Nothing prepares you for being surrounded by death.

I reach into my pocket, hand closing around my phone. Then I remember: Milo really is going. There will be no last-minute freakouts, no showing up at Shirin's telling me he can't go through with it. He's already at the airport, about to do the biggest thing of his life, all on his own.

I have to do the same.

I slip the phone back into my pocket, then crouch down and rest my palm on the uneven stone.

'Hey.'

I'm not expecting a reply, but the clang of silence still hurts.

The rain hits harder, turning the grass and dirt at my feet to mud. I stare at her name again, too choked up now to even whisper. Maybe she can read minds ... well, hopefully just in this moment.

So, I'm here. Hi, Mum. Hey. Sorry it took so long. My feet slip in the sludge. *Crap! Sorry. Um ... what's new? Actually, no, that's dumb, forget that. Okay, now I'm just a dork standing by herself in a cemetery in the rain. The thing is ... I really am sorry. I should've come earlier. You think that too, right? But I do love you, more than anyone, and nothing will ever change that, and I guess I kinda hoped you already knew it. I know, I know ... I'm lazy.*

A bolt of lightning cracks through the sky.

I shriek and topple backwards into the mud.

A laugh sneaks out. Then another. This would only happen to me. Wet through to the skin, I struggle to my feet then slog through the muck until I'm at the edge of her gravestone.

Fine, I was too scared to see all this again. I know I should've come when Dad did ... or when he stopped coming. I've just been trying to be strong, like you. All I want is to be someone you'd be proud of ...

I pull the umbrella further over me as the rain buckets down. I shake my head at the absurdity of it all.

I must look like a friggin' drowned rat now ... Mum, are you mad? Actually, don't tell me. We'll just pretend everything's perfect — like that time I went to Michael Hadid's house party when you thought I was going to a sleepover at Jill's. You knew that one, right?

Thunder rumbles, so heavy and deep it sounds like the sky's about to cave in on itself.

I don't know what else ... oh, I walk dogs now — get paid and stuff. Turns out it's a real job. Who knew, right? And Dad's trying. Well, he's away a lot still, but he's starting to. His girlfriend is great. You'd like her. Heaps, I think. Is that weird? Probably. Sorry ... again.

By the way, you're stuck with me 'cos I'm going to keep coming back here, if that's alright with you. 'Cos I hate that I let you down every day I stayed away.

A tear squeezes out.

Then another.

And I've missed you every day.

Then another tear, until they're mixing with the rain and flowing down my cheeks. As I cry, I imagine her watching me from wherever she is — this silly sight of me alone in the pouring rain in the middle of a cemetery — and a muffled little snort of laughter slips out as I wonder if she really is sipping on a strawberry milkshake. I've thought it so many times I've almost convinced myself it's true.

I wipe at my nose with the back of my hand as salt from my tears licks at my lips. *This is so gross. Oh, Mum, I bet you're thinking, pull it together, Layla, you're making me look bad in front of my friends.*

The sky cracks again, causing me to jump, and a fresh shower of rain pours down. In the distance, a row of trees slope to one side in the wind. I fiddle with my bracelet from Milo, spinning it around my wrist.

I kissed someone, Mum — don't tease me — and it was kind of amazing, but then it was also kind of a disaster. He left Durnan today, so that's that, I guess. Unless he comes back, but I don't think he'll come back.

Fine. You win. It was Milo. I know! But don't worry, things'll be okay for me here. Max the dog's got me. And I'm hanging with Amvi Prashad again — remember her? I think she used to eat sand at preschool.

I crack up at the memory, then scan the cemetery again, for once hoping I'm still alone.

Yeah, Durnan's good. I've got this feeling like ... well, like anything's possible. Probably sounds stupid, but you won't tell anyone, right? Who am I kidding? You were always a blabbermouth. Guess I know where I got that from, hey?

A gust of wind whips my umbrella inside out. I yell in protest, but my words get snatched up in the swirling storm as I battle to hold onto the handle. The umbrella sways, dancing in the sky, refusing to follow orders. An extra strong gust comes through and the umbrella snaps, wires jutting in every direction. I wrestle with it against the wind, laughing 'til my cheeks ache.

Milo

Layla: *Sorry, big day. You still there?*
Milo: *Yeah, boarding soon tho. You OK?*
Layla: *I'm great. Hey, I've decided to rate us 4 stars out of 5*
Milo: *No final star? Brutal*
Layla: *Always room for improvement*
Layla: *You can go to Hollywood and find me one*
Milo: *Deal*
Layla: *I'll meet you on the Walk of Fame. PS: Fine, 4.5 stars. PPS: Rule 5 alert. PPPS: You still owe me a blimp!*
Milo: *The blimp was mine! And stuff the rules*
Milo: *Hey Lay, they're calling my flight so I've gotta run. Bye again, Chicken Girl*
Layla: *Til we meet in the middle, jerkface. It's sure been something*

* * *

My stomach hasn't stopped churning at the thought of leaving Durnan. It churned all the time Mum stood next to me in the check-in line, as I dragged myself through the gate for boarding, as I crammed my backpack into the overhead luggage compartment. Fine … fine! My stomach hasn't stopped churning at the thought of leaving *her*.

Shaking my head as I suss out the movie selection on the flight, I tell myself to get over it. Harden up. Remember why I'm doing this.

Why am I doing this?

I pull down my tray table, and rip open the packet of chocolate-coated almonds Mum bought me for the trip — a substitute for no birthday cake. I pop one in my mouth and crunch through it. Better than grinding my teeth down to chalky dust.

Jesus. I'm going overseas for the first time ever. This is what I wanted. *Want.* I should be thinking of London and travel and adventures — adventures I can't even begin to imagine. I shouldn't be thinking of her. Not Layla. Not now.

Thousands of girls, she teased me. Yeah, right.

The woman to my right yawns, then takes my armrest hostage, her enormous fluffy jumper prickling against my bare arms.

Elbows pinned to my sides, I check my phone. There are no new messages. Just the final goodbye from Layla. I read it again. My stomach whips and I try to convince myself it's due to the old man spluttering phlegm into his fist to my left and the twenty-three-hour flight in my ridiculously near future, but I don't even believe my own bullshit any more. Okay, the old guy's phlegm isn't helping.

It's like my brain doesn't get that Layla and I were floating together in limbo.

Because we weren't together. Not together-together. Not in a way that anyone else in Durnan will ever gossip about over bunches of kale at the Saturday farmers' market. There's no *Layla loves Milo* carving on the eucalyptus tree at the river. We never walked down the main street holding hands, or stuck our tongues down each other's throats in the back row at the cinema before the lights even went down. We never won an award at the Year 12 formal telling us we were destined to be married forever.

As far as everyone in Durnan thinks, Layla and I mean nothing to each other.

Except I don't give a stuff about what everyone in Durnan thinks.

I pop another chocolate-coated almond in my mouth and plug in my earphones, hoping I can drown her out with a song.

For the next five minutes and four seconds, my mind gets stuck on a loop of the moments in the past month leading up to this one.

Mum not letting me out of her sight for two days after I told her about London.

Dad ripping my map in half, then taping it back together the next day like nothing had happened.

Trent barrelling into my room every day to see if I was up for another marathon video-game session.

Then the six-hour drive this morning to Sydney International Airport, where the four of us took turns attempting small talk about what was waiting for me and what was to come for them.

At the gate, Mum cried and held me close when I told her I'd miss her, causing a scene in front of the other passengers like I knew she would. She begged me to message her every day so she knows I've not been stabbed and left to die in front of Westminster Abbey. After shouting her two coffees and a choc-chip muffin, I negotiated her down to three times a week with a face-to-face video chat thrown in once a fortnight — and told her to lay off watching the nightly news and gruesome detective shows.

Always one to keep up appearances, even in Sydney where he knows a whopping zero people, Dad told me he was proud of me for taking a risk, like this was his plan for me all along. He fidgeted with the locks on my backpack, telling me a crook could rip them right off and I should have bought the more expensive ones at the travel store, then he ruffled my hair before making a final dig while Mum was in the bathroom. Something about hoping I'd 'find myself' overseas like Paul Chamberlain's daughter did before she studied medicine. Gritting my teeth, I let his words wash around me rather than absorbing them into my skin.

Trent gave me a quick hug and a few slaps on the back, a crooked smile and a filthy joke to finish before I walked through the gate: a quiet understanding that we're all good.

'Pray for me, bro,' Trent muttered, gesturing to Mum and Dad bickering behind us.

I laughed out loud then, as I do now thinking about it.

The plane rumbles to life and the woman next to me gasps in surprise. I tug at my seatbelt to check it's tight enough.

'Sir, please put up your tray table.' A beaming flight attendant leans towards me, almost choking me in a cloud of flowery perfume. 'And turn off all electronic devices — we're preparing for take-off.'

'Sorry,' I say, looking down at my phone. 'One sec.'

Layla's message is still on the screen: *Til we meet in the middle, jerkface.*

I type out a text — another goodbye, more personal jokes, a try-hard attempt to prove how much I'll miss her, miss whatever the hell that was. Music pounds in my ears as my thumb lingers over the message, aching to link us one more time. But I just stare at the words. I stare at the words until the man beside me sneezes and I look up, catching a hint of blue fading into the grey clouds through the tiny window.

Someone taps me on the shoulder. 'Sir, I said it's time to put up your tray table and turn off your phone,' the attendant says in her sugary voice. 'Shall we make everyone on the plane wait? Or are you ready to join us for the flight to London?'

Cheeks reddening, my thumb trembles over the send button. But then my eye catches Layla's words again: *It's sure been something*

I swallow.

Then I delete my unfinished text, watching the letters disappear one by one until there's nothing left but a flashing cursor. Everything that can be said has been said.

'Yeah,' I tell the attendant, turning off my phone so I can't re-type the message. 'I'm ready.'

If, like Layla, you would like to chat with someone, you can get in touch with one of these wonderful organisations:

BeyondBlue: 1300 22 4636 and beyondblue.org.au
headspace: 1800 650 890 and headspace.org.au
Kids Helpline: 1800 55 1800 and kidshelpline.com.au
Relationships Australia: 1300 364 277 and
relationships.org.au

ACKNOWLEDGMENTS

First, a big thanks-a-million to the HarperCollins dream team: Lisa Berryman, Cristina Cappelluto, Eve Tonelli, Nicola O'Shea, Pam Dunne, Michelle Weisz, Holly Frendo, Bianca Fazzalaro, Jacqui Barton, Hazel Lam and Helen Littleton (for opening the door). Your hard work, vision and kindness continues to amaze me year after year.

Here's looking at JT: the big beautiful brains behind the title *Remind Me How This Ends*. I'm grateful every day that I signed up to that one wrong university subject because it led me to you.

To my darling friends and family, especially McMills FamBam: thank you for always being there with support, love and Beau-man cuddles. Little Nettie and Big Al, I wouldn't have limped over the finish line without your cheerleading. Special mentions also have to go to some of my sunniest word-wranglers — Kimberly Gillan, Simone McClenaughan, Rachael Craw, Ellie Marney, Rebecca James, Nicole Hayes, Trinity Doyle, Fleur Ferris, Erin Van Der Meer, Sam Faull, Holly Richards, Jeremy Lachlan, Sarah Ayoub, Allison Tait, Lauren Sams and Will Kostakis — for always knowing what to say to help me find the light. Also a shout-out to Kate Forsyth, Charlotte Wood and Ali Manning for helping me to lean into this experience in a new way.

Finally, to my readers: thank you for letting me share my imagination with you — before, now and always. Here's to many more adventures together.

Gabrielle Tozer is an internationally published author from Wagga Wagga, New South Wales. Her debut YA novel, *The Intern*, won the State Library of Victoria's 2015 Gold Inky Award, and its sequel, *Faking It*, is also out now.

Based in Sydney, Gabrielle loves sharing her passion for storytelling and creativity, and has appeared at numerous festivals, schools and conferences around Australia. She has also been featured on *Weekend Today*, Triple J and ABC Radio, as well as in *The Sydney Morning Herald*, *Dolly*, *Girlfriend*, *TV Week* and *Cosmopolitan*.

Remind Me How This Ends is Gabrielle's third YA novel. Her first picture book, *Peas and Quiet* (illustrated by Sue deGennaro), and her short story 'The Feeling From Over Here' (featured in *Begin, End, Begin: A #LoveOzYA Anthology*) hit shelves in 2017.

Say hello:
gabrielletozer.com
instagram and twitter: @gabrielletozer
facebook.com/hellogabrielletozer

Also by
GABRIELLE TOZER

The Intern
Faking It
Peas and Quiet